CLOUDED HELL

JR GRAY

ISBN-13: 978-1530525515
ISBN-10: 1530525519

Cover Design: Rebel Graphics
Image: Dollar Photo Club
Editor: Silla Webb

I burned myself to the ground and ashes became my ink.

ONE

REMI

Four hundred sweaty bodies packed into this room, and you could've heard a pin drop. My boots clicked on the concrete floor. It could have been a scene right out of a movie, the way the two shirtless guys circled each other, faces torn up and bleeding, hands in front of their faces, with scraps of wrapping covering swollen and bruised knuckles. I could smell the aggression.

It smelled like money.

I'd been gambling on anything and everything since I'd been given the run of the neighborhood at six. I'd grown up in Vegas, but it wasn't silly cards I was interested in. I loved contests, where real skill was involved. I craved the tension a match brought to a room full of people. I could feed off the energy.

I watched the two thick men trade punches. One was a fair amount bigger than the other, muscled through his arms down to his massive hands. He brought a knee up just in time to block a quick kick from his opponent who I presumed to be the owner of the dive bar I stood in.

I'd had him described to me, dark hair, six feet four, and piercing blue eyes, but those details could have matched half the room. The harsh fake light defined the high arch of his cheekbones even under all the blood. I'd done my research, but there were no pictures of the guy. What told me it was Dante was the swath of planets tattooed across his left shoulder. It dripped down the back of his arm like a tragic afterthought. Everyone knew the tattoo. It was talked about, though no one knew what it symbolized. I studied anyone I planned to use. Information was gold in this business.

He was beautifully deadly, just my type. I'd been looking for him for a long time.

I took the long way around to the gambling window, keeping my eyes on the fight. Dante was quick, but I'd be surprised if he pulled off the win. It was well-known heavyweights tore up lighter guys for a reason. They could hit a lot harder and destroy even faster men. The line, at the window, had thinned when the fight got going, and I only had to wait a few moments to buy a ticket. The odds were in the opponent's favor, so I put money on Dante.

I slipped into one of the rows and took a seat on the bleachers, kicking my feet out in front of me. It had been a long day, and my body was feeling it. I was almost thirty, and struggling with control was taxing.

Dante dodged a fist coming at his head and hit the other guy three times in the span of seconds. The crowd roared, surging like a massive organism with one mind. He didn't pull back to avoid getting hit. He pushed the guy back with punch after punch, giving his opponent plenty of opportunity to hit him back. It was a—unique strategy. Ballsy even. Most boxers tried to avoid getting hit, unless they were masochists.

His opponent landed a right hook to Dante's jaw causing him to stumble back a few paces. The guy charged Dante. My heart skipped a beat. I thought Dante was done for, but he regained his stance and fought off the attack.

"Fuck." I sat forward, resting my elbows on my knees. The heat and tension in the room pressed in around me, collectively choking off all the oxygen.

Dante snarled, baring bloody teeth, and my cock twitched. I adjusted, eyes never leaving his sweat-soaked skin. All his muscle was on full display, the V of his hips cutting right down into his low-slung shorts. I wanted to be the one opposite him in the ring. I wanted him to hit me.

Dante's body shuddered right before he attacked. He slammed his fist into the guy's temple, and the big bloke went down hard, shaking the floor when he landed. It didn't even need to be called. It was clear he was out cold.

Dante raised both hands in the air and growled. But he didn't stay to celebrate. He ducked out of the ring and went right to a commanding woman who had legs a mile long that disappeared under a skirt that hugged her ass. She held a drink out to him, and I waited. Girlfriend? He was bisexual, or so I'd been told.

She didn't touch him as they exchanged a few words. He turned and walked toward the employee door, and she followed. They disappeared, and as the crowd moved around me, getting more drinks, leaving, and cashing in tickets, I sat.

Now that I'd seen the operation, I was sure. I could be me here. If I played it right, I could steal away and hide, even if only for a short time. But he'd never know I'd been here already. It would give me the upper hand.

I could taste the freedom already.

TWO

DANTE

It was late, even the last stragglers on Bourbon Street were long gone. The bar wasn't a tourist attraction. This was where the locals hung out. We got our first rush as the other places closed, and on fight nights when the rest of the city appeared dead, the Inferno was alive. A few patrons sat and nursed their beers, content to close down the place. I sat behind the bar, having let my employees go home to their families. I stayed. I had nowhere else to be.

My attention had been on the same man all night. He sat in the back with a bottle of Patrón to himself. The remnants of Absinthe ringed the bottom of a glass pushed to the side, and his ice had long since run out, but he didn't ask for more. In a place normally reserved for locals, he stood out.

While the bar had been busy, he had been talkative and playful with a dry wit I found myself drawn to. I'd watched him turn down more than one advance.

He had his feet kicked up on the bench across from him with his arms draped over the lacquer-coated table. A shadow of scruff adorned his jaw, and the top two buttons of his polo lay open with his collar not quite lying flat. He had money. Everything he wore, albeit wrinkled, was expensive. He looked unbelievably tired for someone so young, beaten down to a point a lifetime of sleep wouldn't fix it.

I looked away from him when the bell at the front door dinged, signaling the departure of the last two customers, leaving only him. I should tell him to go. I opened my mouth to speak the words, 'Get out, so I can go find my bed.' But what use was making him leave? I wouldn't sleep. I'd given up on finding more than a few hours a night a long time ago.

Ducking out from behind the bar, I stopped myself. I wouldn't go over to him. It wasn't me. I collected the glasses left over and then hand washed them, looking up at frequent intervals to check on the man. There he sat, checking his phone and still nursing his Patrón. Watching him, I realized, I didn't think he ever looked at me. Not once had he met my eyes. I was curious. It was my downfall in all things. I had a need to understand. I poured myself a drink, content to wait him out.

My metabolism could handle quite a bit of liquor, and this man was getting close to my limit, but he never seemed drunk. When the last of the glasses were clean, I approached him. My intrigue had gotten the best of me. Tourists kept to the well-known areas of New Orleans, and I wanted to know what had him in the middle of the God forsaken outer limits of the city. So many of these neighborhoods had been deserted after Katrina. It had been the perfect place for me to hide in plain sight.

I took the seat across from him and he glanced up. Goddamn it. I should've learned my lesson after I married the last out of towner who came through. I hadn't. He had intense dark jade eyes with a defiant storm brewing behind them. The set in his shoulders gave away so much about his personality.

His eyes were bloodshot, and he smelled slightly of wet pavement after the rain, the sea, and ink.

"Evening," I said.

"Or morning." The man slumped back in his seat, and I could feel him appraising me.

I shoved a hand into my disheveled black hair, mussing it more. "Plan on spending the night in here? If you want, I can turn off the lights and make up a bed for you on the bench."

The hint of a smile turned up the corners of his lips. "Only if you promise to read me a bedtime story and tuck me in."

I wasn't entirely sure if he'd said *tuck* or *fuck.* I'd fuck him in. My cock grew half hard behind my jeans. But I wasn't about to let him know I was hard for him.

"If you're looking for a daddy, you've come to the wrong place, handsome... not the way I roll."

His face broke up in a smile. "Damn, and here you look just the part if I was say two or three. What are you, twenty-five?"

"Thirty."

"You're not that much older. It kinda kills the daddy image." He winked. "But if you want to tan my ass, I won't object."

My cock was aching now. He would look so damn pretty covered in my welts. I shouldn't be drawn into this trap again. I arched one of my brows, and he wore an amused smile. I could tell he wanted to get under my skin. We fell silent, and he offered me his glass. I took it and sipped the tequila.

"This shit is vile." My lip curled up as the taste permeated my tongue, and I passed it back to him.

He chuckled again. "If you're trying to get rid of me, I

don't plan on sleeping, but there is a hotel up the road I'm booked in if you feel so inclined as to kick me out."

He had just the hint of a California drawl as he spoke, much different than the southern accents usually heard in these parts. I had been right about him not being from 'round here.

"I can just take a bottle with me." He tapped it on the table.

"I have to be back here in a few hours to get the weekend shipments, no skin off my back if I sit here or at home 'till then. I don't sleep much as it is." I slung one arm over the back of the bench, mimicking his body language.

"I'm not going to get you in trouble with your boss, am I?" He held his pinky up, like a prick, while he downed the rest of the glass.

"Dante," I extended my hand. "I own the place. So stay as long as you like."

"Remi." When our hands met, he furrowed his brow, but his shake was firm. "Are you a poet?"

"My mother was a fan of the Divine Comedy. I don't think she was expecting the devil when she used the name."

He raised his brows, but I didn't explain more. He nodded, picking up the bottle and pouring the last bit into his tumbler.

"Then I've no need to make this drink last."

I flicked my tongue over my teeth as I watched him suck back the last of the alcohol. "Want something else?"

"I'll take another hit of la fée verte and another glass on ice if it's not too much trouble." He offered his glass to me.

I slid out of the booth, and he got up to follow me, bottle in hand. I sensed his eyes boring into my back, but he averted them when I slipped behind the bar and turned on him. The Absinthe went first into the traditional glass, and he watched as I laid a special spoon over the top before taking out a cube of sugar. Next I grabbed a tiny pitcher of water from the fridge below the bar and dripped it over. The cube dissolved and ran over the side of the spoon gradually, dripping into the contents of the glass. Finally, I stirred the contents and made up the Patrón before setting both glasses, along with a glass of JW for myself on the bar. He slapped down a twenty and waved off any change.

"Let me buy you an Absinthe too." He picked up the glass, pinky again lingering in the air, this time drawing my attention to a silver band around his ring finger.

So much for killing a few hours with a good fuck. "I pretty much stick to whiskey, thanks anyways." I always kept my head clear when I wanted to play and even more so when I had to resist. I'd given up the green poison years ago.

"Well how the hell am I going to get any information out of a sober bar owner who owes me nothing?" There was a glint in his eyes as he said it.

"I'd say I'd answer your questions for a blow job." I imagined those pale pink lips stretched around my girth and his piercing eyes staring up at me as I said the words. "But I've made a point not to sleep with married men, since the last time it blew up in my face." I offered him back a grin.

He scoffed and tucked his left hand under the bar. "Not married..." His eyes dropped down my body.

I leaned forward, resting my forearms on the bar, drawing us closer, ignoring his comment. "That's what they all say, rings or not." I tapped my empty ring finger and picked up my drink.

He chuckled but didn't comment further. I threw back

my drink and set the glass in the sink. I'd tried before to drown the pain in meaningless sex, but the appeal had worn thin. His ring bore no real weight to my decision. It was his blatant denial that turned me off.

"Stay as long as you like, I'm going to go get some work done. Just holler if you need anything." I ducked out from behind the large bar that sat in the middle of my place and headed toward the hallway in the back, which housed the bathrooms, supply room, and my office. I settled down behind my desk in my huge chair and kicked my feet up on it. Grabbing a stack of papers off my desk, I started reading the material left there by my manager. She fucking loved her paperwork. God, I think I would drown in it if I skipped a day.

Footsteps drew my mind away from the documents, and I glanced up to find Remi leaning against the door frame.

"Can I help you?" I asked when he didn't say anything.

"About that question...."

I waited.

"I stopped here for the night in hopes of finding a person... or dungeon I'd heard whispers of..." he trailed off, searching my face.

I knew exactly what he was talking about, but I kept my expression neutral. "Oh?"

"Since you're the owner, and this is where it's rumored to be, I thought you could tell me if there was any truth to it." He stepped into the room. There was no sway to his step, but the signs were apparent, he was drunk.

"You'd have to tell me what the rumors are exactly." I dropped my feet to the floor and sat up.

He pulled out one of the chairs opposite me and sat down. "This is a fight bar?"

"That much is true. We don't hide it."

"You're one of them?"

I nodded. "I used to box, before I..."

"Retired?" left his lips before I could finish. I knew he didn't believe me. "Then it's got to be true."

I tossed the stack of papers down on my desk. "I'm not sure what you're talking about, but most rumors about us are true." I winked.

"Then where the fuck is the BDSM club it's rumored you run?"

There it was. "Who said I run one?" I was going to skin him alive. This guy was a stranger, and if he could find me then others could, which was bad. I was long out of the game anyway, but I didn't need people sniffing around.

"I wouldn't have come if I didn't need it." There was a pleading tone to his voice as he rubbed a shaky hand over the back of his neck.

I tried to ignore the need in his voice, but parts of me couldn't shut it out. "And what is it you think you need?"

"I need to be owned, to completely submit, to give everything over," he said in a throaty tone, eyes never leaving mine.

There was something about a man who could lay it all out there and not waiver that got to me. I got up and walked around the desk without replying, taking a seat on the edge nearest him. "On your knees."

He complied in an instant.

"Tell me, boy, why me?"

He kept his eyes downcast and back straight. He'd had training, and the complete compliance did something to me. "Because it needs to be on the down low, Master."

That word stirred a dark part of me, a part I had to ignore while questioning him. It wasn't the typical 'sir' most used, he had gone for broke. That word, if he only knew how it rooted itself deep down in my mind and started to breed ideas there. Or maybe he knew exactly what he was doing. I'd never collared a submissive, and all the boys I had played with had called me Sir. To me, being called Master took it to another level, a dark level.

"Why do you need to hide what you are?"

"I have good reasons, Master," he said barely above a whisper.

"Explain yourself or get the fuck out of my bar."

"I can't." He looked at the floor and rolled his shoulders forward.

"Out."

He swallowed and looked up to meet my gaze. "In my circles, I am a Dominant."

It was clear now. I could see it all. He was on a business trip and had driven way out of his way, to bumble fuck, to find what he was scared to let anyone see.

"You're married, or have a collared mate?"

He shook his head and slid his thumb over the ring on his finger. "No."

"Don't lie to me." My voice dropped till it was a sinister whisper.

"It's a symbol, I'm not married." His jade green eyes spoke more than he said. He loved her or him.

"They give you permission?" Something inside me stirred, and I knew I should say no to him. I shouldn't go there, but after the year I'd had, and his death, something so easy would be hard to say no to. I needed to not think. Someone without the risk of feelings, cold, and purely for the release of it. It sounded too good to be true.

"Yes, we are open, but they have rules."

They? Was he leaving out gender or did he have more than one? I didn't ask. I didn't want to know. I didn't want details. "How long are you here?"

"As long as I need to be. I can't go back till I have things under control." He flexed and unflexed his fingers. The edge showed clearly. "They told me to take care of it before I show my face again."

That made me raise my brows. "Have you been denying it that long?"

He sucked his lip into his mouth and nodded, dropping his gaze back to the floor. "I can't there. My circle thinks of me as someone else." His cheeks flushed a little.

My hand snapped out, grabbing his chin and roughly tilting his face to mine, forcing him to look me in the eyes. "I don't want someone who is ashamed of who they are."

He swallowed hard, and I caught the movement of his Adam's apple. "Yes, Master."

"What are your limits?" I released his chin, shaking off the feeling that this one was going to break me, instead of me him.

He leaned over to rustle through his bag. His hand came back with a crumpled and folded stack of papers. I took it from him and flipped them open, seeing it was a standard limit sheet. I scanned it for his hard limits. He had none.

I pushed my tongue into my cheek. "You can't be a masochist." There weren't many of us.

"You should be able to tell. We can always see it in others." He smirked, there was the hint of his dominant side playing out.

He was a switch. I groaned low, causing my chest to rumble. He was already mine in my head. I held him in my hard stare, and I did see it, maybe I had all along which was why I kept talking to him. Not many could take my sadism.

"It's easy to spot our kind. When I give over, you own

me, anything you want. My sole purpose is to please you, Master." I could smell the arousal coming off him in waves. It was my turn to swallow hard.

"But yet you see yourself as weak. Why is that?"

He shrugged one shoulder. I could already tell he was going to lie to me. "I hold respect in my world. People look at you different when they know you submit."

"It takes more to give yourself over." I knew that because it was something I could never do. Even with my own desire for pain. I took it out in the ring and never let anyone have that control over me. It took a level of trust I didn't possess and never would.

"I know we feed that line of bullshit to every sub. But people look at you different. If you don't agree, I'll parade you around on your hands and knees for a while, then you can see how your people look at you."

My lip twitched and pulled back in a silent snarl.

"I didn't think so." His words were dry, but there was a hint of a tease in his eyes that gave him away.

I reared back and smacked him across the cheek. His head cocked to the side, and the sound resonated through the office. He didn't make a sound, but his eyes pressed closed, and he hunched forward to rest on his hands. I could see the bulge in his jeans. Either pain training had him hard instantly, or he really was what he claimed to be.

Shit. I was a weak man faced with his kind. Our kind.

I lifted my hand and pushed it into his dark tousled hair. He purred at the gesture, and I could see my hand print forming in red on his face. The mark on him, my mark, rooted deep down in my mind and threatened to take over. I knew there was no way I was going to say no to him tonight.

"I don't do SSC," I said at length. I'd seen his affinity

for edge play on his sheet, but I had to put it out there.

"This isn't some billionaire's bedroom. I'm not looking for you to save me. You saw my list."

I nodded. We played along the Risk Aware Consensual Kink here. It was dangerous in the eyes of some, but he was right. We weren't in some billionaire's bedroom where one hit from a flogger would fulfill his need. He needed to be beat down and broken to quiet his mind.

"Where is the club?"

I stiffened. It had been a long time since the club existed. I'd torn it down out of spite years ago. "It doesn't exist any longer. If we play, it's just with me."

He had a look in his eyes I couldn't quite place. It wasn't disappointment, but it was something.

"This won't ever be more than a D/s relationship. I can't do more again." I had no heart left to give. I had locked it away.

"That's good because I'm unavailable." He paused and then went on, "You can't fuck me."

"It wasn't on your limit sheet."

"It's not my limit," he replied.

"I wasn't planning on it anyway." I couldn't risk a connection. Not with him. I could already tell he had an addictive personality. I needed to get my sadism out and feed the animal. He couldn't be real. He was a means to an end for me, a toy, and it was perfect because once he got his fill, he would go back home. "You're merely using me to get what you need?"

"And you're using me to get out that blackness I see in your eyes," he shot back.

"We're using each other."

I didn't have the strength to deny it anymore. I put on a face every day, and it had been a long time since I had touched another person. Was it so wrong to want to share my blackness with him?

THREE

DANTE

"To your feet," I barked.

He got to his feet in an instant but kept his eyes down.

"You said you have as much time as you need?"

He nodded.

"Then go sober the fuck up." I walked past him and out the door to my office, leaving him standing there.

I walked right to the back to open up the cellar doors. I had a truck coming any minute to bring supplies for the fight tonight. I unlocked the fading green doors and pulled it open to reveal a dark concrete stair heading down into blackness. I walked down the stairs, letting my eyes adjust to the low light before I flipped the switch. I was met with a door. I entered the number into the keypad to open up access to the storage area, or so it looked from first glance. There was a large walk in fridge and freezer to one side and then an office. I slipped through the false wall that lead to the staircase down into the underground space where we held the fights.

The reason I'd bought this space was because it used to be a speakeasy back in the day. This was the room they'd used to distill alcohol during prohibition. It suited my needs perfectly. Because of the large tanks the room used to house, it had twenty foot ceilings. I'd put up stands and boxes for higher paying patrons. It was a work of art and as good as a cash printing press.

"Boss?" I heard Liv's voice from the top of the stairs.

"Down here. You can go crawl back into bed if ya want." I turned to find her standing before me. "Quiet little shit."

"You didn't hear me, did you?" She beamed up at me.

Goddamn, she was smoking hot, even at five thirty in the morning. She was old southern beauty. I imagined she slept with her hair in rag curls to get it looking like that every day, but fuck it was worth it. She also had this thing for pencil skirts which accentuated her bigger hips.

"Oh I heard you coming a mile away in those pretty little heels, doll." I flashed her a wink and watched her squirm. There was no doubt in my mind the attraction was returned, even if the dynamic had changed.

There were a lot of parts of me, all the lower ones in fact, that thought about bending her over every surface in the bar to fuck her until she couldn't walk, but then the rational parts of me knew she was the best manager I'd ever had, and if I fucked her she would never come back. So I didn't fuck her, not before and not now.

"Why are you still here, boss?"

I could have sworn she used that word to taunt me, but I was okay with it. "A good looking stranger."

She gasped softly, having been around for the tail end of my melt down after *he* died. "You and strangers."

I half shrugged. "When you've fucked everyone in town..." I trailed off. I didn't need to explain to her. She'd seen it.

"Was he good?" She followed me back up the stairs. "I

have no sex life because I work for this prick who doesn't let me have any time off. Well, that and other things." She gestured at herself then said, "I need the details."

"You're beautiful, don't sell yourself short or act like you don't love the paychecks," I shot back.

She rolled her eyes

"I wouldn't know." I walked up to the truck idling in the parking lot. The driver sat in the truck with a joint. I tapped on the window, and he rolled it down. I slipped him a billfold of dead presidents, and he tucked it away in his pocket.

I had a deal with the factory, and it suited me quite nicely. There was no way I could account for the amount of patrons or liquor I sold on fight nights, so a lot of it went under the table. It was a good thing the fire marshal had a gambling addiction.

Liv and I got to unloading the truck. She brought the boxes to me, and I carried them down the stairs. After they were all loaded and put away in the freezer, Liv ducked into the office. I leaned against the door watching her work, my thoughts lingering on Remi.

"I have a meeting set up for you tomorrow."

I stared at her, waiting for her to continue.

"It's with Caci from Vegas." She paused, waiting for my reaction.

"How did you get him?" I'd been trying to get this for months with no success.

"The market is oversaturated there, and he wants to find new areas for his guys. I happened to persuade him."

I was surprised, and it showed.

Her eyes glinted as she looked up at me. "You're welcome, boss."

"What's his first name?"

"I only have his last. It's Caci."

"Tomorrow?" I asked.

"Yes, Sir." She returned to scanning the file she was looking at when something struck me.

"Tell me how the hell you unload the truck three mornings a week with those heels on?"

She looked at me over the stack of papers she was leafing through and then bent at the waist to retrieve the folder of petty cash from the bottom drawer to show me. "I have two guys who usually come help me. When I saw your bike still here I told them I didn't need them." She tossed it back in the drawer and went back to what she was doing.

"Guys without jobs?" My brow pulled in.

She nodded.

"Pay them double next week. I'm sure they were counting on that cash." I turned to go.

She called after me. "I already paid them this morning. Way ahead of you, boss."

I grinned and shook my head. She was too damn good at my job.

The sun was high in the sky by the time I left. I felt my pockets for my sun glasses. Nothing. I must have forgotten them inside. I squinted past the glare as I climbed the stairs out of the basement and walked right into Remi who was standing there. We both righted ourselves, and I stepped back, sliding my hands into my pockets to wait for him to speak.

"I slept for a couple of hours, had breakfast, and went for a long run. I'm sober." He dropped to his knees as he said it and looked me right in the eyes. I could see he was telling the truth. God, I wanted him, but if I gave in right away, who would be in charge? I walked a circle around him. He'd changed his jeans. They were still expensive looking, and yet he was still kneeling in my parking lot. What else could I make him do? My arousal stirred. I took my position in front of him, feet spread, arms crossed.

"Why?"

He looked startled. "Why what?"

"Why should I?"

The way his body tightened, I knew he had a temper to him. He was used to getting his own way. More than used to it, he expected it.

He got to his feet and looked me in the eyes. "You may be able to read me, but I can read you just as well. You need it as much as I do. I can feel it coming off of you in waves."

He wasn't wrong, but I wasn't going to admit it. We stood chest to chest in a standoff.

"Let's go before I decide this is a bad idea."

FOUR

DANTE

Remi wore enough of a smile to let me know he had won, but not enough for me to send him back to his hotel. I wanted to smack it off his face, but I'd save it for later.

I turned, and he stayed on my heel. He headed toward the back of the parking lot as I got on my bike. I pushed the starter and then pulled out onto the beat up road. I had to weave to avoid potholes. I was convinced the city was going to ignore this district until it rotted off the face of the earth. Maybe then they'd bulldoze it and start afresh. My bar was about a fifteen-minute drive from the river district where I lived. I could have moved the bar over here. I made more than enough money, but then I risked contamination from the tourists.

When I married Masen, he'd insisted on building us a house, moving out of the 'ghetto' as he liked to call it. That's what I got for marrying a lawyer with old family money. It had been a hell of a fight, as I preferred my old house, but he'd wanted something more along the lines of what he'd been accustomed to in his penthouse in Chicago. The results weren't bad, and I had stayed after he left. My chest ached at the thought of him, and I buried him in the back of my mind where he belonged.

I parked my bike out front and climbed the stairs of the large wrap-around porch. I didn't wait for Remi as I opened the front door. I never locked it. People knew better than to come into my house without an invitation. I shuffled up the stairs and lead him toward the stairway to the third floor. We'd put a playroom there when we redid the place, making it a good size and out of the way. I got to the landing outside the playroom, and I turned on Remi.

"My first rule is when we are together you are not allowed clothes." He did his best to keep his expression blank, but his lips twitched up.

I opened the door and stepped into the room. It wasn't massive, but it had everything I could need easily at hand. He stopped at the threshold and pulled his shirt over his head. Folding it, he set it aside before he toed out of his sneakers and pushed out of his designer tattered jeans. Those were folded too and went with the shirt on the floor next to the door. He wore nothing under the jeans, and his cock was already standing straight out from his hips.

"Next rule is you will always remain hard in this room unless I tell you otherwise." My eyes landed soundly on the far end of my table of toys. It had been a very long time since I played without limits, and I could already taste it in the depraved corners of my mind.

He kept his gaze lowered, and his eyes scanned the wall of toys as he walked to the center of the room and dropped to his knees. I stifled the groan that threatened to leave my lips. He was too good.

I picked up my favorite crop, one that was reinforced with steel. I held it with both hands behind my back as I inspected him. He had two full sleeves of individual pictures woven together, as well as other tattoos littering his torso and legs. They were beautiful, aligned with his muscle like his body was designed for them. He was on the thin side of what I normally liked, but not twink-y. A worry line creased his brow, and the stress showed in his tight shoulders. He looked exactly like he'd said, a man who'd denied himself far too long.

I smacked the crop into my hand absentmindedly as I made a circle around him. I scanned the room, thinking. I hated the same old type of play. It got boring. Instead, I wanted to feel the pain dripping off him, and to taste his fear on my lips. It needed to be nothing he'd ever experienced.

My gaze landed on one of the road construction horses I had stolen off the side of the road one night many years ago. I'd turned it into a toy. It had shackles drilled into the base, cold, unforgiving steel cuffs, and the wood itself was rough because the orange paint had worn thin in many of the places. If Remi struggled too much, it would give him a wicked burn on his hips and up his abs. He'd begged for pain, and I was in the mood to give it to him.

I let my eyes fall closed and inhaled. It would be too easy to lose it. I was going to have to keep myself reined in. Taking a deep breath, I picked up the horse and stood it in the center of the room.

"Come here."

He did so without objection, pressing his hip bones into the harsh wood. I bent to shackle his ankles in place. I saw Masen there for a second, and I turned my back to him. If I could get through this, maybe it would be easier. There were so many maybes. Maybe I should get the fuck over it already.

"Extend your arms and grab the top of the horse," I said after setting the other horse about the right distance from him.

Remi took my turned back as disinterest, and I could read the disappointment on him. Good. He needed to be knocked down a few pegs. He glanced over at the crude piece of wood. His fingers barely curled around the top of it. I took some twine and looped it around his wrists, securing them. I could easily undo them, but it would be hard to escape, not that I was expecting him to try.

"We are going to play a game, and if you are what you claim to be, you shall earn your release. If not, you will be punished."

He groaned, long and low.

"Now, I want you to keep your back straight for me like a good boy. I don't want to see you sag in the middle."

"Yes, Master," he purred, adjusting his grip.

I ran the crop down his spine then around the curve of his ass. With his legs spread as they were, I had a glimpse of his tight entrance. I was going to have to keep reminding myself he wasn't mine to take. That he was only a toy to be beaten and sent home to his subs.

"Good boy." Thinking better of it, I laid the crop aside and moved to stand where he could watch me. I tugged at my belt, releasing it from its clasp before pulling it free from the loops of my jeans. I halved it and smacked the thick leather into my hand. The sound cracked through the room, and he didn't flinch. He looked hungry for it.

"I know you claim not to have a safe word, and that's fine, but for my own peace of mind, say 'forfeit' if you need things to stop."

"Forfeit?" For the first time, he broke out of the slave-like trance and looked me in the eyes.

I stared right back at him.

He nodded.

"So if you need to use your safe word, you're forfeiting

our agreement." I didn't even try to hide the sadistic smirk I wore. He wanted the full dominant effect, so I would give it to him, down to shaming even his claim of not needing a safe word.

Another groan rolled through him, and he squirmed, whispering, "Yes, Master."

I came up behind him and gave in to the urge to run my hands over the curve of his ass, and I had to drag my teeth over my lip, resisting my desire to do more. Instead I lifted the belt over my head and across my face as I widened my stance, getting ready. I waited, counting off ticks in my head. I could hear the pace of his heart and how it quickened and see the pulse in his neck. I loved making a boy wait for it when they knew what was coming. When I got to twenty, I snapped my arm down, laying the leather directly over his bare cheeks. The combined sounds of both the belt meeting skin and his erotic moan made a low groan build at the base of my throat. I stifled it, not wanting him to know he was getting to me.

Without hesitation, I struck him again and again till a light sheen of sweat caressed the back of my shoulders and my brow. Grabbing my shirt at the back of the neck, I tugged it off and wiped my face with it before casting it aside. The strain was evident in Remi's glistening body. His breathing hitched, but his back remained straight. I ghosted my fingers over him then grabbed him by the back of the hair, his green eyes meeting mine.

"Good boy, you're so beautiful when you submit."

The struggle fled his face at my words. "Thank you, Master."

I had a wall of toys, but none of them appealed to me. I wanted my hands to be the means of his pain. I smacked over his already reddened cheek and left my hand to linger there, massaging over his flesh. He moaned softly, and I pulled back, not allowing myself to push my control. I hit him again and again until my fingers hurt and my arm ached. His sounds filled the room, and I knew he'd have trouble sitting for days, but I wasn't done.

I had a new toy, well, an unused toy. It had been sitting in a drawer for years waiting for someone who would never come home. I slid open the drawer and ran my hands over the box that sat inside. It had been handmade to fit me. I pulled on the glove and flexed my fingers. Tiny spikes were riveted through the soft leather all over the palm.

They weren't sharp enough to break the skin, but they would leave a patchwork of marks embedded in his flesh. The idea left me hard and breathless. He would go home and carry the marks for days. He would see them in the mirror, and he would want more. An image of him pleasuring himself because of them filled my mind. I groaned low in my throat.

"Are you going to jack off over there as mental torture?" Remi's voice was raspy, even if he was trying to fight it.

"I was thinking about it, but my new toy will be so much more fun to use on you." I turned, holding up my gloved hand so it hit the light, revealing all the tiny spikes.

He whimpered, and the sound was music to my ears. I reached around him and gripped his cock, lightly stroking over him with the blunted metal. His breathing hitched, and his eyes rolled back in his head. He kept his back straight, but he let his head fall to hang between his shoulders.

I pulled my hand away, not wanting to push things too far.

"Please," he gasped. "Don't stop. Let me come."

My dick strained against my jeans. It took every ounce of control I had to step away from him. Every cell in my body revolted and tried to get back to him. This went far past desire. It was otherworldly what I felt for him. I took my need out on his abused ass. Smacking his soft skin over and over with the glove, letting myself go for the first time in a year.

When I stopped, both of us were breathing hard, and I leaned in closer to inhale his scent. It was clean and salty. I wanted him.

I tugged my knife out of my back pocket and cut the ties that held his hands. He almost fell forward as his fingers slipped off the horse. I caught him around the middle and helped him off. His abs were red and chaffed from the wood. When I lowered him to his knees, he fell at my feet, resting the side of his face on my boots. I looked away and dropped the glove next to him.

"You clean off all the toys we use—with your tongue."

"Yes, Master." Not a moment of hesitation.

I could hear the low groan from his lips as he picked up the leather and painfully slowly licked it from end to end, then reversed it and did the same. As he neared the end of it, he looked up, and images of how his tongue would feel on me flashed through my mind. My face hardened, and his smirk returned. He kept my eyes as he licked it over, paying special attention.

Evil little fuck. He knew he was pushing my buttons, but I'd asked for this.

"When you push my buttons, you will be punished."

"Then you're going to be punishing me a lot."

DANTE

"So be it." Even as I said the words, I had a feeling he would keep pushing my buttons because he wanted the punishment. We both wanted it.

He liked the back and forth as much as I did. If he thought it was in his best interest to misbehave to get my hand, he would in an instant. But I was better at this game than he was, and I would find ways to punish him that were pure torture to his mind. He lifted the glove up for my inspection, and I snatched it from him and set it aside.

"Go lay out on my table. I am going to give you welts you can see in the mirror when you leave here."

He sat back on his heels and looked up at me, fingers absentmindedly stroking down his chest as he pushed to stand. He turned his back on me, showing off his ass before he laid out on the stainless steel I used as my table. There were places for cuffs and other bindings there, but I didn't need them.

"I want you to hold on to the edges of the table and spread your knees wide. Don't let go, do you understand me?"

He nodded and as I got near, he reached out to skim his fingers over my leg.

"Do you think I meant later?" I snapped, stepping back out of his grasp?

He shook his head. I turned my back on him and lit a row of candles. The flames flickered and reflected off the centers of his wide eyes when I turned back around. He had taken the position, and his dick was standing straight in the air with his knees pulled up and laid out to the side, giving me plenty of room to work with.

I held his gaze as I turned the candle between his thighs. He braced for the searing pain of the wax, but it never came. From the angle I stood, it looked like I was pouring the wax on his balls, but in reality it hit the metal between his thighs an inch away. His chest heaved when he realized this fact, and he searched my face. I stepped around the table and lowered my face so it was an inch from his.

"When you disobey me, it won't always be pain you get. I know what you want, and denial can be more harsh than even my cane." My breath blew over his lips, and I could see in his eyes that he believed me.

"Please, Master..."

I moved the candle next to his face and let him watch the wax drip down on the slab. He squirmed and groaned as his fingers tightened on the metal. He pushed his feet against the steel and lifted his hips off of it as a low whimper left his lips. He was milking reactions from me, and I tried my best to shut them off. He was already too good at pushing my buttons. I didn't want him to have the satisfaction.

"Please what?"

"Anything... touch me," his words were barely more than a whisper, and I set the candle next to his head.

"You won't get anything, even your own release without begging. I want to hear it all."

"Yes, Master." He pursed his lips for a moment, and I waited. "I want the wax, please, I'll do whatever you want. Anything."

"Anything is a dangerous word with me."

"I know, but you're worth it."

I arched one of my brows. "Am I? And how would you know that?"

"I've been watching you for a few weeks. Never enough for you to notice me until last night, but I've wanted you." His voice was low. There was need there.

I searched my memory for a glimpse of him, but I had nothing. How could he have hidden so well in plain sight? "How?"

"I didn't make a scene like I did last night. I couldn't wait any longer. I knew it was you. I had to take the chance." He searched my face for approval.

I didn't give it to him. "If you want the wax, I want a show. I want to watch you fuck your hand."

"Now, Master?"

"Yes, good boy for asking." I tightened my grip on the candle so I wouldn't touch him.

He released his right hand and brought it down to his cock. Wrapping his fingers around his thick base, he watched me as he stroked over himself. I turned the candle over his chest so he could see a drop of wax form on the edge.

He moaned and threw his head back, cracking it against the slab. He started pleading incoherently, and every sound he made went straight to my cock. It hardened behind my zipper, painfully so. I counted to ten before I let the first drop of wax fall, and I moved to trail it down the center line of his abs. That really got him going, and he started pumping into his hand, lifting his ass with each stroke, slamming his fist over himself.

"You do not get to release here unless I've given you permission." I growled when I saw his body clench and stiffen as he brought himself to the brink.

His hand rolled over his cock, and a clear drop of fluid seeped from his slit. I licked over my lips, barely resisting the urge to bend and lick it off.

"Here in your playroom?" His voice was strained and laced with pleasure.

"I can't tell you what to do with your submissive, but in the great state of Louisiana. When you are here you are submissive to me, as long as this lasts." I moved between his legs and let the warm wax drip down his sac. His moans were unmistakable. I could tell he was floating.

"Yes, Master," his words were half groaned. "I'll be here for work at least one week a month."

"Do you have an objection to my rules, boy?" I snatched the crop off the table behind me and swung it underhand to smack his sac over the hardening wax.

He howled in pain, and his dick jumped. It was written in every movement that he was holding off his release. His Adam's apple bobbed in his throat, and he pressed his eyes closed for a moment.

His palm faltered, and he opened his eyes to meet my gaze. "As long as this lasts? Do you want this to continue?" He sounded so hopeful. I thought about dashing those hopes, but I couldn't really have said no if I wanted to. I needed him.

"You please me—and I don't want someone who will get attached—so come to me when you need me."

"It will be my pleasure, Master."

He was too perfect. I was waiting for the fissure. I had to find a flaw so I wouldn't get attached. I calmed myself and grabbed a fresh candle. This time I held it high, and his eyes followed, but I didn't move to pour it. I made him wait.

"You have ten seconds to come when I order you to, and if you don't come within that amount of time, you don't get to." His chest heaved with every breath, and his hand started to slow on his cock.

I brought the crop down over his pec. "Don't slow it down. How fucking worthless are you? Learn control, boy."

"I'm going to be allowed to come?" There was pleading in his tone.

"I never said that." I poured the hot liquid around the base of his cock, and it pooled in the trimmed patch of hair he had there. Every time his hand slammed down, he hit the wax.

His body arched off the metal, and his muscles tensed. I could hear his sharp breaths, causing his heart to beat faster, and mine matched it, but I stayed calm on the exterior. Long moans parted his mouth. I pressed my eyes closed.

"Dante." The way he said my name was pure sin. No one called me that. It was always Bane or other choice words. I loved the way it rolled off his tongue in a whimper.

"Come for me," I ordered, unable to take my eyes off him.

His hand flew over himself with abandon, and he followed the rule to the letter, letting himself explode all over his abs and his hand. I could see how powerful, the release was written in his body. He gasped silently as his eyes rolled back in his head. He jerked, and his cock pulsed with one final intense wave, and the last of his release

dripped down his head. I bent forward but stopped myself.
He's not yours, Dante.

I wasn't fit to be with anyone else. It was better this
way. I got what I needed and didn't have to involve
feelings. Maybe if I told myself the lie I would start to
believe it.

"You will eat every drop of that." *So I don't give into
the temptation to taste you,* I finished in my head.

He brought his fingers up to his lips and licked them
clean. I had to turn away and take a breath, noticing for the
first time that his tongue was pierced. I grabbed my
aftercare kit and set it on the table next to him. He would
have welts at the very least from all of the play, and I
wanted to treat the burns from the wax.

He sat up and shook his head. "You can't." He got down
and dropped to his knees. "I'm sorry, Master."

My brow creased in the center as I stepped around the
table to pinch his chin between my index finger and thumb,
forcing him to look up at me. "I can't treat your wounds?"

He shook his head, and the sadness behind his eyes hit
me like a knife to the chest. "No, not even that. My
submissive was clear about it."

My hand fell away from his face and dropped to my
side. It took every ounce of my control to rein in my
temper. "Then you are dismissed. You know where to find
me when you are in town again."

He climbed to his feet and turned his back, leaving the
playroom to collect his clothes. His back was riddled with
angry red marks from my belt, and his front was covered
in tiny blisters from the wax. The sight of my marks on him
stirred a primal desire for ownership. One I hadn't felt in
years. I flicked my tongue over my teeth, resisting the urge
to put a permanent mark where everyone would see it. That

kind of mark meant so much more than I was allowed with him.

I was awake long after he left, lying back in bed staring up at the ceiling. Sleep rarely came to me easily. I don't know why I even tried anymore. I should have gone for a run instead. When I let two or so days pass and ran myself to exhaustion, I usually could get in more than an hour or two.

I closed my eyes, begging for sleep when I heard the latch on my door click. The stairs creaked with footsteps. I resisted the urge to sit up in bed. If it was someone coming to kill me, it was in my best interest to fake sleep and catch them off guard. The figure's shadow darkened the doorway, but it was too dark to make out his features. My lip curled back in a silent snarl. I would kill him.

DANTE

But I realized quickly it wasn't the ghost who haunted my nights. This was a new ghost entirely. He'd come back. I stayed still, and he crossed the room to stand over me, looking down on me for a long minute before sitting on the edge of the bed.

"Dante," he whispered, and there was an edge to his voice. "Are you still awake?" He was soft and not at all the playful, fighting submissive I had seen earlier.

"I am." The words were so unlike me, but they flooded out of my lips before I could stop them. "Are you hurt?" I sat up, setting a hand on his thigh, squeezing it lightly.

"I can't keep my promise." He laid his hand over mine and dropped his forehead to the crook of my neck. "I just can't." His voice broke.

"Which?" My thumb stroked over the back of his hand.

Don't do it. What, I wasn't even sure, but I repeated the line to myself.

"I need—" He exhaled out a sigh then picked his head up and turned to bring his knee up onto the bed so he was facing me. "I need—" There was so much behind his pause. It was everything while saying nothing at all. "—I need aftercare. It's not right without it. I feel like I'm trapped in the high without the rush."

"It is one of the most important parts of coming down. I was shocked your submissive would deny you it." I traced over his fingers.

"I want to come down in your arms, Master." He let out a shaky breath. "I want to sleep beside you. It may be what I need more than the pain, and I've never realized it."

I leaned in and took his hand in mine, but he pulled it back like I'd burned him.

"Fuck. Pain used to be enough. I can't control it anymore." His head slumped forward, and he scrubbed a hand over his face.

I took his hand from his face and held it in mine again. "You need to be weak." It would be too easy to fall for him. I felt it in every look, every minute I spent with him. I couldn't let myself go there again.

"I need to be owned. I need someone to be strong for me." He swallowed, hiding the need in his voice. "He doesn't want me to form a bond with anyone, and he knows how much that part means to him, but..." he trailed off, but he didn't have to finish. I knew that to a submissive, the tender side of the dominant as well as the praise was what they needed most.

Few were like him and got off on the pain. No, not only got off on it, but needed it to function like he did. Physical pain was a way to cleanse one's self of the mental anguish, but that was sexual as much as mental. The aftercare was the rebuilding after the breaking. Without it, there was nothing. I wanted it as badly as he did. It was arguably the more important half of it, and we both knew that, but he was right, it was also how the bond was formed.

"Have you collared your submissive?" I asked, not really sure I wanted the answer.

He shook his head. "He wanted the rings, but I told him I could never be with just one person. He won't ever just be with me either."

He didn't have to say it. I knew why. "Because you're hiding what you are." I was starting to suspect the dominant was all for show.

There wasn't a hint of denial on his face.

"Get permission." I slid out of bed and went to my master bath, flipping on the light. He didn't move from where he sat, but his gaze never left me as I gathered supplies.

"Master?"

I looked back over my shoulder from where I stood in the bathroom. "If you think I'm kidding, get out. You will get permission."

"I don't need it." He set his jaw and stood up, crossing his arms over his chest. It was almost cute.

I turned on him. "Then why didn't you stay? Or let me fuck you?"

Reluctantly, he pulled his phone out of his pocket and stared at it. He swallowed hard, pushing a button before bringing it to his ear.

"Kai," he paused. "Yeah, I know it's late." He rubbed a hand over the back of his neck and paced. I'd never had a jealous bone in my body, but here I was feeling a twitch of it for this man he called, who he went home to.

I needed to shut it down. I had to protect myself.

"I have to do this for me. It's not the same without the aftercare. It won't ever be the same. You know what you get out of it, do you really want to deny me it?"

He listened for a few minutes.

"Believe me, I'll be better when I come back." He hung up the phone and tossed it on the nightstand before looking me in the eyes. "It's done."

"You got permission from all of them? That was quick."

He held up his hand and touched his thumb to the ring he wore. "Kai is the only one who matters. The rest I just play with at the club. Kai has a collared submissive of his own to worry about."

Shock hit me hard. "He's a switch, but you can't be?"

"He's my business partner. People assume we share his submissive since he's a switch as well. They don't know about him either."

Every detail I pulled out of him tangled the plot. He didn't have baggage. He had a whole fucking plane full of bags kept in their own neat little suitcases, and I'd put money on the fact he liked to keep them all separate.

His little world was way too complicated. "I don't want to know. You are here for the night to serve a purpose." I turned my back, gathering the rest of the things I needed. I exhaled slowly and then spoke again, keeping all emotion from my voice. "Lay out on the bed and let me take care of that to start with."

He grabbed his shirt by the back of the neck and pulled it off, this time tossing it to the floor without folding it. He stretched out on my sheets, and damn, did he look good there. The long johns he'd changed into sat low on his hips, showing off the dimples in his lower back. I resisted touching him, instead laying the things out on the bed.

The low light cast shadows over his beautiful body as I came up behind him, grabbing the bottle of ointment to pour some on my fingers. Gently, I spread it over the worst of his welts and marks. Taking advantage of what was before me, I used the opportunity to trace my hands over the lines of his muscles down to the hem of his pants. The ink he had complimented him like he'd been hand painted by a master. I suddenly wished he was naked again.

I took the vitamin K cream and spread it in the few places the skin had broken, as he let slip a barely audible moan. I pressed my eyes closed. I wanted to keep my hands on him, and it took every ounce of willpower I had to not do more. He shimmied on the bed a little and hooked his thumbs in the back of his pants, inching them down.

"My ass has the worst of it." He looked back over his shoulder again, and his eyes betrayed him.

"Now you're taunting me." I growled, getting out more cream against my better judgement.

"Look for yourself," he said slyly.

One look and my cock was stiff behind my shorts. My breath caught in my throat, and I rubbed my palms over his cheeks, pressing my eyes shut so I didn't have to look at him. Desire hit me and coursed through my veins until I was stricken with need for him.

"Roll over, and let me get some aloe on the burns." My words were forced, but he didn't seem to notice.

He looked back over his shoulder at me again and shook his head. "I want some of the marks to stay longer."

I knew why, but I wanted to hear the words from his lips. "Oh?" He started to shrug, but my lips curled back in a snarl. "Say it, boy."

"Because I am going to get off to the sight of them after I leave."

I grabbed myself, and I was glad he was laying on his stomach and couldn't see how much he affected me. I laid down next to him, finding his eyes half closed.

I had to have him.

SEVEN

DANTE

The sun was much higher in the sky than I expected, casting broken rays through my blinds when I woke. I blinked away the foggy feeling in my mind and stretched. I felt—rested. It had been so long since I'd slept. I grunted, lifting my arms over my head to stretch, flexing and rolling side to side before noticing the bare spot in the bed next to me. I traced my fingers over the wrinkles in the sheets and dropped my head to inhale the scent lingering on the pillow. *Him.* I could breathe easier. The crushing weight that had sat on my chest for months eased. When had he left?

It was better he was gone. I slipped a hand into my shorts and pressed the heel of my hand into my cock. It was hard to control myself in the morning— I stopped myself. I couldn't linger there in his memory, any memory. It had been a good distraction but a distraction nonetheless.

The clock read after nine when I looked over. "Shit."

I had a meeting in an hour. I rolled out of bed, hitting the floor in the plank position and did push-ups to rid my mind of the cobwebs. After a shower I felt more like myself. I needed to be on my game this morning. I was running out of willing men. I had everything else, so if all went according to plan, we would both make money, and I would bring some much needed funds into the poorest in my employment, funneling that cash into jobs at my bar for the destitute. As it stood, I gave as many people jobs as I could afford to, without shutting the place down, but I needed to do more.

I dressed in my nicest pair of jeans and a gray button up, with a blue and silver tie Liv had told me brought out my eyes. Ties had only one use in my mind, and looking pretty wasn't it. I put on the belt I'd used the night before, running my fingers over it as the memory saturated my mind.

When I got to the bar, I ditched my bike by the back door and found Liv was standing in the upstairs stockroom, looking over order sheets. She looked up at me with her dark eyes and a smile on her lips.

"How are you?" She moved to brush her fingers down my arm, but I stepped back out of reach. The light touch reminded me of Masen and how he couldn't keep his hands off me. Maybe I hadn't noticed Liv did the same before, but now it was like a wound that never quite closed.

"I slept."

She narrowed her gaze, leaving her hand outstretched for a moment before pushing her red-brown hair behind her ear. It curled into ringlets at the ends, and she wore it almost to her ass. "Drugs?" She sighed. "I'm going to smack Rick—"

I cut her off with the shake of my head. "I didn't take anything."

A tiny winkle formed in her brow, and I could see the wheels turning. I didn't have to answer to her or anyone.

"I'm going to go to my office and wait for Caci."

"He's already there, Bane."

Fifteen minutes early, I liked him already. My father

had always said on time was late. I backed out of the storeroom, passing the kitchen. The floors were dark hardwood, and the walls were a forest green, fitting the backwoods southern feel of the state and perhaps intensifying my redneck image. The place was dimly lit for 'atmosphere,' but I had a better reason, giving folks many dark corners to sneak off to. A man leaned back casually in one of the leather chairs facing my desk with his fingers tented.

There wasn't a wrinkle in his charcoal designer shirt despite the angle he sat at. The color complemented his tanned skin tone, which didn't surprise me since he called Vegas home. His dark hair was cut in that messy chic way rich people paid hairdressers out the ass for.

I closed the door and inhaled as I walked around the large, hand-carved beast of a desk that was the centerpiece of the room. Turning to take a seat, my line of sight landed on him, and I had to struggle to withhold a gasp.

"Remi," I fought to keep my tone even. He had changed, not the shell of a broken and needy man who begged at my feet the night before. He was all affluent dominance, almost smug, like the entirety of his air had morphed.

"Dante." He wore a knowing glint in his eyes.

"Mr. Caci, Remington Caci." The words left my mouth with more calm than I felt.

He came from an old crime family, and I shook my head, not having been in the headspace to connect the dots yesterday. There were more reasons than he'd let on why he didn't want anyone to see him as submissive. It wouldn't just have been bad for business, it would have been detrimental if it was known he liked to take a beating, or a dick in the ass for that matter.

I scoffed. It seems he'd done his own research and

found more uses for me than the business avenue.

"You should have stayed. I could've made you breakfast." I reached into my desk and took out a bottle of Jack and two glasses, masking all of my surprise.

"And ruined the chance to put you off guard?" He took the glass I offered and set it on the edge of the desk. He looked relaxed and sated.

"Touché. But I'm harder to rock than that, handsome."

His gaze dropped as his lips turned up. "Hard as a rock. You should have taken care of that before the meeting."

"Did I say I hadn't?" I set my hand over the crotch of my jeans and smiled at him. "The image of you on your knees does things to me."

His lip turned up in the barest hint of a snarl, but his gaze stayed where I put my hand. "Cocky fucker. You're used to the world bending for you."

"It does. You seemed to enjoy it. No?" I slid my fingers over my half-hard length before letting them fall away.

"That ego needs to be taken down a peg or two." The words were dry yet playful.

"Going to do it before or after you beg me to beat you?"

"Before... after... and maybe even during, just to make your life hell. But you'll keep coming back for more, Dante." His hand went to his tie, and he smoothed it down as his eyes dropped to the material around my neck. He crossed his ankle over his knee as he sat back in the chair, comfortable in my office. "Now tell me why we should do business together."

Confidence exuded from his pores. If I had thought it hard to believe he was anything but submissive last night, I saw it now. Years of practice faking it.

"Because we both stand to make money, and your market is tapped out in Vegas. There is nowhere for you to go out there. I've done my research. You could make a whole lot more cash here." I tossed the binder of spreadsheets across the desk to him. "There is money in this city, you know it or you wouldn't be here. Cut the bullshit."

He caught the binder and set it on the desk unopened. "What's stopping me from taking this, opening up my own place, and cutting you out?"

My lip twitched as I repressed a snarl. "You think my people will come if you cross me?"

He half shrugged, but I knew he got my point. "Nor do I want to live in this hell hole. No offense."

"None taken."

A smile flickered at the corners of his lips. "I see you've done your research, but tell me, why me?"

"Because I think you're underrated. I don't just do my research on my business ventures, I do it on people as well. I know you get things done, and you work hard. It's becoming increasingly difficult for you to keep underground fights in Vegas. What better place to move than the haunted city of sin?"

"NOLA has the same laws we do in Vegas. I was thinking of branching out toward the west coast."

"People don't go to the gold coast to bet. They go there to drink and lay on the beach."

"Or maybe it's just an untapped market." He adjusted his seat, almost taunting me with his jabs.

"Are you willing to lose money on that chance? Or will you make a smart move with someone who already has a bar packed nightly?" I sat back and watched him, keeping my expression neutral.

"But I'd make half the money." He folded his hands in his lap and stared back. If he carried half the respect I thought he did, I could see why he thought he had a lot to lose by telling his circle he was submitting.

"Half of something is a lot better than half of nothing." I kept all but the faintest edge out of my voice. "Plus, you're not risking any capital."

He got to his feet and slid his hands into his pockets. "Show me where because this place doesn't look like it will work to me. You've got no structure, and with that huge damn bar in the middle of your floor plan, I don't see it."

I laughed at him as I stepped around my desk, leading the way down the hall to the locked door at the end. I punched a code into the pad beside it and waited for the click. When it sounded, I pushed the door open and flipped on the light. He took the stairs two at a time and I followed, exiting to the large room in the basement. It was the same square footage as the bar above, but it was empty except for a newly constructed ring in the center. The walls were whitewashed cinder blocks, and there was a secure steel reinforced room off to one side with bulletproof glass, which handled the gambling side of things as well as the bar.

He spun in place giving a low whistle as he took it all in. "Bleachers. Simple, but it gets the job done."

He walked around, and I kept my place, letting him explore. I had a feeling he'd been here before, even if he said otherwise. He did say he'd been watching me for sometime.

"There is no bar," he said after he had made the full turn.

"I have girls serving. It's sexier." I licked over my lips. "Imagine ringside girls in short skirts with trays. "

"Does nothing for me." I could feel him undressing me with his eyes, and I stood there giving him a good view for it. "They are going to haul drinks from upstairs?" He took a step forward, closing almost all the distance between us. "Bad business plan."

I let him linger in my space for a moment before turning on my heel. I entered another code which made the door slide into the wall. It led into a hall. I bypassed the locked door which led into the secure gambling intake, heading for the large service bar. Everything was brand new, state of the art, and clean. I had an amazing staff. We just couldn't use the space as often as I wanted since we lacked fighters. It was a good idea. Underground fighting was all the rage at the moment. I could tell he was impressed.

"You have this thought out. That much is clear." He walked back toward the ring. Laying his hands on the ropes, he parted them and stepped inside.

"I've been doing this for years. I just need fresh meat."

He turned on me and waited. I followed him into the ring as he took off his suit coat and laid it over the ropes to one side. He loosened the knot on his tie as our eyes met. I arched a brow. The bright fluorescent lights cast shadows on his face, giving him an almost sadistic look. I could see it all: him tied to the ropes, bound and bloody after a fight with me. I would take all the damage he'd done with his fists out on his ass. There was nothing that made me harder than a fight. My veins stood out on my arms, and I rubbed my hand over them so he wouldn't notice.

"Your assistant told me you were going to fight as well. Are you telling me I should send you a guy without a demonstration?" His tongue ran over his teeth, and I tore my gaze away from the knot at his throat before my growing erection gave me away. "You could be useless, and I could be wasting my time."

He pushed every button like he knew me. "Looking to

get your ass kicked, boy?" My words dripped with condescension.

Unlike him, I left my tie where it was, half hoping I would end up choked with it. When his eyes dropped to it, I thought he had the same idea.

"That cocky?" He kept his hands at his sides as he approached.

"It's not cocky when you can back it up. Let's see if you can even hit me." I smacked his face and backed off before he could think to return the blow.

Bouncing from foot to foot to warm up a little, I rolled my neck and watched him. I saw the flair of arousal in his eyes. He stalked closer, and by the way he walked, I could tell he was a boxer. We carried ourselves differently. He kept his hands loosely in front of his face, not quite in fists, throwing a left when he got in range. I dodged as he jabbed with his right a split second later. I was ready for it, but he was quick, and we both landed blows at the same time. The burn from where his fist landed spread over my flesh, and I groaned, even more aroused. Remi pulled back and clenched his teeth, hiding the pain well.

The air was thick between us as we sized each other up. This wouldn't end well. We both liked pain too much. I had to change the way I fought. Most bare-knuckle fighting in an underground ring like this was won on strategy. I was on him, not giving him a second to recover. I threw blow after blow, landing most of them and not bothering to block the ones he returned. I would win this fight a lot easier going quick and hard. My knuckles hit hard flesh and were soon bloodied. My body could take a lot more damage than his could, and he hit with less power than I did. Every strike of his made me harder as it bruised and tore my skin. He fed the masochistic beast, and it only made me want him more.

A snarl ripped from his throat when I landed another hard blow to his jaw. His head cocked to the side, and blood splattered over the floor. I thought I had him, but I was so wrong. He dove at me. I wasn't expecting the blatant and desperate move. All the air rushed out of my lungs as I slammed into the unforgiving floor with him on top of me. Part of me wanted to roll him under me and fuck him into the mat, and the other part wanted to finish what we'd started. It was a war between my cock and my anger.

I tried to suck a breath, but my chest wouldn't expand.

Remi gripped my tie with one hand, reeling it in, tightening the knot into my throat, while his other fist went for a swift jab to the nose. The crack resonated through my skull and made my vision blur for a moment. I could taste the blood dripping down the back of my throat, but it only served to fuel me.

I closed my left fist and slammed it into his flank. He laughed. He fucking laughed.

"Fuck it." I swung my fist out, hitting any part of him I could connect with as I worked on getting myself into a position to gain the advantage. We rolled and fought, tangling limbs and flailing arms, beating each other bloody. He rubbed his sweat covered skin over mine in an almost pointed way. I grew harder by the minute. My anger turned to lust. It would be so easy to pin him to the mat and then sink inside him.

In one swift motion, I flipped him under me, landing with the full force of my body weight on top of him. Both my hands fisted in his shirt as he kept trying to hit me, landing blows to my arms and shoulders I barely felt. I forced his thighs apart, pushing my knees between them, spreading him wide open. I lowered my head and snarled low and throaty in his face.

"Still want to keep playing, doll?"

His eyes flashed with something like he was warring between his two halves. "Yes, Master," he gasped at last, and if I hadn't been hard already, I would have been in an instant. Between the scent of our mingling blood, and the show of submission, I needed him. I rubbed my stubbled jaw over his cheek then pulled back to look him in the eyes, gauging his reaction before I did anything stupid.

He bucked his hips up into mine. I pressed down with my body, pinning his ass to the floor. He did nothing to hide his erection.

"Shit," I muttered.

The desire to grind into him overwhelmed me. It would be so easy.

I wanted to keep up the pretense of the contest. I wanted to fuck him into the mat, with him struggling and fighting back the whole time. I pulled back, breathing heavily, not from exertion.

He fisted a hand in my shirt and dragged me back down. I thought I imagined it—but then he rocked into me.

"We should go talk numbers and how soon you can arrange fights for me." My tone was more even than I felt.

He tilted his hips this time purposefully, and I could feel every subtle movement as the thin fabric between us did little to hide his arousal. "No more business talk today." He leaned up, and I anticipated his kiss, but instead he rubbed his jaw over my collarbone. With a groan, I collapsed over him. He had accidentally stumbled on one of my few weaknesses. He fisted a hand in my hair and pulled my face up.

"Like that do you?" The grin he wore was as wicked as him picking up his head to rub over the spot again.

Every exchange with him would be a battle.

"Fuck you," I growled, but he was impossible to resist, and he knew it.

"If you insist," he said dryly.

I lunged back to smack him, ripping my shirt from his grip as I did. His head cocked to the side with the force of the blow, and his hand fell from my shirt, going to his already red cheek. His cock twitched between us, and I rolled off of him, pushing my hands into my hair.

"I have the feeling you're going to be the death of me," I said.

"At least you'll enjoy the ride."

EIGHT

DANTE

"Come get a drink with me."

I looked over at him, still lying there rubbing his cheek. "Why do I think I'm going to regret this?"

"Because you probably will." He got to his feet and grabbed his jacket, draping it over his arm. I laid looking up at the ceiling. I had two paths in front of me, and I knew I'd regret going either way.

Remi offered me his hand, and I took it, letting him haul me to my feet.

"What are you thinking?"

"Have you ever wondered what direction your life would take if you'd chosen another path?" I wasn't about to answer his question. It was too much of myself to give away.

His pupils flashed wider, betraying him for a second before he got himself under control. "Every day," he said under his breath. He, for the first time, looked weak standing there.

I stepped into him, wanting to put my arm around him, but his entire demeanor changed. He'd hidden it all away. It was too late, though. I'd seen it, and I wanted to see more.

"Are we going upstairs?"

He shook his head. "No, I want to go someplace you don't rule."

"Rule?" He was entirely right, but I hid my smile.

"Yes, rule, and don't give me one of your innocent looks. People worship you here. I want to go to a place you're unknown." He started to fix his tie, and I wanted to bat his hand away. He looked sexy all dressed up, but there was something telling about disheveled Remi.

"You'll be hard pressed to find it."

He laughed, and I wasn't sure if I should be amused or terrified by his calling my bluff.

After we'd cleaned up, he took my hand, and I let him lead me up the back staircase and out into the parking lot. It was still early, but a light drizzle had set in, darkening the sky. A horrendous, blinding yellow Jeep sat in the parking lot, and I stopped when he walked in its direction. He stopped short, tugging at my hand. A glance over his shoulder at my horrified face had him pause.

"What?"

"I am not getting in that monstrosity."

His lips twisted up at the corners. "Why not?"

"Nothing yellow is respectable."

He burst out laughing and curled at the middle like he was having a fit.

"I fail to see anything funny." I crossed my arms over my chest, and he kept going. Three minutes later he had tears in his eyes and was gasping for air. "Are you finished?"

"Maybe?" He broke out laughing again, and I threw up my hands. "Come back," he said as I turned to walk toward my bike.

I paused, more annoyed with myself for letting him push my buttons than him for laughing. "Yes?"

"Get in the Jeep."

I scoffed. "Good luck with that line."

"Come on, Dante. I want it to be a surprise."

"Can't you surprise me by pointing me in the right direction?"

It was his turn to cross his arms and stand defiantly.

I took a step back toward him. "What made you accept a yellow Jeep from the rental car company, anyway? Were they all out of everything else?"

A crease formed in his brow, and a low growl rumbled in his chest.

"I can't imagine it was the price. I'm sure you could have requested a Rolls if you wanted it."

His scowl deepened. I was clearly hitting a nerve, even if it was unintentional.

"Are you strapped for cash? You could have asked me to come pick you up."

Rage flashed in his eyes, causing a spark to run down my spine. My body was alight with arousal. I realized I loved getting to him, loved figuring him out.

I was fucked.

"I requested it," he said through gritted teeth.

My mouth dropped open. I was utterly shocked. I thought I read him well. "How did I miss this yesterday?"

"You were too busy staring at your assistant's ass while unloading the truck to notice when I left."

I nodded, and he rolled his eyes.

"You don't have to be jealous. I won't ever touch her."

He looked genuinely surprised. "I'm shocked you haven't already."

"She's too good at her job, and I wouldn't want to lose

her."

"Ah." He pulled open the door to the yellow thing. "Coming?"

I opened the passenger side door. "I am humoring you because you amuse me, and I want to see the type of place you think I won't feel at home."

"This sounds like a challenge." He shoved in the clutch and threw her into reverse.

"I own a bar devoted to illegal gambling. How do you think I feel about a good challenge?"

He studied me for a moment. "We are going to gamble today."

"I don't care for traditional gambling."

"Not what I mean." He pulled out onto the road and headed south toward the business district. "I mean a series of personal bets—between us—with high stakes."

"I have no need for your money." I turned toward him, sitting back against the door.

"Nor I yours. I'm sure we can find other things to wager."

"I'm listening."

"If I take you to a place you aren't God, I get one thing from you. Anything I want."

"Anything is a word I don't mess with lightly," I said.

NINE

REMI

I wanted this, and I wasn't even sure what I'd ask for yet, but to have a trump card was priceless. I could almost taste his answer. Victory was in my reach. I had to get him to agree, then I would decide what I wanted. It was too easy.

"If anything is too rich for your blood, how about you give me one night of any type of play I want."

"I refuse to shit on you," he deadpanned.

"You know how I feel about that." I returned with a flat look.

"What do I get in return?"

My body buzzed with nervous energy. There wasn't much I wouldn't already do for him, so the wager seemed unfair, but I wasn't about to let slip as much. "What do you want?" What he asked for would be telling anyway.

"If I win, I want information. I want the truthful answer to one question I chose to ask."

The blood froze in my veins. He'd found the chink in my armor, so to speak. "Deal."

He extended his hand, and I took it.

He leaned back and eyed me. "You think Bourbon Street scares me?"

He was trying to intimidate me. He had to be. I called his bluff. "It's not so much that I think it scares you as I would imagine your reach and hold on the life here is limited."

"You're right on me avoiding this area of town. I'm sure your research told you as much, but my influence is far and wide." He looked so smug and relaxed, but I had an advantage.

I turned onto Canal Street and pulled into the valet of the Boston Club. It was nearly impossible to get a membership to the club. Having the Caci name had its perks. His face told me nothing. He stepped out of the car and walked around the front, gesturing for me to lead the way. If he was trying to act calm until he was outed, he was doing a fantastic job of it. We walked right up to the door without a flicker in his expression.

"Shall we use your key or mine?" he asked, holding up a large ornate skeleton key made out of what I was sure was titanium.

Shit. I held onto hope he was still a nobody here. The bet had been so selective it should have been easy to pick a place he didn't reign.

"Be my guest."

He slid his key into the lock, holding my gaze as he clicked it over. His lips curled up into the hint of a sadistic grin. "Last chance to take back the bet."

Now as a man who was brought up in Vegas, I knew there were two types of raise in poker. The confident raise and the desperate raise. The confident kind was used to scare your opponents, because who would throw away more money when they had shit cards? But it was a scare tactic, one Dante was probably using on me right now.

"I don't back out of bets."

The mechanism in the door clicked, and he pressed it open. It opened into a marble hallway and lost beauty. The mansion was designed and built by famed architect James Gallier. Few got the pleasure of seeing some of his lesser known work like the Boston Club, and it lived up. The crown molding was all original and hand carved. A massive, ornate staircase drew the attention of the room. Every detail had been thought out and executed to perfection. A butler stepped around the corner and half bowed to us.

"Mister Bane, it's a pleasure to see you. The other members are currently in the card room, dining on a late lunch while playing a hand." He turned to me and nodded his hand. "The youngest generation of Caci, I presume? We haven't had the pleasure of an introduction."

I tightened my jaw so it didn't hit the floor.

"Fitz, this is Remington Caci. Remington, this is Fitz Frank Herbert, he oversees the club."

"It's a pleasure to make your acquaintance," Fitz said with an air of superiority.

"Likewise," I returned. I looked at Dante in an entirely new light. I couldn't imagine him stepping foot in this building, let alone having a membership or using it regularly.

"We have a lobster bisque, and I can pull your regular bottle, Mister Bane."

"Are we drinking?" Dante asked me like he wanted me to concede then and there.

"Why not? Since you have a regular."

"Thank you, Fitz, that would be exquisite."

"Shall I show you to the card room?"

"No, thank you." Dante took me by the arm and led me down the hall and further into the exclusive Boston club.

"My name gives me access to this type of cloak and dagger shit, but I've never cared to use this one or any other, and I would have pegged you as the same."

Dante's gray eyes searched my face, and he pursed his lips. We paused in front of a set of French doors I assumed led into the card room.

"I used to be a different person." He didn't offer anything further, and before I could question him, he pushed open the doors and stepped into the room.

It was everything I would have imagined the place to be and nothing all at the same time. There were straight back armchairs with men in cardigans smoking cigars, but it was also less formal than I would have pictured anything of its ilk would have been. There was about twenty or so people standing and sitting around tables and a few others scattered in chairs. There was soft chatter everywhere, laughter, and lots of money.

It was dripping from the walls, displayed in clothes, on hands and wrists and necks, in purses, on the tables, and even walking over the floor. There were no missed opportunities here. Dante was none of this, and yet when he walked up to the table, he was welcomed as one of their own. Claps on the back and handshakes all around.

"Tell me you're playing." An elderly gentleman goaded him.

He held up his hands, offering a warm smile. "I'm going to watch for a bit, enjoy the company."

What I could only describe as a cougar grabbed him by the arm. "Bane, I was starting to think we'd never see your face again."

"You're always welcome to come to me, Ruth."

She waved him off. "Stan and I are entirely over the bloodbath scene. At one time it made me feel alive, but now I find it so ghastly."

"It is rather brutal. What have you two moved onto, then?" He was poised and controlled as he spoke.

"We are dabbling in some long-term bets."

"I'm intrigued," he replied, and either he was feigning interest brilliantly, or he really was.

"We have a nice little group here who bet on anything you can think of. We, of course, have a non-biased professional setting the odds, and then we take wagers. My latest is what the new royal's first word will be. It's exhilarating. Stan has taken a higher stakes approach and placed bets on when Snowden will be apprehended and how Julian Assange will leave the Ecuadorian embassy in London. They've just ceased guarding the door, so it's getting exciting for him. I don't trifle with such things as politics, but it's a thrill nonetheless." She went on, but I tuned her out. I knew my father had a hand in this new frontier of parting the wealthy with their money, and I had no interest in it.

All the money in this room was ill-gotten, and for those reasons Dante could find a home here, but he seemed so averse to any show of wealth. I had to know more. He finally escaped the cougar as our meal was served, with promises to play a round of Boston as soon as he finished.

"I concede, but I want an explanation."

"I was thinking double or nothing."

I was a sucker for raising the stakes. "Go on." I leaned closer.

"I get any two pieces of information I want, or you get two requests."

"No."

"No?" His brows raised. I had him off guard, right where I wanted him.

"If I win, I get one request and one piece of information, and the same for you."

"I see what you're doing. I can roll with it." He adjusted his seat and dipped his spoon into the bisque. "What are we wagering on?"

I scanned the room. He was giving me the advantage by letting me choose again, and I wouldn't blow it. I needed to go with my roots if I had any chance. I knew he'd have the upper hand in almost anything in this room, as well-known as he was. So I went home.

"Play me in seven card stud."

"The Vegas boy wants to play poker?" He shrugged. "If you can wrangle a deck of cards away from these people, be my guest. Although they may hang you for wanting to play poker in this holy place." He was amused, and it worked to my benefit.

"Best out of five?" I asked.

"It's your game."

I abandoned my soup and cleared my throat, about to make a scene, which to my favor I was quite good at. "How would y'all like to have some live action gambling?"

It was as quiet as a church, and I had them.

"My friend, Mr. Bane and I have some business to settle. If you'll allow us, we'd like to use a deck of your cards."

A deck was produced, and we explained what we were about. After the initial scoffs, they called in Fitz to make the odds and went about betting. I took a seat across from Dante, forcing myself to sit still and resist any and all of my tells.

"And here I thought the showmanship I'd heard so much about from your family had skipped a generation."

I snarled at him under my breath. He laced his fingers

behind his head, and he couldn't have looked more calm if he tried. It was an act. Maybe his act was a tell. I had at least two rounds to figure him out. Odds would have it I would be dealt superior at least one of the two, and when it came down to it, the two after that would be most telling.

"We have placed the odds even, because of what we know about Mr. Bane, and because of your heritage and upbringing, Mr. Caci." Fitz spoke with no emotion. "The members will now have five minutes to ask of you what they will and to assess you, within reason."

We stood before the small group like cattle to be slaughtered. They poked and prodded us in turn, and a few of the older gentlemen stared into my eyes for a few long moments, trying to spook me, I guessed.

"Did your father raise you soft?" A gentleman with a cane barked at me.

I bared my teeth. "He named me after his favorite gun, what do you think?"

The man narrowed his eyes and scoffed.

I didn't hear most of what was asked to Dante, which disappointed me. I would have liked to hear the questions those acquainted with him would have asked.

I rolled up my sleeves and set my jacket over the back of the chair. Dante loosened his tie and crossed an ankle over his knee when he sat, looking poised and dapper, like he could have owned the room had he wanted to. I'd underestimated him before, and I couldn't again.

Others sat to join in on the game, and the first hand was dealt. There was money on the table, but neither Dante nor I cared about it with so much more at stake. The onlookers muttered, but I forced them out. I couldn't let any of them get in my head, and they would try. Playing the room was as important as playing the dealer and opponent.

The first round went to him, but I learned a valuable lesson. He went in hard then called or raised in small increments. It was a ploy to weed out the dealer or the faint of heart who sat in on the game with us. I wasn't buying it.

On the second hand, I was dealt a pair of jacks. Nothing to scoff at. So I matched his style going in steep. He called, which was ballsy because he had shit in his showing cards. My next card didn't help me at all, and he was also dealt a dud as far as I could tell, but he raised. My hands started to sweat. It had to be a bluff. Two of our companions folded, but Dante stayed strong for the next two cards. I still had only a fucking pair, but I wasn't going to bitch out now. Not when he wasn't showing shit.

I called and waited for him to flip. It went around the table. The cougar had a pair of fives, so she was out. I showed my hand, and Dante got this look. His top lip curled up, and his eyes glinted in the low light as he flipped over his card. The bastard had two pair. Three of the cards had been face down. What were the fucking odds, minimal, but now I was down two games to nothing. I would have to win the next three hands to take it.

I was fucked and not in the way I wanted to be.

TEN

REMI

The others at the table took some scattered hands, and I was able to win two. With every card dealt, my heart jumped. I mentally logged each one laid face up, quickly tallying what must be left in the deck or face down. Another round to one of the bystanders and my pulse went up ten points. Dante sat back and adjusted his seat, spreading his knees out.

Two hands to two, and the bastard was half hard. He met my gaze and smirked before he tore his gaze away to peek at the face-down cards he'd been dealt. The tension pulsed in the air as the crowd around us took last minute bets and cash exchanged hands. More money than most would see in a lifetime flowed through the room. Dante called as the first card was laid face up. He had to have good cards. He was playing cautiously. By the end of the deal, half the deck would be on the table and face up, with scant few left to guess at. Poker wasn't just a card game; it was mental and psychological.

Dante licked over his lips and kept watching me. I felt like his prey. I resisted the urge to shift under his gaze. His demeanor hadn't changed. Either he had it in his head a win was imminent, or he was bluffing, but his bluffing had been so different in the beginning. He called the next raise, and I wanted to growl at him to give me something to go on. I carefully kept my face neutral.

The next card brought a big raise and two folds. Dante wouldn't fold. I knew money didn't matter to him, even if he was by no means even close to the wealth in this room. Only winning mattered to him, and he was going to sit here and call me out until the cards showed who the winner was. I could toss as much money as I pleased into the pot, and it wouldn't hurt me. I needed to be smart about this.

I raised on the last card and stared him down as he rechecked his cards and sat back. He could have been sitting on the beach with a tropical drink in his hand for as relaxed as he looked.

"All in."

The table gasped, and the room exploded with voices. He was so callous with them, shoving the neat stacks of chips toward the center of the table, causing them to topple and spill, and then he was back to resting against his chair.

I didn't have to check my cards. I had a flush. Nothing to scoff at.

I let the others fold or go in, and when it came around to me at the head of the table, silence set in as they waited to see what I would do. I used the pause to my advantage, letting it settle over us. Dante's eyes found mine as I called. A collective gasp spread through the crowd. I left my chips where they were. No need for a dramatic show. I flipped my cards before the dealer could and waited. One by one it was shown I had the better hand, until it came to Dante.

His lips twisted up at the ends, and he got the same smug look. My stomach dropped to my feet. How the hell could he be so much better at cards than I was? He wasn't a gambler. All the research I had on him told me he wasn't.

My brain searched for an explanation as he flipped over his cards one by one.

Shock hit me like a truck. He had a flush with a nine high. Mine was ten high.

"Good game," he said, rising to his feet.

If I stood, I would have staggered. I'd won. My mask was slipping. I had to compose myself. He strolled right up to me and pulled me to my feet.

"I look forward to seeing what you come up with." His warm breath fanned over my jaw as he leaned close to say the words.

My hands found his hips, holding him there. "No expiration date on this one."

"No, of course not. What fun would it be if there was?" He lightly skimmed his nose under my jaw, and my entire body came to life. He'd had me fully naked, bruised nearly every inch of me, and yet standing here fully clothed was more intimate.

"You say that like you're going to enjoy this."

"I plan to." His retort was so smug, and it had the desired effect. He tilted his hips and brushed himself over me, watching for my reaction.

I groaned in the back of my throat. Only one thing mattered. I needed him to touch me. Using my grip on his hips, I tried to force him closer. He didn't budge. I dug my fingers into his jeans. A dark chuckle resonated through him, rumbling his chest.

"Harder, baby."

He was infuriating, but I did as he asked.

"Good boy."

My chest swelled, and I again tried to get him to press up against me. I craved the touch, the friction, the contact. The bastard didn't move.

"Touch me."

"Not here." He pulled back.

"Please." I knew what the word did to him, and I threw it out like a life preserver.

He shook his head and stepped out of my grasp. With his back to the room, he adjusted and then put on a face. Cash was being passed around and backs clapped. I was left with a tent in my slacks to try and hide. It was a good thing no one paid me any attention.

The submissive in me wanted to beg Dante back, but the other part of me wanted to order it. Frustration pounded in my temples. I would go insane before I left. Dante would see to it. I was at war with myself, but this wasn't the type of war anyone would win. Both sides of me would burn to the ground.

And yet I wouldn't stop myself.

Fitz stepped into my path and held out a briefcase. "Your winnings, Mr. Caci. We don't have an account on file for you, so I took the liberty of packing your winnings up."

There was half a million in cash in the case, and he handed it off like it was nothing, and compared to what he saw daily, it was nothing. Dante had inserted himself into a conversation, purposely out of my reach. This was insanity. Everything you need in reach and yet unable to grab. I was not a patient man, and Dante capitalized on it.

Butlers brought in bottles of Krug Brut Vintage 1988, and at six in the afternoon on a Tuesday, these millionaires were going to get toasted with champagne. I politely refused the glass offered to me, staying on the outskirts to observe. Dante played the room, inviting the crowd to his club. It went against my agenda for the evening, but it was business, so I couldn't fault him. I took an out-of-the way armchair and accepted an offered cigar. He moved seamlessly. I'd watched him at his own castle, and he owned he ring, but he also stood out in and amongst the royalty dominating the room, with none of the same barbaric alpha male qualities. It was sleek sophistication.

A clamor started at one end of the room and quickly spread. Phones beeped, and excitement buzzed through the crowd. A sixty-inch flat screen appeared from one of the cabinets, and a breaking news story was displayed on CNN. Something involving one of the Kardashians or that ilk, and I tuned it out, searching for where Dante had wondered off to.

He was nowhere to be seen, and I started to wonder if he'd left me there. It wouldn't surprise me. He was unpredictable in this way. A shadow in the far corner caught my gaze. He'd slipped away from notice.

The attention was off him as the scandal unfolded on the news, and as the wagers were reviewed, Dante looked weary. He was pale, with the life sucked out of him. The question was on the tip of my tongue as I skirted the fringe of the room, but I didn't let it loose. It could be a trap to make me use the question I'd earned. I expected it of myself, so I expected the games from him. Although if this was a fake, he should be in Hollywood. He wore the expression even in his demeanor, like the weight of his bones were even too much for him to bare at the moment.

"Everything okay?"

He made half an effort to plaster a neutral expression on his face. "But of course."

"You look weary."

"Living has that effect on me."

I half laughed. "It's impossible for you to answer a question, isn't it?"

"If I answered all your questions, and you figured me out, there would be no game left to play, and where is the fun in that?" He was right. Maybe he knew me better than I thought he did, and I already assumed he knew too much.

"So the bit of truth is worth even more than the night of anything I want?"

He looked into my eyes, and I could see his soul there. It was draped in sadness and as black as my heart.

"I've found truth is worth its weight in gold, and like panning for gold, you often think you have more than you do. Most people weave tales with a single strand of truth. Plausible for all but rigorous scrutiny." His voice carried the weight of his mood.

"And yet you don't lie."

"I don't see the point. It's easier to tell the truth."

"Or dodge," I said.

He raised his brows and shrugged one shoulder. "I've found most people only listen in order to reply. They don't need an answer so much as something to reply to, so I give it to them."

"Why don't you come here anymore?" I had to assume my information was lacking because it seemed he hadn't been here in years, but he used to be a regular here.

"Is this the truth you want?"

I clenched my teeth, and my nostrils flared. I wanted to know, but not bad enough to waste it. "No, but I'd like to know nonetheless."

"It was one of my husband's favorite places." He grinned at me because he knew the answer would raise questions.

"You ass." Information on his husband had been all but erased. I knew the man existed, and I knew nothing else about him. I didn't know what had happened to him. If they'd split up, when it happened. There was a husband, and then there wasn't. I couldn't even hammer down a date the so-called husband seemed to have disappeared. It was beyond frustrating, and he knew.

No one around Dante talked either. They couldn't be blackmailed or bribed. I know, I had my man try.

"So I'm told."

"Take me home?" I asked.

"I can't."

My brow knit and my face fell. "Why?"

"Because the world doesn't revolve around you?"

His words stung, but I wasn't going to let him know. "Do you want me to go?"

There was a glint in his eyes. I deflated. He was going to kick me out on my ass and not call me back until he had a use for me. I'd asked to be a toy, so I shouldn't be surprised when I was treated like one.

"Come watch the fight tonight." It wasn't a question. I loved the way he ordered me around.

A little bit of hope crept into my mind, but I loved pushing his buttons too much to say yes right away. "Why should I?"

"You don't want to see the business in action? Since you're going to be a part of it."

He had me there, and he wore a smirk to taunt me.

"You assume I've decided."

"I know you have. We can celebrate the partnership after." He wiggled his brows at me, and I resisted the urge to swoon. No man should be so sexy and dominant. He was exactly what I needed but also my damn kryptonite.

"I'm listening?" I held his gaze but didn't give him an inch.

"If you don't want to celebrate…"

Fucker. "How can I know if I want it if you won't tell me what it is?"

"You won't want it, but I do, which is the point."

"You're a bastard." I pulled at my hair. "It's fucking hell being with you. Has anyone ever told you that?"

His grin broadened. "The whole world is hell, doll. At least with me you get a reprieve from the sun."

"So this is hell at night?"

"I like to think of it as Clouded Hell. One of the rare cool days you've got to hold on to when everything else won't quit."

He lifted his hand again, and instead of smacking me like I expected, he cupped my cheek and brought his forehead to mine. I fucking melted, right there in his inner circle of hell, and I wouldn't have changed it.

When he stepped back, the moment vanished. It would always be like that with him.

"I'll see you at the fight."

"Cocky fuck."

He raised one shoulder and walked out of the club. "How are you getting home?"

"I've got my ways."

As I slipped into my rental, my phone started to buzz in my pocket. I knew who it was before I had it out and answered.

"Boy."

I could feel the eye-roll through the phone. "When are you coming home?"

"Do you miss me already?"

He huffed, but I knew he did. "I have someone who wants an appointment."

"Tell him I can fit him in next week." It was almost comical calling his bluff.

"Sure, I'll put him on your calendar so you don't forget."

"Thanks, boy." I searched for words to fill the silence. "How's the shop?"

"Been busy, but you know how it is. The intern is working out well, so that helps."

"Sweet deal." Our conversations were usually easy, but today it felt strained. I wasn't sure if it was him or me.

"Are you okay?" I pulled out of the lot so Dante wouldn't see me lingering. The last thing I wanted was to give him an edge. I'd carefully kept the parts of my life separate and calculated. He couldn't know I knew as much about him as I did, otherwise, he'd want just as much access to me. Access he couldn't have without bringing my house of cards tumbling down on my head.

"Yeah, I'm chill."

I let the silence stretch between us as I headed toward the Ritz.

"I need to talk to you," he said at length. That was the thing about Kai, he couldn't keep anything from me. I just had to give him time to get it out.

"So talk."

He was hesitant. Kai was never hesitant with me. We'd known each other since we were teenagers. He was my best friend.

"Dude, speak."

"I want to talk in person."

A pit settled in my gut. "Okay, I'll get on a flight in the morning." I wanted to make sure Kai was okay, but I couldn't drag myself away before then. I needed another fix before I went back to pretending.

"Okay." He hung up.

ELEVEN

DANTE

Ten minutes until fight time and the buzz of adrenaline was thick in the air. I could feed off the mixture of alcohol-induced aggression and sexual tension the impending match infused into the crowd.

"Bane." A distinct Scottish accent said my name, and Josh fell to his knees at my feet to press his face into my thigh, rubbing it over my jeans.

"I'm not a lucky rabbit foot you can use at your will." I pushed my fingers into his hair.

Josh peeked up, yellow eyes gleaming. "And why not?"

I yanked his hair as he tried to return his face to my thigh, moving toward my groin. "Because you need to get your ass in the ring."

He pulled against my hold on him. "You're ruining my warm up."

"Maybe you should be actually warming up."

"You mean you don't mind giving me a blow job, then?" He bit my inner thigh.

I hissed, jerking his head back. "If anyone is going to be on their knees, it's going to be you."

He pushed his hands into my thighs, spreading them. "It's against my normal pregame, but I can live with it."

He slipped into the space he'd made and grabbed at my fly.

I growled low in my throat, lifting a booted foot to set on his chest. "Get off your damn knees and go make me some damn money."

"Why must you resist me, Sir?" He jumped to his feet and reached into his shorts to adjust.

I couldn't help but laugh. "Fucker." I shook my head and pressed my steel toe into his groin. "Stop acting like an idiot."

"My usual was detained. I'm guessing that means arrested, so I'm a little deprived. You could have let me have my fun," He acted hurt.

"You would have blown me here too." I pressed my foot forward, crushing him a little.

He nodded vigorously, not backing away from my assault. "You know I like to put on a show, mate."

"I'm going to kick your ass tomorrow." I let my foot fall.

He made a lewd gesture and groaned, gripping himself again. "I look forward to it."

Liv ducked into the ring wearing one of her tight pencil skirts and a ruffly top. Red heels drew attention to her long legs as she took the center with confidence. She held the old fashioned mic to her lips. The room fell silent when she spoke. Josh turned on his heel and ran toward the ring. If I didn't know what a good fighter he was, I would have stopped putting money on him a long time ago.

Liv's voice was commanding as she introduced the two fighters, both featherweights. It would be a long fight. Neither was going to pack the punch of a heavyweight, but they were fast. I had pounds of muscle on Josh and could knock him on his ass, but he always got in three hits to my one. He was a machine.

"Who was that?" Remi dropped into a seat beside me. I glanced over. "A friend."

He scoffed, full of attitude. "I could see that." He paused, looking me over. "Is he one of your submissives?"

"He's my training partner." I wasn't giving him an inch.

Caci's upper lip curled up. "And he wants to be your submissive?"

"Surprisingly enough, he's not submissive at all. I'd call him an exhibitionist."

I took my gaze from him and looked back at the ring. Liv had stepped out, and Josh was sizing up his opponent, taking a few jabs to see how fast he was.

"He wants you."

"He was joking around." I kept my eyes on the fight.

"He played if off that way, but he'd have done it if you would have let him. I saw it in his eyes."

I laughed. Josh and I had always played around. "I have a feeling you would think everyone wants me."

"They probably do. You're one of those people."

I didn't give him the satisfaction of looking at him. I did alright for myself, but few caught my attention.

"I knew I was right." He leaned back in his chair and kept his gaze on me.

One of the waitresses brought me over a fresh scotch and took Caci's drink order. I brought it to my lips, watching Josh. He'd taken two hard hits to the face, and one eye was nearly swollen shut. In legal circles, it may have ended the fight, but this was far from legal. We let fights go on until there was a concession or someone was unconscious.

The pulse of the room quickened as they dove at each other again. The fight slowed, and the knocks of fists against flesh echoed through me. Josh ducked a right hook only to lean into a kidney punch. He went down hard, head slamming into the mat. I was on my feet, surging forward with the room as my breath caught in my throat.

I cringed like I could feel it from where I sat. Liv climbed back into the ring to check on Josh, but he was already dragging himself to his feet. His opponent nailed him with a knee to the jaw as he tried to get up, sending Josh sprawling out on his back.

My chest tightened, and I fell back to grip the arm of my seat. He lay stunned for a moment, and I was sure he was out. Liv was in the ring again and held up her hand for the other fighter to stay back. I leaned forward, resting my elbows on my knees. I covered my mouth with my hand as she knelt beside him, pressing her fingers to his neck. He slapped her hand away from his neck and dragged himself up. He turned and spit blood over the edge of the ring, coating the floor.

His eyes were alight with anger as he turned on the other fighter.

Remi grabbed my face, tearing my attention away from the fight.

"What, Caci?" I snapped.

"Why are you calling me that?" He tightened his grip on my jaw so I couldn't turn back to the fight.

"Because here you are my business partner, not my plaything."

He growled and started to get up. I grabbed his wrist, pressing my fingers between the bones to separate them. He moaned, eyes floating half shut. There was something off about Remi. I hadn't found him needy, but he seemed desperate for my attention.

"What?" I asked again.

"I need you tonight before I go back."

"Not the way to get what you want." He still had too many dominant traits he needed to be broken of.

He fell to his knees before me. The fight was so intense no one around us noticed. "Please." The word worked its way through me like needles in my brain. There wasn't a part of me unaffected, and he knew it.

"Please?" I asked. I had to force myself to look at him as Josh landed a few blows of his own. It was a constant chess match of back and forth.

"Please tell me how to get what I want."

I looked him over. "I would suggest some dignity in public, but I think it's above you."

"You know you need to beat me just as bad as I need it," he whispered so he was barely audible above the din of the room.

"I don't think that's the real reason you want me at this moment. You're ignoring business to beg at my feet." I smacked his cheek as he moved closer.

"I have already decided to work with you. I came here tonight for you." He grabbed my thigh and dug his nails in.

"I know. But you're lying." I ignored his hand.

"What do you want me to say?" He spoke through gritted teeth, clearly not used to not getting his own way.

"I want you to say it."

"What?" He looked into my eyes.

"You know exactly what, and if you're going to play games, get out of my sight." I sat back and crossed my arms over my chest, returning my attention to Josh.

My words had the desired effect.

"I didn't like him touching you."

"I know. Why?" It was agony to split my attention. Josh had never lost a fight on purpose. Even when he'd thrown them for money, he did so at the last minute.

"Because I don't want to share you."

My head snapped around. His words caught me off guard. "I'm not the one with other mates.",

He looked at his feet. I turned away. If I kept looking I would give into him. He had this commanding hold on my emotions, playing them like an expert.

Josh moved in and slugged his opponent in the temple. He staggered and looked like he was going to go down but remained on his feet. The guy had to be jacked on something. There was no way he was withstanding so much without any outward sign. Josh went all out, throwing punch after punch, backing him into a corner. I ended up on the edge of my seat, forgetting about Remi.

Josh had him. He landed blow after blow until his opponent was trapped. Now he just had to get him down. I rubbed my hands together, tasting the tension in the air. This was what it was to be alive. Josh struck him in the nose, and it splattered blood, coating them both. The opponent growled and launched himself at Josh, taking them both down to the mat. The guy seemed to thrive on pain, getting stronger as the fight progressed.

He came up on top with Josh pinned under him and let go on his face. My teeth slammed together, and the rest of the room vanished. I forced myself to stay in my seat, but I wanted to kick the mother fucker's teeth in for hurting Josh.

Josh swung wildly, finally getting the guy off him. He dragged himself up and took a shaky breath before stalking toward his opponent. There was cold determination in his eyes. Josh lost all pretense of defending himself as he got near, taking wild shots and leaving himself open as he attacked. Both of them took up the style, slugging it out. Josh started to gain ground, and a grin spread over my face.

"That a boy," I muttered.

Remi was on his feet behind me. He didn't say a word, slipping out of the booth. I let him go as Josh landed on his back again.

He didn't get up. The guy reared back and kicked him in the ribs. Josh curled to his side and raised an arm. I looked away. I'd never seen him concede. He'd allowed himself to be knocked out if the payout was big enough, but not this.

Liv shoved the fighter back as he pulled back for another kick. She snarled, eyes blazing when he came after her. She curled her blood red nails into her palms.

"Try me." Even in heels, she was frightening as tall as she was.

He scoffed and turned to go back to his corner. I could see the relief wash over her face as soon as his back was turned. She dropped to her knees at Josh's side and whispered to him. I moved through the lingering bodies to get to her. She was helping Josh to his feet when I got there. He pushed her hands off of him and doubled over, resting his forearms on his knees as he dry-heaved. He probably had broken at least a few ribs.

She dropped her hands, and if she could have shot daggers from her eyes, I'd be dead. She turned on her stilettos and sauntered away. I grabbed a cigarette from the pack in my pocket and stuck it between his lips. He grunted and jutted out his chin, waiting for me to light it. I held out my lighter, and he inhaled roughly, coughing through his first exhale.

"We need to take you in to see if you have a fucking punctured lung."

"Just take me home to the whiskey, mate."

I knew he wouldn't let me take him to the ER. There

was a pride between us about fighting, but I had to offer. It was already shameful enough he'd conceded.

"Going to ride bitch?" I offered my arm, but he shook his head.

"Fuck you, you can drive my truck."

Josh straightened up and took a few steps toward the edge of the ring. He grunted as he ducked between the ropes. I followed after him, shaking my head. Stubborn fuck.

He wouldn't even let me help him into his truck, and I ignored the puddle of blood he vomited out the door after he got inside. Josh lived about twenty minutes outside of the city, in an area I liked to call the redneck danger zone. I could hear the gators sliding out of the way as I pulled into his drive. It was two miles through the overgrown trees before his house came into view.

I pulled his Chevy into the grass in front of his porch, shocked to find there wasn't six to ten other cars on his lawn. I half wanted to start a junkyard there, just to see if Josh would notice. I opened my door and came around to his side determined to help even if he resisted. He stumbled to his porch and then used the rail to haul himself up the stairs.

"You can take the truck back to the club."

"I already put my bike in the back while your stubborn ass was puking." I used his keys to open the front door and held it open for him.

"Thanks for driving me." He limped to the kitchen and opened the freezer. He was straight on a bottle of fire whiskey. He took a long pull then wiped his mouth with the back of his hand.

"You don't have to stay."

TWELVE

DANTE

I took the bottle out of Josh's hand and took a swig. "I'm going to at least stay to see if you have a concussion."

Josh pressed his tongue into the side of his cheek and studied me. "You don't have to take care of me."

"Who would have thought it would have come down to me taking care of you?" I swallowed more whiskey, and my mouth went dry. I took a step closer to him, lingering in his personal space. "Not me." I laughed, trying to break the moment.

He dropped his gaze from mine and pressed his face into my chest. I wrapped my arms around him as he shook with rage and defeat. Josh was the softer of the two of us, and he'd held me through my husband vanishing, or dying, or whatever he'd done. I had a debt to repay. He gripped the side of my shirt, holding on like he could slip away at any moment. I wrapped an arm around the back of his neck and let him.

"What the fuck happened?" he said after a long while. His voice was raw and cracked. He didn't need to lift his head to show me the tears on his face.

I shook my head. What could I say? I wasn't good at comfort. I was good at telling people to suck it up.

"We've all lost fights."

"I didn't lose. I got my ass handed to me." He wasn't wrong.

"It wasn't that bad."

"You're really going to stand here and lie to me?" He pulled back this time and set his jaw.

"You got your ass handed to you, and it was embarrassing. The guy had to be jacked up on something. I've never seen anybody take your hits and not flinch." I stuck my hands in my pockets, not sure if he wanted to be back in my arms or if he wanted to nurse his pride by himself.

He returned to the bottle. "Doesn't change the fact he kicked my ass, even if he was on something. I'm losing my touch." He took another swig, then dry heaved.

"You shouldn't be drinking. Your brain just went through a fucking mixer." The bruises were setting in and turning an ugly shade of purple.

His dark eyes met mine as he pressed the bottle to his lips. "Like you have any room to talk, mate." His accent was highlighted by his mood.

"I'm not going to come back here and find you half eaten by one of those fucking mutts you keep." I grabbed the bottle out of his hand and started to pour it in the sink. He shoved me while trying to yank the bottle back.

I barely kept my feet, stumbling backward, righting the bottle. Josh came at me, so I upended the bottle, pouring it right on his cracked and peeling linoleum. His mouth hung open, horrified I would do such a thing. The nearly full fifth bathed the floor, filling the entire room with its sweet scent.

Josh half turned to grab a dirty dish rag then spun and sprinted at me.

Fuck.

I didn't have time to brace myself and ended up on my back with my best friend on top of me. He wasn't so much trying to harm me, but he wanted me to know he was pissed, so he aimed for spots that would leave bruises. I did my best to miss his fists as I tried to throw him off. We wrestled on the floor, each trying to get the upper hand, rolling into furniture and banging into his cabinets, mopping up the whiskey with our clothes. He was slick with sweat and alcohol and even more impossible to grab. I wrapped a hand around his throat and used my hips to flip him under me. His hand slammed into the floor, and he grunted, pressing his eyes closed as his body went limp.

"Is this done?" I forced my hand up under his chin, only applying a little pressure so I wouldn't cut off the blood supply to his brain or compress his windpipe.

"Yea," he wheezed.

I released my grip and sat back on his hips. "You fucking bastard."

He dug his teeth into his lip. "Thanks."

"Yep." I climbed to my feet and offered him a hand. He took it and looked around the room.

"I'm not cleaning this up tonight."

"The whiskey is going to eat your floor."

"And? It already looks like shit." He pushed past me, going into his living room, and collapsed onto the pea-green sofa left over from his mother's house.

I glanced at my wet clothes and decided I didn't care enough to do anything about them either and followed his example. He laid his head in my lap as soon as I sat.

"Sleep. I'll wake you in a few hours to see if you're brain damaged."

He laughed. "I'm already brain damaged."

THIRTEEN

REMI

The worst part about throwing a fit is you usually know you're in the wrong. I knew I was wrong, but none of it changed how I felt. It didn't stop me from making a scene, nor from storming out like a little bitch. I scrubbed a hand over my face. What the hell was wrong with me?

I punched the wheel of my Jeep over and over. I should have swallowed my pride and gone back in there, but how would I look? Bane was right about everything. In there I was Caci, not his little bitch. Two days and I'd lost my fuckin' head. I couldn't let myself go there. I had an image to uphold, but more than that, I didn't think I could live with myself if I became a full-time submissive.

As sad as it was, no one looked down on submissive men more than I did. I was my own biggest critic. I may hate certain aspects of my father, but no matter how far I ran, and how different I tried to make my life, I was the worst parts of him. It was still early, and the traffic flowed easier than my thoughts back to the Ritz. I found myself in a particular state of self-loathing as I left the Jeep with the valet.

"R?"

Only one person called me that.

"Boy."

He groaned, lifting his lip like he did every time I used the name. Kai stood in his full inked glory there on the curb. He had a cigarette to his lips with his body half angled into the building and one foot against the wall.

"What are you doing here?"

He offered me a drag, but I shook my head. "I told you I needed to talk to you." His eyes told me more than his lips.

I grabbed two fistfuls of his shirt and dragged his body to mine. "Talk to me then."

"Let's go to our room."

I cringed but pulled back and wrapped an arm around him. It felt like a betrayal. After one night it felt like a betrayal. I laughed at myself. I had to get a grip. He dropped his face to my shoulder for the elevator ride. I brushed my fingers up his spine, worried now.

When the door was safely closed behind us I broke the silence. "Come on. This isn't you. What's up?"

He took a seat on the edge of the bed. "I'm going to lose him."

I knew who he was talking about without asking. "He's in love with you. He's not going to leave."

"Yeah, he really is. It was insane to think anyone would take me with all the rules."

"You act like he wants to get married and start a family." I laughed and took a place across from him, leaning on the dresser.

Kai looked up, and his eyes told me everything.

If I hadn't had my ass firmly planted on the desk, I would have staggered.

"Kyle asked me to move in. When I tell him no, he's going to break up with me." Kai grabbed his bare bicep.

His hot pink shirt clashed with his tattoos in the low light. Kai didn't have any large pieces, they were all fist size or smaller woven together, and every single one had a meaning. There was a lifetime of our stories inked into his skin. Some of them matched ones I had on my own.

"He wouldn't. The kid's in love with you."

He dropped his head to hang between his shoulders. I reached out for him, but he pulled away from my touch.

"It's been two years."

"So? What is he, like twenty-three?"

"Yeah, and he's past the sleep around stage. He doesn't get us, and he probably never will." There was sorrow behind his words.

"Why are you so convinced he's going to break up with you?"

"Because he's been hinting at wanting more for months. I kept pushing it off, but then you seemed to be doing worse..." He was taking it a lot harder than I expected. I couldn't quite figure out what I was missing.

"You've got to spell this out for me. What's going on inside your head?"

"He wants more, and I don't have it to give. I love him, R, I love him."

The words settled between us, and I thought about my words before I said them.

"I've known you twenty years, and you think I don't know how you feel about Kyle?" I laughed and pushed off the desk to collect him in my arms.

He leaned into my touch. "What am I going to do when he leaves?"

"You're going to be fine. He's not going anywhere. He loves you too much."

He rubbed his face on my chest. "You think so?"

"I know so, now tell me why you came here."

He blew out the breath he'd been holding and pulled back to look into my eyes. "I had to see for myself if I'd lost you."

"Lost me?" I knew what he was getting at, but I was going to play dumb.

"You've been losing it, and I don't mean like before when you've been gone too long. This time you've been really losing it." I waited for his verdict. We both knew he wasn't finished. He made me wait, and the question was on my lips when he finally went on. "You seem better."

"I'm fine, Kai. You need to stop worrying so much. All this fear of abandonment shit, do I need to put you in Goddamn therapy?"

A smile curled at the corners of my mouth. "Fuck off with that." He punched my arm then tugged his shirt off. I watched him undress, unashamed. He was thin, always had been, what with the surfing and him eating like a damn bird. He laid back on the bed. "I'm fucking tired."

I took a seat on the other bed and laughed. "We taking the first flight out?"

"Yeah..." His voice was laced with sleep as I flipped on the TV. I didn't care to watch it, but I wanted the background noise. I waited until his breathing evened out before I picked up my phone. I flipped through the alerts, and there wasn't a single thing from him. Not even an emoji. Fucker. I resisted the urge to throw my phone at the wall. I wasn't really surprised.

I couldn't believe I was actually considering texting him. This wasn't me. Even as a submissive I'd never gotten to this point. Why the hell did it already feel like he was slipping through my fingers? I needed to get a damn grip. I sent him a message telling him to pick me up outside the hotel. I didn't word it like a request. I had to keep some of my balls.

Bane: You have some nerve.

Remi: Come take it out of my ass.

Bane: You'd like it too much.

Bane: I should tell you I'm coming and never show. That would teach you.

Remi: Asshole. You would too.

Bane: I'm already downstairs.

My cock pressed into the fly of my jeans. I was on my feet in an instant. I glanced over at Kai. If he woke he'd be upset finding my bed empty. He'd just told me he was scared of being abandoned, and I left him there knowing full well what I was doing. If anyone was to blame for fucking up their life, I knew I was. When it all came crashing down I would let it all fall on my shoulders.

Dante was waiting for me. God, I wanted to run to him, but I made myself walk.

He sat in the valet lane on his bike. I knew if I complained about riding on the back he'd leave me here, so I climbed on and wrapped my arms around his middle. He took off without so much as a glance over his shoulder. It suited my purposes well. I had no interest in talking about my display. The faster we got to his playroom the better. I could already taste the punishment.

I was coated in a light sheen of sweat by the time we pulled up outside his place. He stopped his bike and waited. I hooked my leg and climbed off. He killed the engine and followed suit, but he stayed there looking me over. I wanted to shrink under his gaze. I needed to be weak with him, and it began as soon as he looked at me.

"Why are we at the bar?"

"Because I own the damn place, and I already had to

leave to drive Josh home, so I need to show my face as this is my job."

My stomach flipped, and I tasted bile. It wasn't logical, but Josh made me insane. There were probably hundreds of guys who hit on him each month, Dante was charismatic and addictive, and yet I put all my focus on this one guy. I overanalyzed myself constantly a habit I'm sure I developed trying to hide who I was from my father. Dante went right for his office.

He let me step inside before he closed the door. I put on a face and took a seat. It was second nature, and his office was a place of business. He stepped around his large desk and took his seat, not speaking right away. I waited him out, feeling like a child in the principal's office. I'd lost.

"I'm not jealous." He looked like a caged animal. "But you were getting off on the fight. I didn't—"

He cut me off. "At first, maybe, but then I was concerned."

"He's a fighter. He can handle himself." There was too much scorn in my reply.

His lips twitched at the corners. He didn't believe me, and I wasn't sure I believed myself.

"Envy doesn't look good on you." He stood abruptly.

I waited. He studied me for a moment then walked around the desk. I fell to my knees at his feet, satisfied I'd get what I came here for. He could be played as easily as I could. We needed each other. I'd done my research, and I knew this man inside and out.

"You know there is something attractive about how jealous you are."

I smiled but didn't let it reach my gaze as I looked up. "Because you want to be desired, and my jealousy is proof I want you?"

"It's proof you're deranged enough to think I shouldn't have the freedom you do."

"You were celibate long before me," I replied.

"By choice, not because some boy demanded it of me."

"I haven't demanded anything." I looked him right in the eyes.

"Yet." He gripped himself. "I think it's time I fix that."

I shrugged one shoulder. He could fuck anyone he liked.

His fingers brushed over the leather of his belt. "There are a few who have been begging to learn submission."

Heat seared through me. "No." The word left my lips before I could stop them.

"There it is."

I didn't speak. This was different. I didn't know how, but it was.

His lips twitched at the corners. He'd taken my silence as my surrender.

"I'm going to break you like the wild horse you are until you stop saying what you don't mean."

"Are you going to ride my ass into the ground?" I smiled sweetly, ignoring his other comment.

"Have you asked daddy for permission?" His hand never left his belt.

I knew who he meant, but the word got under my skin. "I don't ask my father anymore for permission for anything."

"You know very well I mean Kai."

"What does he have to do with it?"

"You can't consummate the relationship." There was nothing callous about his statement.

"By choice."

"Keep telling yourself as much if it helps you sleep at night."

"Are you going to punish me for my behavior now, Sir?" I batted my eyelashes at him.

He patted me on the head. "Yes." He stepped around me and opened the door.

"What the fuck? Where are you going?"

"I have work to do. I took enough time off tonight. You need to learn patience. You couldn't even sit through a fight without throwing a tantrum to get your way."

He wasn't wrong. I was used to being the center of my submissives' worlds. Even the few discreet dominants I'd had over the years came to worship me.

He left without another word.

FOURTEEN

REMI

I felt like a Goddamn dog waiting in Dante's office for him. I was spoiled. I was used to getting my way, and after two hours of thinking it over, I realized this was probably why my relationships, with other dominants, never lasted. I was always in charge. Everything was in my control. They gave me the pain I needed but not the freedom. I couldn't decide if I loved or hated Dante for this.

I paced for the first twenty minutes and then took to his private liquor cabinet. There wasn't much good in it, but he had a decent tequila which kept me occupied. He didn't own a TV, I suspected. I hadn't seen one in his house nor did he have one in his office. The walls were lined with bookshelves overloaded with well-read novels. There were a few photos scattered there as well, which I studied. Josh and Dante, a picture of his assistant girl. Her legs were a mile long, and she was something else. Even after the change, she was my type, if I'd been interested in girls.

There was another where Dante looked stricken in love. It was almost sad to see, as impending heartbreak hung just around the corner. I didn't know the details, but I knew he was presumed dead. I wanted the story there, but I wouldn't press—yet.

The clock told me I'd been sitting in here for two hours. It was after two, and if Kai woke up he'd be upset if I wasn't there. I walked up to the door and put my hand on the handle.

"Fuck."

I should walk out of here and go back to the hotel, back to the soft bed before the six A.M. flight, but I couldn't bring myself to turn the handle. I couldn't bring myself to walk out the door. I needed another fix before I left. I whirled around, fists clenched, looking for something to hit. My gaze landed on the oak bookshelves. They would withstand a little pounding. I stalked over and threw my right fist into the ornately carved post. Pain washed over me, and it only took seconds for the release to hit my brain. My eyes slid half closed, and I sucked in a breath before continuing my assault of the wood. I hit it over and over until my hand was numb, and I could barely lift my arm. I dropped my arm, knowing there was already a bruise forming over my knuckles. I would feel it tattooing, but now I would be able to wait. I took a seat behind Dante's desk and crossed my ankle over my knee to wait for the bastard. I could outplay him in any mind game he threw at me.

Or so I thought.

It was another hour before he strolled in wearing his smug grin.

"Miss me?"

I shrugged one shoulder, trying to keep my annoyance at bay. If I let it show, chances were he wouldn't give me what I had already waited this long for. It's what I would have done to my submissive. He stopped across from me and looked down his nose. I knew he was expecting me to get up from his chair, but I wasn't about to move.

"I didn't think you'd still be here."

"I knew I was being punished."

"I told you I'd find creative punishments."

"I know." The bastard had, and I hadn't even put two and two together until now, but I wasn't going to tell him so.

"Remove your slacks." He rolled his sleeves, and I whimpered.

I licked over my lips as my hands automatically went to my belt. He took a seat, knees spread, eyes never leaving me. I stepped out of my slacks and stood there in front of him, cock on full display, hard as he liked me, and waited.

"Over my knee." His lips turned up at the corners.

My mouth fell open. He was such a bastard. He couldn't really expect me to—could he? There was no indication he was joking. I lingered to call his bluff. I wasn't sure which would be more humiliating, being spanked over his knee or handing over the little pride I had left and submitting to it when Dante was joking.

"If you want to go back to your submissive." Dante shifted his weight like he was going to stand.

"No." I took a step toward him.

Dante got to his feet and looked down his nose at me. "Did you forget how to submit overnight?"

I pressed my eyes closed and shook my head. More like I'd forgotten how to put my mask back on once Dante had stripped me bare. I wasn't sure how to return to my normal life. I didn't want to have to fake it anymore.

I dropped to my knees. It was a standoff. I'd been beaten, but I'd never been broken. This is what I'd been missing my entire existence. He held the key, and he was going to make me work for it. He didn't even look at me, like I was beneath his notice, and I adored him for it.

"I'm sorry, Master."

His head tilted slightly. "For?"

I bit back a groan. Nothing would be easy with him, and it was exactly what I needed. I'd been praised my entire life for skating through, and it meant nothing. This, this meant more.

"For doubting what you requested of me. For breaking the rules." I wanted to pick up my head. I wanted to look into his icy stare so he could see what he'd already done to me, the arrogant prick.

He sat back down, and I exhaled. It was a silent approval for my words. I hid my smile, keeping my head down as I pushed off the floor.

"No."

I froze.

"Crawl." His words dripped with condemnation.

My cock leaked precum. I was painfully hard which only made his request more embarrassing. He knew I was enjoying my humiliation. I took my time going to him, making him wait for what he wanted. I would submit, but I was going to make him earn it as much as I had to.

I came around the outside of his thigh, rubbing my face against it. He slid his fingers into my hair. The touch was everything, and before I could get my fill, it disappeared.

"Over my knee."

I draped myself over his thighs, feeling more exposed than I'd ever been. He would tear down my walls brick by brick until I was fully open to him. I wasn't even sure he knew he was doing it. He'd grown accustomed to total control and expected it now. He couldn't know how hard it was for me to give it. How he left me in shreds afterwards but craving more.

I landed there over him, but nothing happened. Doubt

seeped into the cracks in my foundation, and I sank. I was here for the pain. I'd put it off too long, and I knew the little control I once had was all gone. I couldn't keep functioning like this.

The first smack landed, and he didn't stop. He landed hit after hit on the back of my thighs and my ass, warming the skin. The light burn spread out from the point of impact and engulfed me. He increased the force, and I lost myself in the sensation. I would have bruises for weeks, and I'd cherish every one. His hand stilled, and the weight of it on my ass hurt. My body felt like jello. I didn't want to move.

"You are so sexy like this."

My chest swelled. He massaged over my ass so I felt his marks. If I could have, I would've pressed into his touch. I dreaded leaving. I didn't want to return to my life because it wasn't anything but a lie.

"Thank you." My voice was raspy.

He skimmed his fingertips up my seam. I wanted him there. It could've been the innocent gesture of giving comfort after such a beating. He may not even want me like I wanted him. Arousal flared through me. It was impossible to ignore as he traced patterns between my thighs and under the curve of my ass, getting acquainted with every intimate part of me. My cock begged to be touched, swelling against his leg, until its pulse was all-consuming. I rutted against his leg, getting as much friction against his jeans as I could manage. His fingers dipped lower, skimming over my taint.

I moaned through my teeth, feeling his cock press into my abs. He wanted me. I turned my head and bit him through his jeans hard enough to leave a mark. His fingers curled around my thigh, guiding me to straddle his lap. I set my hands on his chest and looked down into his eyes.

His pupils were the size of dimes. He was practically feral. I rocked my ass over his erection to poke the bear, so to speak.

"I thought this was only about pain." He slid a hand between us letting it hover over my groin.

"It was." I didn't know what it was about any longer. It would be so easy to leave my life in ruin and give into him.

I dropped my forehead to his, but he didn't close the gap. He slid his hands up my back, drawing me closer so my chest pressed into his. My lips parted, and I drew in a breath of him.

Petrichor. He smelled like earth after a long rain.

I didn't belong here.

"Dante—"

He dragged the pad of his thumb over my lower lip. "Don't say it. Just go."

I wanted to bite down on his thumb, to suck it into my mouth, but he was right. Neither of us had to say it. This wasn't right. I slid off his lap and stood before him without shame. I'd left it with my dignity on the floor. I stood rooted to the spot, unable to move. He rose and straightened his jeans, seemingly unaffected as I died inside. He took a step and then two, inserting himself right back into my personal space.

His mouth hovered over mine. I'd never wanted to kiss anyone so bad. My veins ached with need. I swallowed past the lump in my throat, trying to find words, anything.

"Dante—" I said again.

"Tell me what you want!" A callous demand. He didn't know what he asked. He wouldn't have to give up anything to be with me. I would have to face the layers and layers of lies I'd built up around myself.

His breath was hot on my lips, and I could almost taste

him, or I imagined I could.

The word was on the tip of my tongue. I wanted him. Needed him. I was desperate, but I couldn't do it like this. Not to Kai and not to Dante. The soft touch of his fingers trailed down my neck as we hovered in purgatory. If I stepped back I would be in Hell, but if I gave into him, it would only be a brief taste of Heaven. I couldn't let it last. I wasn't allowed to be who I was with him.

"May I go?" Each word killed a part of me. I forced myself to step back. "I have a plane to catch." Kai was waiting for me. It had to be nearly five in the morning. If I stayed any longer I'd miss the flight. Part of me wanted him to grab me and take what was his. I wanted to feel possessed.

He crossed his arms over his chest and jutted his chin out. "You may." It was a challenge.

I squeezed my hands into fists. My ass hurt, my dick ached, and instead of being satisfied like I'd been the night before, my heart was heavy with a vision of a future I would deny myself.

"Go on then." The words cut me.

It hurt, even if it was what I'd asked for. God, how had I become such a fool for him?

I dressed in silence and then walked to the door to save face, but once past the threshold, I ran and didn't stop.

FIFTEEN

DANTE

Two weeks had passed, and I hadn't spoken a word to Remi. He handled all the business details through his assistant and cited personal reasons for being out of the office so much. I'd had Liv check into the tattoo shop he owned and worked at on the side. It was a cover for his illegal dealings, as well as the way he laundered money, much as my club was to me. But he wasn't even there.

I didn't seek him out. I wouldn't let myself go to him. I needed him to come to me when he was desperate again. There was power in desperation. It was the first step in really breaking him down and getting inside his mind as he had tried with me. Actually, if I was honest with myself, as he had done to me. Goddamn, as I had let him do to me. I didn't just want to play with his body, I wanted to fuck his mind. I saw no point in wasting time on someone whose mind wasn't worth seducing.

I thought tonight would be that night. I was going to ignore him as much as possible until he begged, as retribution for leaving me this long without a word.

I pulled on a pair of shorts, forgoing a shirt or shoes before ducking out my door. I ran all the way to the bar to warm my muscles for the night's fight. It was 'opening' night for the new guys, we were packed to the brim, and I had to fight my way toward the bar. I wasn't sure if they wanted to see the fight, or gamble as there was nothing better to do on a Thursday night in this godforsaken part of the world. Or perhaps they wanted to see the Alpha get knocked around by some out-of-towner? No matter the reason, they would all line my pocket.

"They here yet?" I asked the bartender as I passed where she was mobbed, struggling to get everyone served. I had six extra girls on downstairs, and we were still swamped.

"Yeah, downstairs getting ready, boss," she yelled over the din.

I walked that way, rolling my shoulders. I made my way down the stairs, and the noise hit me in the chest like a physical blow. I paused, taking it in. I could taste the tension in the air and feel the energy pulsing on my skin. It had been much too long. I was grabbed before I could continue.

"Bane."

I looked back into Josh's dark eyes and waited for him to go on.

"This guy is big—"

I cut him off with a look. He didn't release my arm.

"Bane." He was pleading.

My lips twitched up at the corners. "And what if he kicks my ass?" A little taste of death never hurt anyone…much.

His fingers dug into my arm. "If you die—"

"You'll dig me up and kick my ass?"

It earned me a smile. "And then I'll burn your body and piss in the ashes."

"Classy. Can I go, Mother?"

He growled but released my arm, calling after me, "I

hope you get your ass handed to you. Then you'll know what it feels like."

"Nobody can hurt me worse than him." I saw the pity in Josh's eyes, and I turned away. Masen had already ripped a hole out of my chest with his bare hands. They said the wound would heal with time. It didn't heal, it festered, tainting everything in its reach. I was left with an all-consuming empty space in the center of my chest. Eventually, I got better at hiding it, and the world moved on. I moved from distraction to distraction. Remi was like a drug. He numbed the pain, and I could breathe. I was anxious to play again. I was anxious to act on the plans I'd made for him over the last two weeks. I had to hold myself back or I would end up spoiling the shit out of my new little masochist.

There wasn't an open seat in the house, and most of the standing room was packed too. There were sweaty, writhing bodies everywhere. This was my kingdom. I put on an indifferent face, expecting to see Remi staring back at me from his fighter's corner. Standing there instead was his business manager and some tatted up punk. An asshole by the look of him. It didn't matter, he was shorter than I was by a few inches, but he had about fifty pounds of hard muscle on me. He was blond with a choppy cut and high cheek bones. Josh was right, it looked like Remi wanted me to get my ass kicked. A smile twisted over my lips at the thought of sending Remi's prized fighter back to him in a box. He was a dick, and I was a fucking sucker for enjoying it.

I rolled my neck and stepped into the ring. Liv was at my side, stepping in next to me to announce the rules. She met my gaze before she said anything. I could read the worry there, and I ignored it. She wouldn't say anything to me in public. She knew better.

After a pause, she went on with the rule. There was only one. If the opponent stopped moving, we had to get off him. Others were left unsaid and generally followed, like hits to the balls and biting, but hell if you wanted to get dirty, I'd allow it and give it back. Liv stayed to ref while Remi's business manager slipped out of the ring. I already hated his face. It was too bad I couldn't have a little piece of them both.

"This is it?" The guy looked over at the manager.

I was already pissed Remi didn't show, and now this bastard was going to shit talk in my house? I shook my arms out and then stalked toward him. He chuckled as he stood his ground, throwing a fist as I got close. I dodged to the side and put all my weight behind my arm, twisting into the hit. My knuckles slammed it into his temple. He went down like a limp rag doll. I thought about kicking him, but I had more honor than that. The odds had been slightly in my favor going into this, and I would've made more money off the bets had I let it go on longer and showed some weakness, but this tasted so much better.

I stepped over the body, looking down, I knew he wasn't dead. I could see his chest rising and falling.

"Get up." I backed off to give him a minute. I didn't want the easy win. I wanted the bull. Josh lingered in my periphery, shaking his head.

When my opponent faced me again, he was raging. If he'd been a cartoon, steam would've been coming out of his ears. He came at me, and I was ready. He wasn't just thick, but quicker than I would have guessed. He landed a blow to my flank that would leave a pretty bruise before I could get out of his way. I circled around him, looking for a weakness as we traded blows. My breathing slowed, and the room around us vanished. Pain and focus took over. I lived solely inside the ring, analyzing every movement. I threw a left hook, checking him in the jaw, and followed it with a quick jab from my right as I dodged. He caught me with a quick left, and I should have backed off to avoid it, but I didn't. I drove forward, throwing hit after hit, taking each and every one of his, letting him hammer them into me, and giving them back faster than he could throw them. His breathing started to stagger.

I was going to end it. He already had a concussion, and another hard hit to his face would do him in. I fell back half a step to draw him forward, letting him think he'd gained some ground. One step, then two. His lips twitched up as he thought he'd found my weakness. How wrong he was. I launched myself forward from my back foot, bringing my fist around to land on his cheek bone. His head cocked to the side with the force of the blow and he went down, this time out cold.

Liv called the fight, but I ignored her. Walking right up to Remi's manager, I grabbed him by the shirt. "You tell *him* not to waste my time with a piece of shit like this again. If he doesn't have any real fighters, the deal is off." I released him and turned my back, walking out of the ring, needing some sort of stress release. It wasn't coming in the form of Remi at my feet, so I needed another victim.

I sat in my office long after hours, staring at my phone. Remi would know by now. I wouldn't call him. I wouldn't go to him. It took a full lockdown of my self-control, but I wouldn't do it.

SIXTEEN

REMI

If I hadn't seen the video of the fight, I wouldn't have believed it. I clicked the button on my laptop to rewind it, to see the way his body moved. I gripped myself through my shorts and glanced over at Kai. He was busy inking a full back piece, and I doubted he'd even take a break for another hour. He couldn't see me from where I sat. It would be so easy.

I trailed my fingers over the places Dante had left marks. I could almost taste them, even if the bruises had faded. I'd looked at them in the mirror over my bed and fucked my hand every night since I'd left. I groaned as I slipped my hand into my shorts.

I squeezed my shaft, digging my nails into the sensitive skin. I had to bite back a hiss of pain. Kai could easily walk out and see me. The rooms in the shop were three-quarter walls to divide the space with wide open doorways. Maybe I wanted to be caught. I kicked my feet out, watching a bead of sweat drip down Dante's neck. When he threw a punch his muscles tightened, and it took me back to him swinging his belt. The sound of his fist hitting flesh was close, so close, to the way the leather sounded against mine.

I shouldn't be imagining him touching me, but it was impossible not to. I wanted his hands on me. I wanted him to mark me with them. I was hit with the sudden realization he'd been acting when he was in the ring with me. He hadn't even gone at half speed. He was a monster when he fought. It took every ounce of self-control I had to keep from getting up and into my Jeep to drive to the airport.

I used my free hand to unbutton my shorts and slide down my zipper, freeing my cock. My hand crested my head, and I tightened my grip. Dante landed a blow to his opponent's cheek. Even in the video, I could hear the break. I rewound the footage to watch the hit again in slow motion. The sheer power drove me to fuck my hand faster. I wanted him to look at me with the same intensity.

"I was starting to think I'd never see your dick again." Kai stood in the doorway.

"Fuck." I tightened my grip on my head as my orgasm died where it had started. My balls ached, and my stomach turned with the ruined release. Little was more painful.

He laughed as I grunted, pressing my eyes shut.

"You've been standing there waiting, haven't you?"

"Your O-face is pretty easy to read, bro."

I banged my head against the wall, breathing through the pain before putting my dick away.

"I thought you were working."

"Taking a smoke break." He slipped a cigarette between his lips and lit it.

"Can you not in here?"

"Need some help, boys?" The guy Kai had been tattooing wandered in. I knew his face. I'd seen him around. I was pretty sure Kai had played with him a time or two.

"Think we can convince him to get his dick back out if

we both get on our knees?" Kai asked him, his voice playful.

"I've got work to get to, plus you should really finish and wrap up his back before fluids are exchanged." I made to step around them, but he mirrored my movement, blocking my path.

"It's just a blowjob, handsome. Plus, I think you'll like me on my knees...Sir." He dropped down as he said the word, looking up at me with soft brown eyes and slightly parted lips. He was everything my type used to be. Or still was if I could get my head out of Dante's ass.

"I really can't." I locked eyes with Kai before making my escape.

It was time for a trip to see Pops, even if it was the last place I wanted to be.

It was blazing hot by the time my flight landed. There wasn't the constant influx of fresh ocean air like Cali, which made Vegas stagnant in comparison. It wasn't just the air that was stagnant, the people were stagnant too. People and dreams came here to die. All the locals had a worn out and used look the neon heap of scrap metal caused. Few could escape it when twenty-four hours of pleasure were offered at every turn. My father taught me at a young age that everyone had a vice and a tell, the trick was figuring it out to use it against them. Figuring people out happened to be my father's specialty.

I was thirty-two to zero with him, but it was only a matter of time. I slung my bag over my shoulder and caught a cab. I might be able to avoid seeing him if I kept my head down for this trip. Dante had destroyed the men I sent his way, and I needed better specimens. I knew just where to find them. I told the cabbie the address and sat back to sweat. Either the guy's air was broken or he wasn't willing to waste the extra gas to put it on. In any case, I would sweat through my dress shirt by the time I reached my destination. I didn't dare change into the tees residing in the bag next to me. There were rules when I was in Vegas.

Where I was going was in the opposite direction of the strip. The drive gave me a lot of time to think over my life choices. It was a conversation I didn't want to have. My phone buzzed in my pocket, and I slipped it out to see Kai's name on the screen. I ignored the call and turned it off before shoving it into my duffle. As much as I liked manufactured confrontation, I hated actual confrontation. I leaned my head back and closed my eyes. Everything felt outside my control, and I had to fix it.

The cab pulled up outside a rusted out warehouse. The roof sagged in places, and the paint had been long ago bleached to an off-white color by the harsh sun. There were a few cars in the parking lot, and most fared the same as the building. A washed out place for washed out people, but I knew something most didn't.

"Sure you want to be left here?" The cabbie looked me over as he said it, and I knew what he was thinking. I was too soft to be left in a place like this.

I flashed him a smile as I handed over the fare. "I'll be alright."

"If you say so, buddy." He took the cash and didn't offer me my change.

I slammed the door behind me and crossed the gravel lot. Digging in my pocket for my keys, I found the one I was looking for by touch. It was familiar, as many times as I'd been here at four A.M. I slipped it into the lock and tugged at the door until it gave. One of Sammy's things, he never changed the locks.

I let the door swing closed behind me as my eyes landed on the man himself. He stood with his back to the door, watching the ring in the center of the room. Inside was nothing like the outside. Every piece of equipment, though well used, was in pristine condition. Feet padded into the track overhead, and a few guys with headphones on hit bags off to one side of the room. It was well past the peak hour and too early for the after-work crowd. These were all probably guys who worked the night shift at the casinos.

I waited for Sammy to notice me. Walking up behind a man like him would get me laid out, and I didn't much want bruises from anyone else. Ten minutes passed and Sammy hadn't turned. The men in the ring started another round, and the time bled out. I dug into the patience I'd learned here many years ago and slid my hands into my pockets.

I checked my watch as Sammy started a third round. He must be torturing the two in the ring for something. He'd barely let them catch their breath. Sammy chided the fighters from the sidelines. Little comments and corrections. The man never raised his voice. I should thank Dante for the extra lesson in waiting I'd had, or I might have grown annoyed with Sammy. Nothing seemed like a long wait after the night in Dante's office.

"Well, you proved me wrong," Sammy said in his soft tone. I almost couldn't make out the words.

"I'll take any edge I can get."

"Get yer ass over here." Sammy waved me over without looking back.

I strolled over, taking my sweet ass time to make a point. "How you been?" I took a place next to Sammy, standing in front of the ring to watch the two men slugging it out.

There wasn't a ref in there with them, and in this ring there weren't any rules either.

"Got no complaints." Sammy looked over at me for the first time. "Getting soft."

"Sitting sixty hours a week with a needle in my hand will do that."

"What a waste." We fell into a comfortable silence until Sammy called the men off each other.

"Clean yourself up then hit the track." As the two men walked away, he turned on me. "You're here for my guys?"

I didn't care to hide my intentions. I could recruit guys under Sammy's nose, but I wouldn't be allowed back if I did. I knew better.

"Yeah. I need a few bodies but not the normal type."

"If you want prize fighters, you know here ain't the place to find 'em."

I scoffed. "We both know you could train prize fighters if ya wanted to."

"I'd get bored."

"So why are you here? You know I put my own guys up." He didn't have to say it. We both knew what he meant.

"I'm not looking for bodies for Vegas. I've got enough people to feed the circus here."

Sammy adjusted his stance and slid his meaty hands into his pockets. "I'm listening." At a glance, anyone might assume Sammy was fat, but under his shit his 'gut' was actually hard-packed muscle, and his thick neck and arms were the same. I'd always assumed he dressed the way he did to throw people off, as men his age usually couldn't keep their muscle tone the way Sammy had. It was either steroid induced or dedication, and as well as I'd known Sammy over the years I still wasn't sure which.

"I've started a new operation in New Orleans. I have a partner there."

"Spit it out. Give me the nets." Sammy leaned back into the ropes and crossed his arms over his massive chest.

"My pool in Cali is thin. I'm working on a few other areas, but I figured I'd see if you wanted some cash thrown your way." The best way to handle Sammy was to dangle the bait and then leave him to come to it. Too much pushing would spook him. "But if you don't have enough guys, don't worry about it."

"If you think I don't know your game by now."

I raised both hands palms up. "I'm not trying to insult, boss. I got a good thing here, they just fight more than we do."

"How many?"

"I need a guy or two a week."

Sammy's large forehead creased as both his brows shot up. "You only do a fight a week here if you're lucky, I know, I keep track of these things. I get two guys in a week. If you don't have enough of your own guys to fight there too, how many fights a week are they running?"

I held up two fingers.

"He runs two nights a week?"

I slid my tongue over my teeth. "Sometimes three when he can get the guys."

"He's got no competition there?"

"Nada."

Sammy dragged his hand over the lower half of his face. "Those damn rednecks got nothing better to do than beat the shit out of each other. Huh?"

I laughed. "You got that right. They sent my last one back to me really fucked up."

Sammy tilted his chin down. "Did you send some pussy

to test the waters?"

"Na, I sent a fucking heavyweight to fight the owner. Guy had at least fifty pounds on him."

"You're shitting me?"

I pulled out my phone and showed him the video.

"Fuck, I've got a few guys who need their asses handed to 'em. Now don't you go telling them I said that." He laughed to himself and pushed off the ropes.

"Let's go to my office. We'll see what we can work out."

With the door closed behind us and Sammy sitting behind his desk, he went to work. The place was a sty, half his floor was covered in stacks of books on the art of fighting, piles of papers he needed to file, more than his secretary would get to in a lifetime. He had boxes of shirts and gloves. Boxes sent to him by sponsors he'd never look at twice. I was shocked there was an empty chair for me to sit on. I took a seat and he leaned forward, lacing his fingers, leaning on his forearms. He liked to be intimidating. I'd known him too long, and after seeing my father shoot someone in the face on my eighth birthday, I didn't know what fear was anymore.

"What's the cut for my guys?"

"Same as here. I'll pay for travel and rooms."

He gave a low whistle. "You've got yourself a sweet deal, don't ya now?"

He rubbed his tongue on the inside of his lip. "What's my cut?"

"I'll throw you a finder's fee."

He gave me a flat look. We both knew I was undercutting it, but if I came in and offered him the sun and stars, he'd doubt it and then ask for more. I wanted to keep as much of my green as possible, and he wanted to part me with as much of it as he could. Friendship didn't extend into negotiations. "How much of the house are you taking?"

"I'll double the fee I'm giving the guys, and you know it's good for them to get the experience. You said it yourself."

Sammy sat back. "How much of the house are you taking?"

"Five percent," I lied, and he knew it. He would expect no less.

"I want half of it."

"Fuck no." I was really getting twenty, but there was still no way in hell I would give him more than a percent. He wasn't doing shit but sit on his ass and loan me bodies.

"One, and don't ask for more."

"Fine." He held out his hand, and we shook. "Now that the business is outta the way, let's get you in the ring and see how lazy you've gotten."

I rose to my feet. I'd been ready for this. I needed my head cleared. Sammy was my trainer before I knew I needed a dominant. I had to have it before I faced my father. It had been far too long. I'd been stupid to stay away from Dante this long. I had to keep walking a line, getting what I needed but not giving myself over to Dante. I wasn't sure where the line was anymore, but I'd blown past it.

"Where the fuck have you been? I got word you got into town two days ago." He stood and buttoned his jacket, then pulled me into a hug. It was warm and everything it shouldn't be. I returned the gesture, and we both fixed our shirts when he pulled back. It was so ingrained in me to be this way when I was here.

"I was taking care of business."

One brow twitched as he returned to his seat. His gaze shifted across the room, and I knew what it meant. "Not done playing, I see."

I shut my mouth tight, glad when one of the girls came to take our order. I didn't give her a second glance even though she wore less than the girls on stage. Only the best for Caci Sr.

"A double Patròn on the rocks," I said, turning back to my father.

His eyes were on the girl. If she were a third his age I'd be shocked. She batted her lashes at him and pressed her palms into the table, leaning over to shove her breasts together. The position of mistress was almost better than wife, and everyone in this room knew it. One of the many reasons I left.

"Scotch, dry." He waved her off and watched her shake her ass as she walked away before he turned his attention back to me. "She's one of my favorites."

"I can see why," I said, dryly.

He sat back, studying me. I stared him in the eyes and didn't flinch. My father was a large man, in height and girth. His hands were folded on the table in front of him. My stomach turned. He looked calm, but there was a reason he was who he was. As soon as I could walk I'd been in a suit. This was a man who pressed his own clothes before dressing every morning. Appearance was everything.

"When are you going to stop playing games and take your place?"

Never.

"I do what I need to," I replied wearily. It was going to be one of those days.

"You do what suits your fancy. I can't keep up this pace forever, and then I'll need you to step in." He was already pushing sixty and kept up just fine.

"Let's not speak of such things."

"We are going to speak of it." His voice dropped, and he leaned forward so our faces were only a foot apart. "We are going to speak of it now, after you ignore my calls for a week. You have my name and my money, boy. Don't act like you have the steel balls of a self-made man when you would be nothing without me." He sat back, his upper lip curled in a sneer.

Ten years ago the speech would have scared me straight for a few months. Now I had such little regard for my life. I stared back.

"I don't touch your money."

Both his thick brows shot up. I dug my phone out, logged into the app, and held the statement out to him.

"Haven't in years." I tossed my phone down onto the table. "Granted, I used the capital you provided, but you'll notice it's in the account too."

I should shut my mouth. I shouldn't have come in the mood I was in. My mistakes all could have been prevented had I not been so stubborn, but it was nearly impossible to change a lifetime of breeding overnight.

"If you choose to live in poverty and leave my money sitting there, I guess this is your choice. But you're blood," he said blood like he said gold. "The blood running through your veins is Caci blood. You have a responsibility to me and your family." He glanced around again, checking to make sure there wasn't anyone listening in on our business. He held privacy in high esteem. He'd shot men for less. "You have a responsibility to carry on *my* name."

"You don't have to worry about the bloodline." I'd slept

with a few dozen women in the city, and I'd made sure he knew about it. There couldn't be any doubt—could there? I schooled my features and tapered my words as the server approached. "I'm twenty-seven, I don't need to settle down just yet."

She stepped in so close to set my drink down in front of me, I could feel the heat from her tits in my face. I snapped my teeth, and she squealed. My father burst out laughing.

"This kid of mine is a womanizer." He said it like he didn't have four mistresses already.

She giggled and rubbed up against him as she placed his drink on the table. He grabbed her ass, and she gasped. She'd have bruises from his grasp. All of this might have been shocking had I not been in strip clubs since I was three years old. His antics bored me now. He smacked her ass as she sauntered off.

"No one likes to settle down, but it needs to be done."

"Is this a prelude into 'you need to move home, son'?" I shocked myself as the words came out.

"I know you needed your freedom, as all children of a certain age do, and I've let you have it, but it's time to take on a bigger role in the business and forget this cage fighting nonsense." He paused. "It's not like you can't still have all of the same things on the side. You'll have to be a little more discreet out of respect, but we all do it."

There was nothing to say. I picked up my drink and pressed it to my lips. He wouldn't take 'no' for an answer. I wasn't going to give up fighting. It had been my salvation in this world, and I wouldn't have survived without it. It wasn't even the open relationship I was against. Clearly, I'd lived in one for years with Kai. The women in these situations had no choice. They fell in love with the men and stayed for the money. Maybe they deserved it if they tolerated the sleeping around 'respectfully,' but I couldn't do it. No one had even made me want to stay until Kai, and that wasn't a marriage. It was a friendship with benefits. He understood what I was, knew what I had to hide. He was my real family.

I drank. Drink after drink. As fast as the server would bring them. She didn't mind the running either. It meant she had more time with my father, and since he was paying, she'd have his money too. I tasted bile on my tongue. My stomach was at war with the Patron, but I kept pouring it down my throat. Each thought that entered my mind dragged me down like a weight tied around my neck. The more time I spent here the more therapy I would need, and I couldn't split myself between three places. I would have to give at least one of them up to do as my father asked, if not both.

Other men would kill for this. A private room at the nicest strip club in Vegas, if there were such a thing. Money, women, power. I was mortal, and I enjoyed the perks at times, but I had my own money now. I wasn't any happier than I had been when Kai and I first moved with barely five-hundred-dollars between us. I tried to find my calm in the memories of Dante, but it wasn't enough. I couldn't survive without the pain either, but it didn't make me happy. It took the edge off.

Realization hit me. My entire life I thought I needed the pain, craved it even, couldn't get through a day without it. I'd got more than enough of it with Dante, but now I knew pain wasn't the only thing I needed. I needed to let go of everything and be freed from my mind. Dante held the key. One taste, and I knew I was addicted. It would never taste the same with anyone ever again.

I was fucked.

I had to go back.

SEVENTEEN

DANTE

Lights flashed in my rain-streaked windows and I looked up, unable to make out much in the glare. I wasn't expecting anyone. When the engine died, my eyes adjusted instantly, and I could make out a yellow Jeep.

I stepped out onto my porch and crossed my arms over my chest. The car was a rental, which meant one thing. Him. I was a little surprised it had taken him this long to come back. He stepped out like he owned the place. His suit was rumpled, and he was missing a jacket, leaving him in a soaked shirt and a vest. I groaned even though he looked like death. I wouldn't show it, but it put a warm spot in my chest to know he came to me like this. I wanted him to need me.

"Look what the storm dragged in," I said.

"I thought you said I could come and go as I pleased?" he replied, pushing his fingers through his disheveled hair, but he didn't approach me. I had said as much. I wasn't used to someone who could stand on their own two feet.

"I did, but we had business you should have handled yourself. It's been six weeks. Are you avoiding me?" I tried and failed to keep the edge out of my voice. I was usually good at hiding my emotions.

He took a step forward, flashing me a smile. "I was busy?" He turned his statement into a question.

"Your cute bullshit may work on your submissives, but it won't work on me."

"Sorry?" He did it again.

"Neither will ending everything with a question. You're either sorry or you aren't. Don't ask me."

He pursed his lips, and I could tell he was trying not to grin. "Forgive me, Sir." His eyes pleaded with me as he dropped to his knees on the wet drive.

"If you're too busy, why are you here?"

"I'm sorry," he said again, more sincerely this time.

"You were so eager when you were here before. I want to know what happened."

His Adam's apple bobbed in his throat, and he didn't say anything.

I turned and walked back into the house, closing the door most of the way behind me.

"What are you doing?" he called after me before I could get it shut.

"Until you decide you want to talk, you can wait out there." I risked a glance over my shoulder and saw the fear in his eyes. I knew he remembered my office. I have the patience of a saint and the conscience of the devil himself. I would leave him on his knees all damn night, and he knew it.

"I was conflicted." His words came through the slit in the door, right before it closed.

I counted to five and then reopened it. "About?" I didn't venture outside. He'd give me what I wanted or he'd stay there.

"About how I feel."

"Go on."

He dropped his head. I waited.

"You don't speak to me for over a month, and you think you can just show up and I'll allow you to fall at my feet?"

"Dante, I was..." He slumped in defeat and his hands met the porch, his head hung limp between his shoulders. "I tried to deny to myself, and to Kai, how much I need you." When he looked up at me again, agony was written on his face.

"And now you will be denied by me." I knew he'd never be mine, and I had to stop trying to convince myself this would work. No matter how I felt about him, I had to let go.

He fell forward to his forearms and pressed his forehead to the ground. "Forgive me. Don't make me suffer anymore. I've already suffered more than you can imagine for the past month." His muscles and the hang of his body were riddled with the pain he claimed. He was either a great actor or his words were true.

I didn't want to believe him.

"Maybe you should find someone who has time for your waffling."

"Kai made me leave. He told me he couldn't deal with me anymore unless I got what I needed." He picked up his head to try and gauge my reaction.

"You said that before." My face was unwavering stone. "Maybe you two can find a dominant who will take on both of you and your bullshit." It was mean, but I was past caring. I couldn't allow myself to have feelings. Feelings always lead to disappointment.

"I won't leave again. I promise you." He crawled to me and dropped his face to my boots. "Master."

I pressed my palm into my chest where it ached. Could I keep doing this knowing he would leave again? He could make all the promises in the world, but I didn't believe he could really be with me. He couldn't surrender. He would lose too much. I was betting Kai held out for this same reason.

"Go find someone else," I spat my words, showing the anger I harbored for his actions.

"I tried." He turned his head away, resting his cheek on the arch of my foot. "It's impossible. No one can give me what you can."

I stiffened but didn't pull away. I knew my resolve wavered. I gave him something no one else did. His words worked their way down into my sub-conscience and wreaked havoc.

"If you ever do this again, we are done. Do you understand?" I couldn't deny my need to take care of him anymore. I wanted to give him everything he needed. I wanted him to be able to let go and hand it all over to me. "I'm not wasting my time if you're looking elsewhere."

He slid his hands up the back of my legs, coming up on his knees. I waited a moment before looking down to meet his gaze. He wore a cocky grin. He loved to win. Oh, how I wanted to dash that from him.

I wrapped my long fingers around his throat, yanking him to his feet. I brought our faces millimeters apart. "Tell me what you need."

"I need to be nothing."

"Oh, you've always been nothing." I chuckled darkly. "But you're my nothing."

He went limp in my grasp, leaning into me. "You know how many times I've imagined you saying that?"

"Every night you went to bed without me?"

He didn't answer, and I released my grip on his throat. "Your penance starts now."

His head snapped up. "Master?"

"You heard me."

His arousal grew behind his slacks. He was as easy as I was. It would be our downfall.

"What do you want from me, Master?"

"Go lie in the middle of the floor in the playroom. I want a show."

He swallowed. "A show?"

"It's not your place to ask questions. You know better."

He lowered his chin and nodded before turning to take the stairs up. He was king of the ring in his world. Now he was going to be my boy on his knees in mine.

I peeled off my Hanes' tee as I walked up the stairs, tossing it aside. My jeans were slung low on my hips, and when I got to the top, I flipped on the full bank of lights, illuminating him in the center of the room where he stood. I toed off my boots, opting for bare feet.

"Why do you still have clothes on?"

He moved his hands to his belt, undoing it before sliding it from the loops. He hung his slacks over the Saint Andrew's cross and laid his button-down and vest next to it. He wasn't wearing anything under. He folded his hands in front of himself and stood watching me.

"You are nothing here."

He set his hands on his hips and stared me down. "It's going to take a lot more than stripping me naked to humiliate me."

I reared back and smacked him so hard his head cocked to the side. He wore my print in flaming red across his cheek when he turned back, but his face said it all.

"Please."

"I don't want to hear your begging."

"Then what do you want, Master?" The cockiness to his

tone burrowed its way into my mind. He needed some humility. He thought he owned the world.

"What I want is of little consequence to you. I want to know what you want and why it took you so long to come and get it."

"I told you I have an image to uphold."

"I don't think you're telling me the truth." I stepped toward him, crossing my arms over my chest. "If you don't want to be here, you shouldn't have come back."

"I need to be here." He lowered his eyes for the first time, and I knew I'd struck a nerve.

"Need and want are two different things. I don't want you here if you don't want it. I have no use for a submissive who doesn't want it."

"Isn't needing it enough?" he whispered.

"No, you have to want it, and you have to be honest with me. Secrets will divide us."

He nodded.

"I expect honesty from you. You have to let me into the darkest parts of your mind for this. I want it all, inside and out. If there is no trust here, then there is nothing." I paused for a moment. "It can't be faked either. If you want this, you have to give yourself over in return."

"I trust you." His head shot up, and he looked offended. "I wouldn't have come to you in the first place if I didn't."

"I must also trust you. This goes both ways. You've made the rules, set my boundaries, and you hold the end with a word, and yet you want secrets?" We stood face to face, and his deep green eyes stared into mine.

"I'm not used to being open."

"You're also not used to actually being submissive."

Shock showed on his face. It had been a guess, but now I knew there was some truth to it.

"I want to submit to you."

"Then you have to be honest with me. I want to know what's going through your mind so I can help you, so I can care for you, so I can be here for you. This clearly isn't about a fuck. You came to me only for the mental aspects of the game we play, and you want to shield your thoughts?" I wasn't sure my words were getting through. He hid as much of himself as I did, but this wasn't the place for it. Life and death were in the balance in this room.

"It's physical..." He really believed it.

"It's not physical, you're fooling yourself. If it were lust you would have had my dick in your ass by now. There is so much more here."

He bowed his head again, and I thought he was working over what I'd said. He could meditate on it while he worked. He was here now, and I wasn't going to waste time.

"Lay on the floor with one arm above your head." I went to the cabinet for my favorite blue rope.

EIGHTEEN

REMI

I tested the binding on my left arm he'd secured to the leg of his play table. He'd weaved the rope over my skin in a spider web pattern, starting around my hand, encasing my thumb, and traveling down my arm. The blue rope contrasted my tanned skin, crisscrossing over the ink. I felt like his art, and a smile crept across my face. It was out of character, and this was a punishment, but Jesus, did he make me feel good.

"Wrap your hand around your cock."

I trailed my fingers over my abs, taking my sweet ass time, because I knew it would get to him. My fingers curled around my base, and I groaned involuntarily as my hips lifted off the floor. He'd bound my ankles to my thighs in a frog tie and cuffed me into a spreader bar. I'd never felt so free.

"Stroke it."

I did as I was told, letting my fingers glide over the smooth head of my cock and back down. Pleasure washed over me, and life melted away.

"Faster."

"Squeeze it."

"Fuck your hand for me."

I lost myself in his commands. The deep baritone of his voice. Nothing mattered but pleasing him.

"Stop." My chest heaved as I pried my fingers from my dick.

My eyes snapped opened. I hadn't even realized I'd closed them. Dante loomed over me, the bulge in his jeans unmissable. I waited for his next command. A grin slithered across one side of his mouth. My chest swelled.

"You're so sexy, boy." He held himself with his arm behind his back like he was hiding something.

It was unusual for him, and I came out of my trance a little.

"But?" I prompted him, too horny to wait for his leisure.

"No, but, you're beautiful, and I want more."

More was a dangerous word.

"I'm yours to do with what you will."

"Excellent." He brought the hidden object forward. It was a good-sized glass dildo. He dropped to his knees beside me, rough jeans brushing against my bare skin. He pressed the tip against my lips. "Suck."

I parted them for him. He shoved the tip to the back of my throat, not giving me time to adjust to it. I wished it was him. His rope on my body and his taste on my tongue. My release only on his whim. Bliss.

He pulled back and pushed forward, playing the glass over my tongue. My cock strained, leaking precum over my inked abs, but I waited for permission.

He ignored the lower half of me, barely touching me as he worked. I wanted to beg for the contact I craved, but it was my rules preventing it. The words were on the tip of my tongue, but I swallowed them back. He withdrew the dildo and held it out.

"Fuck yourself with it."

A mixture of elation and disappointment washed through me. I wasn't sure why I'd thought he would use it on me. He was following the rules I'd set. I took it from him and met his eyes as I reached between my legs. The cool tip met my entrance, and I sucked air in through my teeth. I'd never fucked myself with anything. I'd had plenty of toys used on me, but this was different. This was putting on a show, only I couldn't act my way through it like I did with everything else. I was raw for him.

With a little pressure, the glass slid past my barrier. I toyed with it pulling back and inching it forward, stretching myself wide open. He watched, hungry. His tongue flicked across his teeth, and a low rumble filled his chest. I watched the struggle behind his eyes. He wanted me as much as I wanted him and that drove me on. I filled myself for his pleasure.

"Can you get off with your prostate?"

I gasped, knowing my voice wouldn't come out audibly so I nodded instead. He grabbed the spreader bar pressing it toward my ass to open me further. I could feel his rough fingers brush against my skin, and then they were gone. He popped open a bottle of lube and drizzled it on the glass as it moved, adding to my saliva, reducing the friction while increasing the stimulation.

"Take yourself there, but don't let go."

I tilted the shaft and pressed the slick head into my prostate. He stayed there, one hand on the bar, the other on my thigh as I fucked myself. My dick stood straight up, begging to be touched.

"Enough." He was breathless.

I made him breathless. I dragged my teeth over my lips and started to slide the dildo out of myself.

"Leave it in, all the way."

I did as I was told.

"Let go of it."

I grunted but waited for his next command.

"Fuck your hand."

"Yes, Master." It was barely more than a whisper.

My eyes started to fall shut, but I made them stay open. I had to see what I did to him. I had to know I was good for him. Sweat beaded on my forehead, and my chest heaved. It only took a few moments to bring myself to the brink, but I didn't give in. I wanted to hold on to the moment. His eyes on me. My skin burned where he touched it. I knew then it would never be enough. I could drown in him, and it would still never be enough.

"Good boy."

His words took me to another level. I was floating on his whim, utterly under his control.

"Come."

I couldn't have held back if I wanted to. At his word my body shuddered, giving him what he'd asked for. I was engulfed in it. Every nerve on fire. My vision blacked as I stroked myself through the release. I kept my hand going past the pain of over stimulation. Finally, my hand fell away.

His thumb rubbed over the juncture of my hip, and he leaned over me. "Such a good boy."

A lazy smile crept over my mouth. I've craved these moments my whole life, this is what I've lived for. For him. I didn't want to leave.

"Now if only you could be this good when it's information I'm after and not your release."

I dug my nails into my palm and squeezed my eyes shut. Nothing would get past him. Just when I'd thought he'd forgotten something, there it was. He picked up his hand

and looked like he was going to skim his fingertips over my stomach, but he pulled back.

"A guy can't even get some cuddling before the inquisition starts?"

He shook his head.

"Untie me first?"

"Why did you stay away so long?"

It was part of the game for him. He wanted more than my body. He wanted my mind. He didn't need to touch me to infiltrate the darkest parts of me. I could tell this was more important to him.

"I had business."

"I'm going to give you one more chance to answer me. You belong to me in this room. Now answer the question. Why did you stay away so long?"

"Let me get dressed then we can go talk." It was enough time to come up with an excuse.

"Are you scared to tell me the truth?"

"Do you always feel the need to get inside everyone's head?"

"Has answering a question with a question worked for you in the past? Because it's not going to work here."

"Dante—"

He took a knife from his back pocket and cut the ropes binding me in quick succession.

"Where the hell did that come from?" I let the ropes fall from me as I sat up.

"I had thought about putting my name on your chest."

Arousal sparked in my gut. "Why didn't you?"

"Because no matter how many times you say it, you don't belong to me here. You come and offer your body, but you don't let me have what counts."

He had more of it than he knew. More of it than I liked.

"That's not true."

"Get out." He dumped my clothes on top of me and turned on his heel.

I scrambled to my feet, still reeling. The high was crashing down on my head.

"Dante..." I called, but he was long gone.

I pulled on my slacks, taking my time. I wasn't going to get away with the things I did in the past. I took the stairs two at a time and walked out the door. It was pissing down rain as I stepped out onto the porch.

I lingered there, wondering if he was watching me from wherever he'd disappeared to in the house. He could turn it all off and be so cold in an instant. It made me doubt all of his feelings. I had to walk out of here with my head held high. Fuck him if he thought he deserved to know every thought in my head. He barely knew me. It wasn't his right to demand, but it was. I'd offered it all to him that night. I'd come to him. I hated when reasoning interrupted me justifying to myself why I was angry. I hated even more that he might be right.

There was a stark contrast between Dante and other dominants I'd been with. Other dominants I'd walked all over. None of them had made me feel like this. None of them made me crave them. Maybe this bastard actually knew what I needed.

I stepped off the porch and hurried to my vehicle. I rested my head against the rain-soaked Jeep and took a breath. If I didn't get myself under control, I was going to march back in there and say something I couldn't take back. I pulled open my door and then slammed it without getting in.

I turned back to the house. "You fucking bastard!" I yelled.

"You don't have to yell." His voice came calmly from on the porch, in the shadows.

I jumped. "Fuck, have you been here this whole time?"

"You're like an elephant, stomping around and not paying attention to your surroundings. You're going to get mugged one day."

I took my wallet out of my pocket and threw it at him. "Who cares? I don't need the money."

He didn't move to pick it up. It was a standoff. I had to swallow my pride and do as he asked. I wanted to. I wanted him. I wanted to climb into his bed and never leave, but I couldn't ignore the rest of my life or abandon Kai.

He must have had the patience of a saint. He didn't move or speak. He watched as the rain soaked me through. Every step toward him was a battle. Every step toward what I wanted for myself was a battle. I'd been in this war with myself too long, and I was tired.

"Can I come back in?"

"Are you going to tell me why you stayed away so long?"

I nodded.

NINETEEN

DANTE

"Go on then," I said. He hadn't left. He'd stayed. He'd stayed here to be with me. I was elated, and I let none of it show. He was like a damn baby bird, and any sudden movement would scare him away.

He took a deep breath. There was fear in his eyes. He could run at any moment, and I'd never see him again. It was better to be rid of him now before he burrowed his way into my heart. I couldn't take another loss, and he was already too close.

"I'm realizing things about myself I'd rather not know." The whisper floated to me on the wind.

"What have you realized?" I wanted to keep him talking, even if he was speaking to himself.

"What I've needed all along."

"The pain is a mask."

He hung his head. "Yes."

"You need it, but you need to let go more."

He dragged his head up and looked me in the eyes. "No one can do it but you."

"There aren't many dominants like me." I'd been told it, and I'd seen it.

"That's why I had to find you." He sounded tired, like

he carried the weight of the world to my door. I wanted him to leave the burden where he stood.

"This isn't and never will just be physical."

His shoulder shook. "I thought it could be." He fell to his knees as the rain hammered down. The droplets slid down his ink and dripped off his fingertips. He was beautiful. Different than my husband had been. He'd been clean cut with only one tattoo. Remi was covered, and every picture told me a story. He thought he hid behind a mask, but he'd really painted a picture if anyone cared to look close enough.

"This brings us closer than sex. It's trust and exposing yourself in a way you never have to with a simple fuck."

He stayed silent.

"You can't handle it, can you?"

Slowly, his head rose. "What?"

"The connection. You've been running from it your whole life. Kai is an excuse."

"How do you know?" he asked.

How did I know? I knew because I'd done the same thing for so long. I'd been doing it since my husband died. I shouldn't be doing this. I knew I shouldn't, as I crossed the porch. I walked right up to him, there on his knees, and wrapped my hand around the back of his head.

Remi was going to destroy me. Masen almost had. Masen was fire, and he'd burned me, almost beyond recognition. I'd been left in pieces, but pieces could be put back together. This man kneeling before me was a bomb, and when he went off he was going to take out everything in his path. I wrapped my other arm around the weapon and hugged him to me.

"I know because I've done it myself. If we both want our lives to stay the same, we have to draw lines."

"Like a contract."

"Yeah, maybe it's a good idea."

He nodded, pressing his face into my thigh. My dick was hard from the contact. I needed rules to follow or I could easily lose myself in this, in him, and I think he was too used to people losing themselves in him.

"Can I come in now?"

He got to his feet.

"This will be on my terms. Do you understand?"

The smirk returned.

"I don't think you do. I think you're so used to getting your way, and you don't really know what giving up control means."

"I'm looking forward to you showing me."

I scoffed and left him standing there as I walked inside. He followed on my heels like a good boy. The hardest part of this, of him, was he knew to get to me already.

"Stand here," I said stopping at the entrance to my room.

He did as I asked, and I slid my hands under his shirt, lifting it up. He raised his arms, allowing me to take it off.

"I don't have my bag."

I gave him a look, and he closed his mouth. Next I took his slacks off again and tossed them on the floor. I walked over them and saw his lip twitch. It was so easy to get to him.

"I have some things that should fit you." I stepped into my room, and he followed. In my closet, I pulled a soft tee from the shelf and handed it over to him. He waited.

"Put it on."

"I never thought I'd have a dominant who'd want me dressed for bed." The sass was back. He rebounded from opening himself up, to putting the mask back in place like an expert. He'd been doing this for a long time. It was more proof of my bomb theory, and yet here I was handing over sweatpants.

"I never thought I'd have a submissive I couldn't fuck."

"Touché." There was a weight carried with the word. A sadness holding onto it as it left his lips. If I looked hard enough I could see the seam in his mask and the areas where it slipped.

"Crashing?"

He met my eyes, and I knew before he confirmed it.

"Come to bed with me, my boy. Let me hold you so you can come down."

When we climbed into bed, he melted into my arms. I think if he could have tied himself to me, he would have. I closed my eyes, and like the last time he was in my bed, my mind went quiet. The effect was remarkable. I wasn't anywhere but with him. My mind wasn't hell. It was cool and clouded here in the shade with him.

I sunk into sleep with ease, for the first time in weeks.

I left him sleeping in my bed. I was conflicted, and I needed therapy. By the time I made it to the bar, Liv had already unloaded the truck and had her feet kicked up on my desk going over paperwork.

"Do you ever sleep?"

Liv glanced up. "I'm superwoman. I don't need to sleep." She wrinkled her nose in the cute way she does. "I sleep from about ten to four. It's enough for me."

More than I did, but I wasn't about to tell her. She needed it. "Admit it, you just hate leaving this place."

"Of course, I do, boss." She said the word boss in a taunting manner. I loved the way it rolled off her tongue.

"You're dangerous."

Her curls from last night were still in perfect shape, and there wasn't a wrinkle in her blouse. "I know, and I like it that way."

I laughed and shook my head. "It's a good thing you're too valuable to fuck."

"You have yourself in enough trouble with your dick. You don't need to add me to the list."

I took a seat across from her and wondered if she knew how right she was.

"I'd bruise more than your ego if you acted like that with me." She side-eyed me in a sisterly way.

I rolled my eyes but believed her. I'd seen her take down a few men with a swift kick to the manhood, bringing them to their knees, and every single one had deserved it.

"Am I really so bad?"

"You have your moments."

I shouldn't have asked the question, but I'm a masochist as well as a sadist. "Moments of good or moments of bad?"

"Yes."

"Bitch."

She flashed me a grin then returned to her work, biting on her pencil in a sex kitten way I figured had to be a punishment for something I'd done to her, or perhaps the universe was punishing me for a past life. Either way, I was going to sit and endure it.

"You're really in trouble with this one aren't you?"

"What makes you ask?"

A tiny crease formed in her brow, and she sighed, setting down the papers. "Never mind. We are fucked for tonight. You need to see if Josh can fight."

"What?"

She nodded.

"We have no one?"

She bit her lip and shook her head.

I exhaled. "He took a big ego hit after the last one. I'm not sure it's a good idea."

"What's the alternative? He fights you and loses, or he fights one of Caci's guys and maybe loses." Her frown deepened.

"I'll just take the fight."

"This would be your third fight in a row." She gave me the stern, motherly look.

I shrugged. "And?" Now that the idea was in my head, I wanted it. It would help clear my head and help me decide what to do about the boy in my bed.

If Liv saw it, I was fucked. I didn't know what to do with myself. He wasn't mine. He wouldn't ever be mine. The rules were clear, and I was so close to crossing a line. I couldn't let him go, but at the same time I knew I couldn't continue how we were going. I was setting myself up to get fucked.

"Lost in thought?"

I looked up from where I sat on the wrong side of my desk. "You were right."

"I know I am." She pursed her dark red lips. "I don't want you to go back to that place."

"I haven't left it."

"Until now." She knew so much more than she let on.

"Am I so easy to read?"

"Maybe not to everyone, but I can tell. I don't think I've seen you sleep this well in years." There was more on her mind, and I needed her to say it. "You can't live life like you were, and you can't go on as you are."

I dropped my head back to hang over the back of the chair. "Maybe this is the only shot at happiness I'm going to get."

She got up, smoothed a hand down the front of her skirt, then walked over to where I sat. She placed a kiss on my forehead. "You don't need him or anyone else to be happy. You're not going to be happy until you let Masen go. If you want to go forward and have any sort of healthy thing with Caci, you have to fix yourself first."

She was right, but I hated hearing it.

"What if I can't be fixed?" I dragged my head up to look at her.

She gave my shoulder a squeeze, digging her white nails into my muscle. "You lost yourself someplace, and I think you can get it back if you want it. But you haven't wanted it for years. You wanted to be in the ground with Masen, and you've done everything but put a bullet in your brain trying to get there."

"I'm not suicidal," I snapped.

"I never said you were, but you haven't tried very hard to live." She stepped back. "Tell me why you're here and not wrapped up in Caci?"

"What if he's not dead?"

"He's dead. Stop chasing ghosts." A line had formed between her brows. I could see the pity there.

I hung my head and nodded. "This ghost is going to haunt me forever."

"Then you'll never be happy." Her fingers drifted up my arm and over my shoulder. They lingered for a second then she walked toward the door. "Have you heard from Josh?"

Shit. "No."

"How long has it been since you heard from him?"

"A few days." Or so I thought. I was a shit friend. I needed to go see him, but Remi was at my place.

She gave me a pointed look over her shoulder.

"He's been taking the loss hard." I really hoped he hadn't drunk himself into a coma. It was like him to disappear for a few days with a bruised ego, but this was going on too long.

"Still?"

"Yeah, I've barely seen him except at fights for a few weeks."

"He hasn't been the same in the ring either," she said.

"No, he's been a different person. I tried to talk to him after the last loss, but he wouldn't speak to me."

She sighed. "Three losses and an almost. He's going to drink himself to death or get himself killed in the ring."

I rubbed my fingers over my temple. "I'll go check on him now."

"You fix your personal life, and I'll go dry Josh out. But when Caci leaves, go see Josh. He's been there for you for a long time, and it's time you repaid some of it."

"I owe him a lot, don't I?"

"You'd be dead if it wasn't for him. I really do believe that." Her words weren't harsh, but I felt them in my chest.

"Stop being right."

"Maybe when you boys get your acts together I can take a break from being right."

"I don't know how to fix this mess," I admitted.

"Only you can figure that out, but I'll tell you, chasing ghosts and not asking for what you want are the two ways not to get it."

I rolled my eyes, but she was gone. It was time to face this and him. If he was what made me happy, why did it still feel like there was a weight on my chest?

TWENTY

DANTE

The sun leaked through the cracks in the windows, glinting across his chest as it expanded and contracted. He had one arm draped over his face, shielding his eyes. I crossed the room and drew the curtains. The room was engulfed in blackness. It took a few moments for my eyes to adjust. I seldom slept during the night hours, so I needed the curtains to have any hope of catching a bit of sleep.

I slipped back into bed next to him and laid my arm over his chest, inching closer, trying to not wake him. The warmth of his body heated my cool skin, and I molded myself to him. I found myself wanting more of this. I'd told myself it would be enough, but I'd been lying. I needed the dominance to keep myself sane, but I also needed someone to make my life with. I'd been punishing myself for so long I couldn't remember what this felt like. I couldn't let it go now, but he wasn't mine.

"What's in your head?" He startled me.

"I didn't think you were awake."

"Your thoughts are so loud they woke me," he murmured.

I drifted my fingers over his skin. "I was trying to quiet my mind before I went to sleep." I had to change the subject, or I risked spilling my guts. "When do you have to leave?"

"Later today."

"Stay." It was an impulse, and I never acted on impulse. He really was turning me inside out, like Liv had said.

He picked up his head to look at me. "Say it again."

"Stay, at least for a couple of days."

A smile spread over his face like a sunrise. He lit up and dropped his forehead to rest against mine. "Now how can I say no?" He rubbed his nose over mine, and for an instant I thought he was going to kiss me. My lips parted, and I inhaled a breath of him. The ink and blood and sorrow hidden under his skin...I wanted it all. Before his lips touched mine he dropped his face to my neck and fisted a hand in my shirt. He went stiff, agony written in his movements.

I didn't say anything, I did what I could and held him. Eventually, he loosened and slid his arm around my lower back to hold me tighter.

"I'll stay," he said at last. "For a couple of days."

I turned into his hair, wanting to press a kiss there, but I stopped myself. He had limits, and he had these limits for a reason. I wasn't going to be the dick who forced anything he didn't want. I allowed only the smile taking over my face.

"Go back to sleep."

"I'm trying." I stretched out, letting him settle onto my chest. It was a lie. I wasn't trying to sleep. I was trying to figure out how I was going to fix the mess I'd made of myself. I didn't know how to let go of the ghost of him I'd let take over everything.

"Your thoughts are loud again."

"How do you know?"

"I'm not giving up my secrets if you're not." He yawned. "Aren't you tired? You haven't slept at all."

I wasn't sure what good sleep was. "I slept two hours."

"If that. You slipped out pretty early."

"I went to the bar," I admitted.

"Why?" He tensed a little, and I was sure he assumed Josh. How could someone with so little to offer be so possessive? It baffled me. Not that I wanted it to change, even a little.

"I went to help Liv with the truck." It was mostly true.

"How's Josh?" There it was.

"I haven't seen him." Also true.

"He's been losing." I could hear the sleep in Remi's voice. He'd lose it if I kept him distracted.

"I know. It's sent him into a downward spiral."

"And what are you going to do about it?" Now he was back awake.

"You don't miss much, Caci, do you?"

His eyes flashed with rage. "How do you think I've stayed alive all these years?"

We fell into silence, and his breathing slowed. Then it hit me, I knew where I needed to start. I hadn't been there in years, and it was time to go.

"Come with me someplace?"

"Now?" he asked.

"Yeah, I think I need to go now."

"Where?"

"You'll see."

TWENTY ONE

DANTE

'Saint Louis cemetery number three', the sign read as I pulled to a stop on the street in front of the famous place. His family owned a large plot here, not that he'd spoken to his father in fifteen years, but it's where he wanted his final resting place to be. His sister visited from time to time. She sent me a message every time she was in town. I ignored them all. It had been about six months since I'd heard from her. Maybe she'd given up. She was the only other person who'd been here with me at the time. I felt a little tinge of guilt about never replying to her again. I stepped off my bike and inhaled the damp air. I could barely look at the place, and he wasn't even in there.

Remi came up behind me and placed his hand on my lower back. "What's this?"

I figured he knew what it was but wanted to hear it from my lips. "It's where the box with my husband is."

He nodded.

"But he's not in it."

Remi turned toward me, the confusion showing on his face. I wasn't ready to tell the story, so I led him into the ancient graveyard. He followed, not pressing the issue. I wondered how much his research on me could have told him. Only a handful knew the story, and it was a different one than we'd told the police.

The tombs loomed over us like individual haunted houses. Some of them long abandoned, while others looked well cared for with offerings from the living. I'd always thought guilt drove most visits to these places, and mine was no different. I'd told myself for so long I'd stayed away because he wasn't really here, but I'd stayed away because I was livid. No, livid didn't even described it. He'd taken away everything with his selfish act.

I found the area his family owned after a few wrong turns. The place was a maze, and a few of the ghosts who haunted it were probably poor souls or grave robbers who'd gotten lost in here. His mother's line went back for a century in this city and at the end of the row, he laid next to her. It had probably been the only act of kindness his father had bestowed on her, letting her come to rest here instead of in Chicago.

There were flowers in front of both his and his mother's tombs. Recent ones, Sara *had* given up. I hung my head. It was a bridge I'd never be able to fix. For the best, but I mourned it now. Remi's fingers traced over Masen's name etched in the marble. He didn't speak. I drew in a breath, fighting the bile in my throat and the weakness in my knees.

"I shouldn't have brought you here," I managed to get out.

"Is this what's been weighing on your mind?" All the games between us were gone. Remi stood before me. He wasn't trying to get anything from me or me from him. He was transparent, well, as transparent as the son of a mob boss with a graveyard of his own skeletons was going to get.

"I've been carrying it since I put the box in there." I pressed my face into the cool stone and squeezed my eyes shut. He wasn't even here, so why did it feel like I was looking at his dead body?

"Why is the box empty?"

There was no official report. I could tell him anything, but I wanted to share this with him.

"Because he was a coward."

He waited.

"He didn't want to dwindle to nothing. He didn't want me to see him like that." I'd never said the words out loud.

"I don't understand."

"He asked me to kill him over breakfast. He set a gun on the counter as I flipped a pancake, right next to the fucking fruit. We had three months, maybe more, and he put a gun on the table and told me he couldn't do it anymore." Tears burned in my eyes. I hadn't cried, not even when I found our bed empty the next morning. I'd had cold determination then and anger since.

"You killed him?" His voice was as hollow as the ground under our feet.

"I wish I had now. Then I'd know his final resting place." I swallowed past the lump in my throat. It wasn't true. I'd never have been able to do it. "I took the gun and threw it in the river. Selfish bastard." I sounded bitter.

"You didn't report it so you could collect the insurance money?" he asked. Now it was a puzzle Remi had to figure out.

"I never made a claim with them. I've never touched a penny of his money."

"His money?"

"You had to have seen it. He had a trust fund, and he

made quite a bit of his own. All of his money, every penny, is still sitting in his account."

"I assumed something had happened to it all. Maybe a gambling debt. The papertrail would've gone cold after he died."

"It's all still in his Swiss account."

"Held by the courts?" he asked. I could see him trying to work through the reasons behind my actions.

I scoffed. "No, no one contested it. I won't touch it."

"So you didn't take his money, and you didn't make a claim on the insurance. Why do you need anyone to think there is a body there?"

"Dignity." I dragged my fingers down the stone so hard I left a trail of blood behind them. "He asked me to."

"What happened, Dante?" He pulled my hand away from the wall.

Thunder sounded in the distance. Some spring we were getting. It was already raining every other day. Wind whipped through the empty spaces between the tombs like a soft whisper from the dead. I'd never be able to hear his voice again. He wasn't even here to haunt the damn graveyard.

"His doctor gave him enough pills to overdose, and he left."

"You let him go?"

My breath hitched. "Do you think *I* would have *let* him?"

"No."

"He left me a note detailing what he wanted done with his estate and how he wanted to hold on to his dignity. How he was sorry, but he couldn't live like this anymore. He wanted me to hold on to the memory of him well. He wanted me to use the money and move on. Start over. Put it into the club if I wanted, or sell it and start over some place if I couldn't get over it. He told me to travel, to meet someone. To love again. But he took it all away when he took away my closure." I wiped my face, suddenly wanting to beat my fists into the swirls of light purple and silver running through the marble until it was smeared with blood.

"Dante..." He didn't know what to say. No one did, so they left it alone. I functioned well enough so they figured I'd moved on, but how could I? I was stuck in the tomb with his ghost. I'd left my soul there when they'd sealed it.

"You don't have to say anything at all. I should have come alone."

He looked at me for a moment, and I expected him to leave. He didn't owe me anything. He wasn't my boyfriend. He was my fuck toy, and I was his means to an end. He didn't walk away, though. He wrapped his arms around me and held me there.

"I may have found the only person on the planet with as much baggage as I have." He squeezed me tighter and went on. "He doesn't deserve your pain. He doesn't deserve this. You can't torture yourself your whole life over his choices. We all make our own, and he made the wrong one. You're right, he's a fucking coward. I can't say what I would have done if I was faced with the same circumstances, but I can say I wouldn't have left an empty box for Kai."

There it was. He belonged to Kai.

"I'm not in love with Kai, and I couldn't do that to him. I can't imagine loving someone as much as you clearly love him and doing that to them. If he loved you one-tenth of what you feel for him, he shouldn't have been able to do it."

My chest swelled and a little warmth crept into the void

there. "He loved me, but he was scared."

"Stop making excuses for him. Stop carrying the weight of it. You have to let it go. Five years is too long to punish yourself for his mistakes."

I pressed my face into his chest while he held me by the back of the head. I collected myself at last. "You don't love Kai? Then why all of this?"

He laughed and pulled my hair. "I love Kai to death. I've never been in love with Kai. It's why we both have always had other people. I just can't imagine life without him. He's my best friend, my brother. He's been there through everything, and I can't abandon him now."

"But he has another submissive he sleeps with?"

Remi nodded. He looked ashamed.

"Then why?" I didn't have to say it. He knew what I was asking.

"Because he's jealous. He thinks if I can have everything he has with me and sleep with a dominant, they won't want me to stay with him, so I'll leave."

Which I might have done had I not known. I was glad I hadn't asked, hadn't pushed.

"We made a pact a long time ago not to ever give it to anyone. We could have others, but relationships don't last, friendships do, so we'd live together and always have each other. Then we'd never be alone and never have to suffer the pain."

"His parents' abused him?"

"That's not the half of it." Remi's throat sounded dry.

If I asked for what I wanted, could I share him? I wasn't sure, but if I wanted more I was going to have to try. Why did life have to be so fucking hard?

"You know what I could use?"

Remi creased his brow. "A sledgehammer so you can

get into the vault and destroy it?" A smile crept over his lips.

I laughed. "No, I could really go for some breakfast."

He looked more surprised than when I'd told him the story. "I don't think I've seen you have anything but scotch since I met you."

"I used to do a lot of cooking." I looped my arm around his shoulders and led the way toward the exit. I felt a little bit lighter. Enough to take a full breath through the darkness.

"Do you think it's safe for me to eat your food if it's been so long? Aren't you out of practice?"

"It's like riding a bike. I worked as a cook for a few years before I opened the bar."

"I know."

I nudged my shoulder into him as we walked. "Don't you like to leave anything to be learned from the person you're letting strip and humiliate you?"

"I learn quirks and tells from people themselves. I like to know all the important stuff going in. I am trusting you with my ass."

"You're trusting me to do whatever I want to you. What could have an impact? I can't get any worse than bruising you from head to foot." I slung a leg over my bike, and instead of going to his Jeep he came up behind me and got on.

"I could risk falling for the guy. I had to make sure he was as unappealing and true to his word as possible. I didn't want some pussy who thought he was going hard and gave me the fake BDSM experience."

He could risk falling for the guy. "And you were sure you wouldn't fall for me?"

"I was until I met you."

I cast him a look over my shoulder but didn't press. I had some eggs to make. No man could resist my cooking skills.

He settled into a chair at the counter as I collected the things I would need from the cabinets and pantry. I was surprised the house was as well stocked with food as it was. Liv's doing, I assumed. She hoped I'd stop living off booze and cigarettes. It wasn't likely to happen, but she liked to have little grains of hope for her boys. I wasn't sure why she hadn't given up on Josh and me yet. With seemingly no social life of her own, it was a wonder she put up with us. It made me wonder—I pushed the notion out of my mind—I had someone else to focus on at the moment. I pulled off my shirt and tossed it toward the laundry room, kicking off my jeans next.

"What the hell are you doing?" Remi asked.

I stretched when I was free of the confines of my clothes and reached for the apron where I'd left it on the hook.

"It's freeing to cook naked. The apron is so I don't burn my balls."

I hadn't picked it up since the morning when Masen had handed me the gun. I pressed through the memory and tied it around my waist. I couldn't let memories hold me back any longer. It was time to get the fuck over it. My hands did the work I wasn't sure my mind remembered. I knew where all the ingredients were, and I didn't need a recipe as I measured out and poured them into a large glass bowl.

"You really have all of this memorized?"

"To be honest, I'm a little surprised I still do." I cracked eggs into the bowl.

"There is nothing sexier than a man who can cook."

The weight between us was lighter, not completely gone but noticeably different. I'd exposed most of my baggage maybe it would inspire him to do the same. Maybe this could work as it was, and I didn't need more. All I knew was I liked having him in my house. I wasn't healed by any means, but it was easier. I set the plate I made in front of Remi and piled food onto my own before taking the seat next to him. We went to work in silence, devouring the food in short order.

"You know the only thing that would make this better?"

I raised a brow, shooting him a glance, daring him to criticize my food.

"If you'd have brought it to me in bed."

I laughed and the mood lightened further. "Who's the slave here? You should be bringing me breakfast in bed."

"I'm a submissive, not a slave." He pointed his fork at me. "And if you make me cook, I may burn down your kitchen."

I gasped. "If you kill my baby, you will die."

"Your baby?"

"The Viking." I pointed at the massive stainless steel, six burner stove. It had two side by side ovens and a grill. It was restaurant quality, and it was one of the few things I'd let Masen buy me over the years. I hadn't realized all the ways I'd kept him around and all the ways I'd let it hold me back from the things I used to love. Liv had seen it. I was the only person I'd successfully hidden it from.

"Is it special?" He cocked his head, looking at it.

"It's high quality restaurant grade."

"My father has one, but I don't think the thing has ever been turned on. He eats all his meals at strip clubs and local joints."

I winced. "Such a waste."

"His whole place is all for show, not that anyone is ever welcome there, but the rumors of solid gold floors make him seem more than he is. At least, this is what he's told me. I couldn't imagine living there. It's like a museum." It was more than he'd said about his father the entire time I'd known him. I wanted to keep him talking.

"Your mother let him design the house?" I knew I shouldn't have said it before it came out of my mouth, but I'd never been one to hold my tongue.

A dark cloud passed over him, and his entire body language changed. "I'm pretty sure he had her killed." The words were dead as they left his mouth. He'd walked into a fog, and I wasn't there any longer.

"He had her killed?" It contradicted what I'd learned in my own research.

"The person you think is my mother isn't."

I recoiled.

He laughed. "My father had a longstanding affair with the housekeeper. Men like him are expected to have women on the side. Even his wife expected it. If they don't, they're considered fags."

"Sleeping with their wife isn't enough?"

"Hardly. It's our culture. One woman can't possibly fulfill a real man's 'needs.' The wife is to provide heirs, but she couldn't. In fifteen years she didn't get pregnant once. So he turned to the maid."

"His wife was okay with it?"

"I doubt she had any choice. I didn't know her well. She jumped off a building when I was five."

It wasn't a shock. The case had been public. The feds had been talking to her and most guessed he'd pushed her.

"So the maid is your mother. Is she still with him?"

"No." He was cold.

I wanted to question it, clarify which 'mother' he'd thought had been killed, but it didn't feel right.

"Shortly before his wife killed herself, I was told the maid had to return to her country. Her visa had been revoked. I looked for her when I figured it all out, and there is no trace of her."

"How did you figure it out?"

He pushed the forgotten eggs around his plate. "I have green eyes. My father and 'mother' both have blue."

"Eye color is complicated. Green and brown can be produced by blue, it's just unlikely."

He gave me a pointed look. "You're too smart for a guy who gets knocked around for a living."

I shrugged. It was true, but I enjoyed getting knocked around, and an office would have felt like a cage.

"I know that now, but when I took high school biology, they were breaking it down, and told me it was impossible. So they basically told me one of my parents' wasn't my parent. At first, I assumed my mother had cheated. I wouldn't have blamed her. It would have been a good reason for her to jump off a building had my father found out."

"What did you do?" I leaned closer to him, wanting to know it all, wanting to see what made him tick. Getting to know him was even more of a drug than getting him naked. I liked who I saw under the front he put out. I wanted to be the only one who knew what was inside.

"I stole some of his DNA."

I gave a low whistle. "How'd you survive?"

"I drugged him." It was a glimpse into Remi's mind, knowing he was capable of drugging his father to get what he wanted at such a young age. A chill ran up my spine. He'd do anything he thought was best for him. Or if he thought he was being lied to. There was no doubt in my mind what Remi was capable of. Part of it had to be genetics. Look at what he was a product of.

"How?"

"In his drink. When he woke up on the floor the next morning I made up a story." He flashed his teeth. "It wasn't the first time he'd had too much." His eyes unfocused. He was reliving the past. There was no doubt in my mind Remi may be the only person on the planet more fucked up than I was, but nothing I found out diminished how I felt. It showed me he was more than the games. He cared enough to tell me.

"Once you knew he was your father, how did you proceed?"

"It was slow and a lot of guesswork on my part. I'll never know for sure unless I find her." He set his fork down with a clatter.

"How can you be sure his wife isn't your mother then?"

"Oh, that was easy enough. I got her sister to let me test her. I told her it was for a school project. She's a hairdresser in Vegas with no ties to the mob, so it wasn't hard to ask for DNA. She had no reason to protect it."

The picture was starting to form in my mind. Remi had left Vegas at nineteen to move to California with Kai. I was sure this was part of the driving factor between their friendship and pact. Neither of them had much family they cared to keep around, and what family Remi had, he no longer trusted. Any teenager would have rebelled and run. It also explained why he never touched any of his father's money. It was better to be self-reliant and self-made. I respected him more for it. He wasn't a spoiled brat like I'd first believed.

"Let me grab the dishes." I picked up his plate and took

them both to the sink full of pots. I had a dishwasher, but I never used it. It ruined the pans, and if I was washing them I might as well do the plates. Masen always thought it was silly, but he'd stood by me and dried every last dish without complaint. I laid out a towel to set the clean dishes on and got to work. Remi picked up his phone and entered his own world while I worked. The silence was crushing.

I dropped my head, taking my aggression out on the pots and pans. There were reasons he was going to keep choosing Kai, and I couldn't compete with it. I was ten years too late. I had to stop investing myself into this. It would be like Masen all over again. He'd vanish before my eyes, and there was nothing I could do about it. I was meant to be alone.

"Aiming to take the finish off those pans?" His arms slid around my waist. Bare hands touching my exposed skin for the first time. I'd always kept him tied up for this reason. It was dangerous for him to touch me. To be this close. Only the thin layer of his sweats stayed between his dick and my ass. "Have they wronged you?"

"They can take the abuse." I rinsed it and set it aside, moving on to the next with a little less vigor.

"Wouldn't you rather take out your aggression on me?"

Yes. No, I shouldn't. "I'm not sure you deserve it."

He dropped his head to rub his nose over the line of my shoulder. "I've been a good boy, Master."

"There is the issue right there."

He smiled against my skin, rocking up on his toes to press his groin into me. "I can change if that's what it takes."

I forced myself to remain still, fighting the urge to force him over the counter and fuck him right there. My hard on pushed against the apron, which left little to the imagination. I was lucky to be facing the sink.

"I think making you wait and suffer a little longer will be more fun." More like he had to wait until I got a grip on my control again.

"I get nothing for agreeing to stay longer?" he whined. It was adorable, and it almost made me want to give him what he asked for, but I wasn't that nice.

"You've already agreed to stay, and I didn't have to bribe you, so you've put all the cards in my hand. Next time you should think these things through and secure terms up front. Amateur."

"God, you're an ass." He snaked his hand around my hip and brushed his fingers over my arousal.

I snapped, grabbing his wrist with my wet hand. "I think I'll go for a run." I pushed him back, and then dried my hands on my apron as I disappeared up the stairs to find shorts.

TWENTY TWO

REMI

I knew I pushed it too far this morning. I'd made the rules, and I was breaking the rules. I had to talk to Kai. I couldn't do this any longer. It wasn't fair for him to have everything in a submissive and expect me not to have anything with a dominant. It would have been better if I'd flown home for it, but I'd already promised Dante I'd stay.

When Dante slipped out the door, I dialed the shop's number and let it ring. I wanted to tell him I was still in Vegas, but I needed to get out from under the lies. If I wanted anything with Dante, I had to do it clean and be honest with both of them about what my intentions were. It was exhausting living a double life, and I couldn't do a triple.

"Ocean Ink," Kai answered.

"Kai."

He sighed and I heard him scoot his chair across the room and shuffle the phone. "Why'd you call this number?"

"Because I figured you wouldn't answer your cell."

He huffed which meant I was right. "You said you were coming home this morning. Are you waiting for the car at the airport?" He knew I wasn't.

"Why do you ask questions you know the answer to?"

"Because I can feel you slipping through my fingers, and I'm angry?" He was the opposite of Dante. He would put what he felt right on the table. I'd always admired it. I wished I could do the same.

"I'm not slipping through your fingers."

"Why'd you call?"

"I think you know the answer to that too."

Silence was his answer.

"This arrangement isn't fair."

"You agreed to it." He ground his teeth. A horrible habit, but I loved it.

"I felt like I'd lose you to Kyle if I didn't."

Another sigh. "Have you ever lost me?"

"Kyle is different."

"So is your whore."

I growled. "Stop calling him that."

More silence. This was the reason I should have flown home to talk to him. He could throw a tantrum like the best bratty sub I'd seen. He knew how to get what he wanted from his dominant. If he'd let me, I would have started calling him princess in our scenes. I already did in my head.

"I need more with him."

"Are you going to move there?"

"No, never." I hoped it was the truth. I wasn't sure what I'd do if Dante demanded it. I probably wouldn't live long enough to see it.

"Okay. Do what you have to do. I don't want to hear about it."

"Thank you."

"Don't thank me. I'm not your keeper."

I pressed my eyes closed. "Then why make the rule in

the first place?"

"Because I'm trying to hold on to the ocean, and it's impossible. I know nothing can stop the tide as it goes out, but that won't keep me from trying like any other fool who's tried to keep you." He hung up the phone. My heart ached, and I probably deserved it. Why did I have to break my best friend to be happy?

I nuzzled into Dante's chest, taking in a breath of him. I never wanted this to end. His breathing had evened out. For a guy who didn't sleep much, a little play seemed to put him out like a baby. I chuckled to myself. I enjoyed the effect I had on him. Now the trick would be to try and force everything out of my mind so I could do the same. Since I'd been trying for over an hour, I didn't think it was going to happen.

"Stop thinking."

"I thought you were asleep," I muttered into his skin.

"Your mental pacing is keeping me awake." His voice was laced with sleep, and I wasn't sure if he was actually awake or talking in his sleep.

"Mental pacing?"

"You accused me of it last night, and it seems you're stuck in your head now with it going a million miles a second."

He was right, of course, but I wasn't about to admit it.

"How do you figure?"

"Your breath hitches when you're overthinking," he said.

I stopped in my tracks. "Seriously?" I hadn't realized my tells were as prominent as his. What a pair we made.

He nodded.

"I don't think anyone has ever noticed that before." My brow creased. I was so naked to him.

"Because most don't pay attention. They don't think about you. They are too busy thinking about themselves. I suspect you've never been with someone who cared more about what you were getting out of things than themselves."

He was probably right.

"I'm right," he said. Cocky fucker.

I growled playfully at him. He tilted his head down and ran his nose next my ear. I was about to utter a witty comeback when sharp pain shot up my spine. I couldn't breathe. I couldn't think. Nothing existed except the pain. It stopped as suddenly as it started, and I gasped. He was laughing, and I looked up into his eyes.

"What the hell?" I asked.

"If you won't get out of your own head, I'm going to have to help you." Another flash of pain, and I was practically purring.

He knew just what I needed. I sprawled out over him as his hands worked their way up and down my body. He alternated between sharp presses to every pressure point he could reach, lighting me on fire, and soft caressing which made me ache for him. His fingertips explored and marked every inch, finding places I hadn't even known could cause pain.

His touch radiated through me, and one thing resonated: ownership. When his hand stilled, my body draped over his, completely relaxed except for my cock. It pressed into his thigh, and the subtle shift of his leg told me he was quite aware. I pulled my hips back, wanting just a hint of friction. Before I could press forward he spoke.

"Behave," he breathed into my hair as he gripped my

lower back.

"How did you know?"

"You're easy. It doesn't take much." His voice was laced with sleep.

My eyes felt heavy, and I wasn't going fight it. There would be other opportunities to push things with him, if I decided to go that route. I still hadn't—

I woke up to vibrating. Strong arms held me from behind, and I groaned, not wanting to wake up. It couldn't be my alarm, that would ring. What the hell was it? I slipped my hand under the pillow where I'd stashed my phone and squinted at the screen when it came free.

Kai.

Shit.

I lifted Dante's arm carefully and slipped out of the bed. I glanced around the room as I hit enter, deciding the bathroom was the best place. I closed the door to the en-suite behind me before I spoke into the phone.

"Hey."

"Where are you?"

"Why?" It was instinctual not to answer. I didn't like that about myself.

"Because I need you here."

"Why?" I felt like an idiot, but it was too early to make any sense.

"Because Kyle broke up with me." His voice cracked as he said it.

"Where are you?" My mind reeled. I didn't want to leave.

"At the beach house." Kai sucked in a breath, and it hitched. I closed my eyes, and I could picture him. Eyes red and puffy. Since we were kids, Kai always took things harder than anyone else. He learned how to hide his emotional side, but it still came out with me, and it always would. I was his safe place, and I treasured the fact. "When I said I wouldn't move in with him he packed up his shit and left. He just fucking left. He said I would never be available. I don't even know what the fuck he meant."

Kai kept rambling, but I knew what Kyle had meant. As long as Kai was with me, even behind the scenes, he'd never fully give over to Kyle. But Kyle didn't know Kai needed to submit as much as I did. It showed me Kyle didn't know Kai at all, and he was letting his jealousy blind him.

"It's really late, but I'll try and book a flight home first thing."

"Just drive home."

It hit me. Kai must think I was still in Vegas. I'd never told him otherwise. "I've been drinking. I can't." My statement was met with silence. "You know how it is. I didn't think I'd need to get my ass home. I'm sorry." And I was sorry. I felt like a failure for not being able to be there for Kai. He needed me, and here I was getting the fix I needed. I was at war between what was best for him and what was best for me. I wondered if it would always be the case. It was starting to seem like it.

"Get home fast, please."

"I will." My heart felt heavy as I hung up. I paced the bathroom. I felt like shit going to climb back into bed with Dante when Kai was dealing with all this alone. I was a dick for taking available comfort when he had none. As late as it was here, there wouldn't be any flights. There was nothing I could do until morning.

I quietly opened the en-suite door and stepped back into

the room. Dante had rolled onto his back, and he had his mouth hanging open a little and one arm covering his eyes. His chest moved in rhythm, and I knew he was still out cold. I smiled in spite of myself. When he wasn't all aggressive and growly, he was adorable. I would never admit it out loud, because he'd probably kick my ass, but it was true. He'd kicked off the blanket, and his legs were spread wide with his boxers askew. I could see the outline of his cock resting between his thighs.

Blood rushed below my belt, and I slid a hand into my sweats to grip myself. Easy, I told myself. You can't go from a call with your best friend upset on the phone to wanting to fuck your dominant. Well, you can, but you'll feel like a douchebag afterward. The human brain was a fucked up thing.

I pressed one knee into the mattress and leaned over to skim my fingers over his length. I'd never gotten a chance to touch him. I was always bound when we were together, and when we weren't playing I was trying to keep up the pretense I didn't want or need him. None of it was true, and it sunk in more each day.

I spread myself out on the bed, my head on his chest and one leg hooked over his thigh. I didn't think I'd be able to sleep again. Kai took up too much of my mind. If he didn't have a submissive any longer would he want more from me? It was entirely possible he wouldn't want me to see anyone else. He'd never asked before, but was it really too far a jump to be made? He didn't like the idea of Dante. I'd had dominants before, but Dante was different and he knew it as well as I did.

I exhaled and tried to push it out of my mind. There was no use thinking about it now. Going over and over it wouldn't solve a damn thing. I wouldn't know Kai's mind until I was there.

If this was the last time I was going to see Dante, I didn't want to leave so soon. I had a decision to make, and it wasn't going to be an easy one, but they never were.

I slept fitfully despite Dante's attempts to calm me. I was up with the sun, booking a ticket. I thought about slipping out before he woke again, but every time I did I risked his wrath, and I knew now it would kill me if I wasn't allowed back. I walked a tightrope of what everyone else wanted, and Dante was my safety net. I needed what only he could offer.

"You said you were staying. Stay."

I looked up from where I sat on the edge of the bed shoving my feet into my boots. "You're serious?" My heart was in my throat.

He nodded.

Kai was all alone. "I can't. I have—business I need to get back for." The words hurt as they left my mouth, and I was fully aware he might not ask again.

He turned his back on me. "Okay."

"Dante..." I trailed off, not sure what I could even say.

"There is nothing to say. You have to go. You aren't beholden to me."

I dragged a hand over my face, an ache settling in my chest. No, I wasn't, and if I kept leaving I probably would never be.

TWENTY THREE

REMI

The car pulled up outside my house. It felt like I hadn't been here in weeks, when in reality it had only been a few days. It was still early on the West Coast. Kai would be up with the sun surfing, as long as the weather was favorable, and it was. I smiled at the thought. It had been way too long since we'd been out together. I stepped out of the car and handed the driver a generous tip when he held out my bag. I put it on my shoulder and climbed the steps. The custom built house was three stories, right on the beach. The top floor was mine, the second Kai's, and the bottom we used for entertaining. I pressed my thumb on the keypad and waited for the click.

When we'd designed the place, we wanted an entirely open concept. There was a view from every room. The scent of fresh ocean air hit me. This was home. This would always be home, so why did my chest ache to be in that god awful city? One of the mysteries of life I would probably never understand.

It was my little slice of heaven. Every pillow was in place on sleek furniture. Large eighteen-inch tiles lined the path to the wall of windows at the back, and my eyes followed it to land on Kai standing out on the deck. I smiled, wider than I should have. I wouldn't have survived if it wasn't for Kai. He was my rock. I loved him. He was my brother and my best friend. I padded silently across the tile, drinking in the image of him.

His shorts hung low on his thin waist, and the tattoos covering his arms were wet and glinted in the sun. He threw his head back and gathered his shoulder length hair to tie into a man bun. I got a completely different feeling when I looked at Kai. I would put him before myself every time. If I needed to take a bullet to save Kai's life, I wouldn't have to think about it. He was my submissive, and I would protect him until the end.

I took a deep breath, dropping my bag by the hidden staircase before opening my mouth to call his name. The words died in my throat as Kyle stepped out from behind him. He was four or five inches shorter than Kai and thicker, carrying himself like a football player, while Kai was wiry in comparison. He wore a wetsuit, pulled down to hang around his waist, just showing off the cut over his hips. Kai grabbed him, and Kyle leaned up to brush his lips over Kai's shoulder. Kai couldn't keep his hands off of Kyle. It had been that way since they'd met, and years later it was no different. Kai was enamored with him. Joy twinkled in Kai's eyes as music and laughter reached my ears. I'd never been jealous of their relationship once, but now I was sick.

My knees quivered. I'd thrown out what might have been the last of my sanity and the good graces of Dante to come back to this. Kai hadn't even called to tell me they'd made up. A black spot started to form in my chest. I was a puppet in their lives. They each wanted me to play a role, and none of them cared if I was happy. Every single person used me, and it was my fault. I'd let them. I wasn't happy, not here, certainly not in Vegas, maybe I never would be.

Kai looked up and caught my gaze. He mouthed the word 'sorry,' but it was too late. For once I did the selfish thing. I did what I wanted to do, and I walked right back out of my house. I wasn't sure where I'd go, but I couldn't be here.

TWENTY FOUR

DANTE

Ghosts followed me. Ghosts lived in my house. Ghosts lingered in the club. This entire fucking city was haunted with my ghosts, built on the bones of our ancestors. I'd built my new life on the bones of the old, and I was starting to think I'd cursed myself. I was about ready to find a priestess to get an exorcism.

I'd sent everyone home and cleaned the bar myself. When I finished I set a bottle of Johnny Walker Blue next to me, determined to finish the thing so I could sleep off this pathetic mood. I tried to refill my glass, finding I'd emptied the bottle. Taking another wouldn't hurt my bottom line, so I staggered to my feet and around the bar. Whoever decided to put top shelf liquor on the top shelf was an asshole. The tricky part would be climbing up on the rungs to successfully get the bottle.

"How much have you had to drink?"

I paused with one foot up and looked over my shoulder. "More than my share."

"No shit, Sherlock." He placed a hand on my shoulder, keeping me on the ground. "Let me get that for you."

I tried to shrug out of his grasp. "I've got it. I'm not that far gone."

"As you slur your words and can barely talk? Right."
He shook his head but let go of me, taking a step back.
"Fine, break your neck."

I grabbed the shelf and hauled myself up. The room
tipped, and I nearly lost it. I wasn't about to tell him he was
right, so I took another step and then a third. Carefully, I
stretched my hand up and closed my fingers around the
bottle right as the ground decided to take a violent pitch,
sending me flying off the ladder. I landed on my ass, but I
curled the bottle into my chest like a baby, saving it.

"The bottle is okay!"

"Fuck's sake. Is this how I get?" Josh looked at the
ceiling, clearly not talking to me. "No wonder no one
wants to deal with me."

"Who the fuck are you talking to?" I climbed to my feet,
using the bar to brace myself as the floor settled down.

"God. Got to talk to someone when you're too
intoxicated to reply."

"I can reply." Even I could hear myself slurring as I said
it.

He raised a brow but didn't say a word, instead grabbing
my glass and a fresh one for himself and holding a hand
out for the bottle. I reluctantly handed it over, and he filled
both glasses.

"You scold me and then join me?"

"You've got the good stuff out. I'm not going to miss
it."

Through my foggy, fucked up, self-pity I remembered
the conversation Liv and I'd had about Josh. Maybe he
needed this as much as I did. I picked up my glass but
didn't bring it to my lips.

"Speaking of which, how are you dealing?"

He raised one shoulder and looked away. Code for not

good.

"Has Liv been by?"

He scoffed. "Yeah, she insisted on cleaning my Goddamn place. Even put my guns back in the safe and made me clean up all the C4. It looks like I'm married or some shit now."

"Stop leaving your C4 around the house. You're going to blow yourself up."

"At least the cats don't try and eat it anymore." He moistened his lips like he had more to say but wasn't sure how to approach the subject.

I didn't want to hear whatever it was, that much I knew.

"We've got to get back to training." I filled the silence with words. It was better than listening to what the depths of my mind was whispering.

He arched one brow. "Because I've lost three in a row?"

He knew it was the reason I said it.

"No, you need to get out of your head to fix that. I need it." And I did. He'd been my fix since Masen left.

He pushed his tongue into his cheek. "Yeah, alright, but you've got to sober up first."

I scowled.

"I'm not shaking your brain any more than you've already done tonight. Why are you drinking?"

I figured he'd shown up because he'd known Remi left, but how could he have? "I felt like it." There was no reason to give him more information than he needed.

"You're lying. To me or to yourself. I haven't seen you this bad since Masen left."

His words made me recoil. They burned. I'd never feel how I felt about Masen about anyone else. "How dare you!" I looked down at the bottle and then back at Josh. I couldn't believe he'd even compare the two. They were so different. They made me feel completely different. I was in pain, sure, but no two pains were the same, like no two cuts were, and no two scars would ever be.

"I'm callin' it like I see it."

"I'm not that fucking bad. I didn't eat for weeks after he left, and I was belligerent."

"Not far off of it now."

"You're so off base." I downed the contents of my drink, denying his words even though I felt the sting of truth. "I don't have to listen to this." I shoved myself away from the bar and staggered toward my office. There was no way I'd get home in one piece. I'd have to sober up on my sofa before Liv came in and yelled at me further. I couldn't even destroy myself in my own bar anymore. What had my life come to?

"Did he leave you?"

I reeled around at his words and came out swinging. I landed two jabs before Josh got his fists up. Half of my punches went wide as he moved. I was at the right level of drunk to know I was too drunk for a fight but too far gone to be rational. He slammed his fist into my ribs as I missed him by a mile then hit me in the kidney. Josh wasn't a large guy, but shit he could land a powerful punch. I grunted and continued to swing, throwing all regard for defense out the window. The pain was welcomed. I only landed one or two to his ten, but it didn't matter. Stumbling, I grabbed hold of him in a miserable dive and took us both to the ground. He landed hard on his back, but it didn't deter him. We rolled around knocking over chairs and tables, vying for the upper hand.

At the same moment, we both lost the will and ended up on our backs next to each other, breathing hard.

"I need more to drink." Josh sat up slowly and then went

for the bottle. He took a swig directly from it. At fifty dollars a shot, he'd just ruined the bottle. I yanked it out of his hand to pour some down my own throat. I couldn't let it go to waste. He grabbed it back after a few seconds, and we went on like barbarians, sitting our asses on the floor drinking.

"You were right. He left."

"For good?"

"I don't know, but he will."

It got worse every time he left. My whiskey told me the answer was no. It told me to call his ass and demand he come back—to stay. I should not be allowed near my phone after a fifth of whiskey. My thoughts drifted in and out when I suddenly remembered. Josh. I glanced around the room, wondering where he'd gone.

He sat to one side, a cigarette dangling from his lips. "He's toxic."

"I know."

"Then why let him come back?"

"Maybe I'm toxic too." I had nothing else to offer.

"Is killing each other worth it?"

"Better than the abyss of loneliness." I really believed it at that moment, whether it was whiskey induced sense was yet to be determined.

"Maybe you're looking in all the wrong places. Ever considered that?" He stood over me, arms crossed over his chest.

"I haven't looked anywhere but inside myself."

He turned and walked toward the door.

"Where did my phone go?"

"No fucking idea," he said as the door swung shut behind him.

I spotted my phone across the room, and as if by the

grace of the devil it started ringing as I looked at it. I was starting to wonder if my entire life was some cruel sitcom to amuse the gods. Pressing a hand into one of the chairs we'd left standing, I climbed to my feet. The ground lurched, and I stumbled.

The door creaked open. I didn't bother to look, sure Josh was returning to get in the last word.

"Forget your balls?"

"I wasn't aware I'd left them."

My head snapped up. There he was, although I wasn't entirely sure I wasn't hallucinating him. I inhaled sharply, giving away my shock.

"Hey," he said. He had the same bag slung over his arm he carried the night before, and he wore the same clothes he'd left in. It was quite unlike Remi. His skin hung on his face, and he looked like he hadn't slept. There was also a sizable bruise spreading over his collar bone, visible around the collar of his shirt.

I hadn't put it there. My chest tightened. I hated the thought of someone else marking him.

"And here I thought it would be at least a week before I was graced with your presence again." The bitterness showed in my voice. Why did I have such a need for him?

"Would you prefer I leave?" The twist of his lips told me he already knew the answer.

I crossed my arms over my chest. "I should tell you when you're allowed here and when you aren't. I have plans."

He checked his watch. "At one in the morning?"

This wasn't going well. Why couldn't I admit what I wanted? Why couldn't I let myself be weak with him? *'Because you've done that and look where it got you,'* I told myself. I walked ungracefully to the other side of the bar to retrieve my phone.

"Going someplace drunk?"

"Do you think it's your business?" The missed call had been from him.

He stiffened. "I've changed my plans to be here."

"I was unaware of your plans to start with, but a text would have sufficed." I started to text Josh to pick me up, but Remi grabbed the phone from my hand. I growled and lurched for it.

"So you're an asshole drunk." He picked up the bottle Josh and I had left on the floor and sniffed it. "But you probably don't drink this much very often." He was right, not often to this level. I liked my head clear while I was at work.

"Why are you here?" I felt better with the counter to stabilize me.

"I missed my flight."

We both knew it was a lie. "You've been gone all day."

"I got stuck in security?"

"You couldn't go to the Motel 6 up the road?" I looked up, flames swirled in his eyes, mixing the green with a hint of orange.

He scoffed barely loud enough for me to hear it.

"Alright, then some other fancy ass shit like the Ritz."

He shrugged.

"Let me get Liv on the phone. I'm sure she can find you a room somewhere." I held out my hand for the phone. Why wasn't I telling him to stay?

"I don't need her." He wore jeans and a tie-dyed tee that made him look more surfer than business man.

"What do you want, Remi?"

He didn't answer.

"Not this again." I bared my teeth and pointed at the

door. "If you're not going to speak, get out."

He dropped to his knees beside me and laid his head against my thigh. Still he didn't speak. I shrugged, trying to push him away, giving off pure ice, but he rubbed his cheek over me seeking any affection.

He laid a hand over my abs, his voice half whisper. "I want you, Dante. You've made me feel."

I paused so I wouldn't say the words on my tongue. Pressing my eyes closed, I said instead, "Our worlds don't fit together. You wouldn't be happy here." It was what he wanted me to say. He had to be sent home.

He turned his face to press against my thigh. "I can't be happy when I leave a piece of— myself— behind when I go." He drew his words out, tasting them before he let them out into the world. "I couldn't force myself to—" he trailed off.

The bruise on his collarbone told me he wasn't saying something. He'd been some place in-between. My mind was too fuzzy to put it together. I'd have to remember in the morning. The blackness called to me. It would be easy to close my eyes and sleep off this night.

Everything in me wanted to tell him to stay. To tell him I felt the same, but I held back. I'd been here before. The definition of insanity was doing the same thing over and over and expecting a different result. It took all my restraint to not touch him. To not pull him into my arms. I had never longed to touch someone so much. So much so my chest ached.

"Why do you think our worlds don't fit together?"

"I live here. I want stability. You ebb and flow, drifting from one place to the next. You only want this," I gestured between us. "When it suits you."

"Maybe I don't want it to be that way anymore." His

words were hushed, but I heard every one. "This is who I am. I've been denying it for so long that I've begun to resent him for it."

"You're used to California and the ocean. I'm a redneck fuck who can't give you any of what you need." I laid my hand on his head, stroking my fingers through his hair. I had to hold myself back. I wanted so much more.

He stiffened and picked up his head to look me in the eyes. "Then come with me. Fuck all of this." He pleaded with his eyes, and I turned away from him. "I have enough money for many lifetimes. You don't need any of this." He reached out and grasped for me.

"I'm not going to California." I shrugged out of his grasp, thrusting both hands into my hair. "I can't. I have my club, my people, my guys."

"I see how you are with me. There is something here."

He was right, and I bit back the harsh retort that threatened to leave my lips.

"Tell me you feel this." He grabbed me again, rubbing his face over my thigh and my groin, and I grew hard under the light touch. I dropped my head back, staring at the ceiling.

I felt it, but I couldn't say it. I wouldn't go. The only thing more stupid than thinking a happily ever after was in my cards would be trusting him enough to give up my life to chase it. It would be easier to say I felt nothing. To deny him and let him walk away thinking I didn't want him so he wouldn't come back. I was too damaged to give him what he needed.

"I wouldn't be happy there."

"Leave Josh in charge. You can come back." There was more pleading to his tone, and it hit me like an icepick to the chest. I was laid bare to him, and he played me with ease.

I picked up my head. "Remi, all he cares about is pain. Someone has to keep him in check. But none of that matters."

"Why not?"

"You would never be submissive to me there."

He choked back a sob and jutted his chin out. "You don't know how I would be."

"Yes, I do."

"It doesn't have to be California. It can be the South of France for all I care."

"I'm not leaving—" Him. I left it unspoken, but I knew he felt it.

"You're going to put this before our happiness?" The hurt showed in his voice.

"This is my life."

He grabbed hold of my shirt, getting to his feet to look me in the eyes. I didn't stop him. I knew I should have, but I didn't. The submissive side was gone. Anger burned in his eyes. "So I mean nothing to you?"

"You left me this morning." I closed my fingers around his wrist.

"I had no choice."

"You are a fantastic submissive, Remi—"

He cut me off. "Don't feed me that line of bullshit. I am worth more than that."

"Am I worth more than the bullshit you feed me?" I pushed my fingers into his hair. He would have been a perfect match for me, even better than Masen. He was funny, full of witty banter, playing with my mind as much as my body. More than that, he was addictive, like a drug I couldn't get enough of. He burned hot through my veins, rooting his way into my head so he was stuck there.

He took a resigned breath. "Do you think in a different reality this could have worked?"

In a different reality where I didn't still ache for the man who'd gone missing. If I hadn't dug myself into this hole I didn't know how to get out of. Or a different reality where our lives weren't complicated by my job and his life— maybe. "I don't know, and what if's won't help us any."

"I want to keep you." He climbed into my lap and rubbed his nose over mine as he spoke in a whisper. He wanted to keep me, and it would be so if I let him. There would be no keeping him, though, even as his dominant. Remi didn't do a thing he didn't want to.

I tightened my grip on him, knowing my prints would be bruised into his skin and ignored the groan that left his lips. Those words burrowed their way into the back of my mind and stayed there. They were going to rot. The image of him staying, the life we could have had, would grow rancid. Ideas caused more harm than memories ever could.

"I won't be one of many." I had a feeling with him I always would be, and I was almost stupid enough to do it anyway. If I kept telling myself that, maybe it would ease the pain that practically cracked my chest in half.

Remi's fingers loosened on my shirt. "They don't matter like you do. Not anymore. *He* can't give me this." He knew all the right things to say. The way he looked up at me thawed the ice in my chest. My hands rested on his hips, and he draped his arms over my shoulders, pushing one hand into my hair to tug at the short ends. The sensation sent a shiver down my spine, and my eyes rolled back in my head.

His nose skimmed over mine, and my lips parted in a silent gasp. Every subtle movement made me crave him, and I gave in, brushing my thumbs over the lines of his hips. I sucked in a breath of him, letting it permeate the depths of my lungs with his smell.

There was a momentary pause in his movement, then I felt his soft lips over mine. They were barely there, and I took the bait, chasing them, pressing my mouth full on to his. His tongue skimmed the seam of my lips, and I parted them more, willing him in. Our tongues met and tangled as I tilted my head to deepen the kiss. His taste hit me and made me want him that much more. He tasted of fresh air, like taking a breath from his lungs came right from the sea.

It was as if he was a new beginning, taunting me. I tightened my grip on his sides, digging my nails into his skin as I grew harder under him. Remi must have noticed because he started rocking his hips over my erection.

Fuck.

I lifted my hands, splaying them out against his chest, shoving him back. "You have to go, because if you don't, I will fuck you, and neither of us can live with that."

TWENTY·FIVE

DANTE

I thought he was going to argue, but instead, he slipped out of my grasp. I clenched my fist at my side, wanting to reach out for him. He kept backing up, eyes never leaving me. When he bent to pick up his bag, I knew he was serious. I reached for the bottle of whiskey, taking my eyes off him. I heard the door open and close and poured myself another double. I never drank it. Instead, I sat and sobered up.

By the time Liv showed up I had my wits enough to help her. She didn't ask, and I didn't offer, but her sidelong looks told me she knew some of it. I had no doubt Josh had seen Remi come in on his way out, and for me to still be at the bar, alone, when she arrived was telling. There were times I wished I could disappear. Flee to an island where no one knew me. No one cared enough to give me a look of pity. We finished in silence, and I was sober enough to drive myself home. I took the long way 'round, letting the early morning breeze blow through my hair. All the rain was starting to drive the birth of spring, pushing away the cold, bringing in new life. The trees all had buds, and I could smell the rich soil coming alive.

It should have been me underground feeding the new

life. Not Masen. The realization hit me. I'd felt it for years, but I'd never put the feeling into words. I resented him for being the one to die first. I'd always thought it would be me. I never took care of myself, smoking and drinking more than my share. He'd eaten clean, gone to the gym daily before work, and generally cared about his wellbeing like I never had. Yet here I stood, walking the earth alone, while he joined the afterlife.

It wasn't fair.

Life wasn't fair.

I turned down my street and into my drive. As I walked around to the front of the house, I saw a figure sitting on my front porch. I paused. He'd taken a seat on the bench at the far side, and it looked like he was on the phone. He had his head in one hand and the phone in the other with his shoulders slumped forward.

My gaze drifted over the ink on his arms, how it weaved over the cut of his muscles. I didn't move. I watched. I was enthralled by him. It felt like I was stealing something private. He took the phone away from his face and brought his hand back like he was going to throw it, but after a few moments, he set it on the step between his feet. He didn't make a move to get up, and it made me wonder who he'd been talking to. I walked to the door, turned the doorknob without a sound, and lifted my foot to step inside.

"Dante," was all he said, but I paused.

I lingered before crossing the porch to sit next to him. "I thought you left."

"I can't."

He hung his head. His bag was half slung over his shoulder, but even that seemed like it had been too much effort. He made no move to get closer. Sitting there, he was— broken— a shell of what he'd been the first time he'd turned up. Everything I'd sensed inside seemed to be thrown into focus. His stature defeated. I couldn't hold myself back anymore. I had no idea what had happened, but I wanted to take it all away. I collected him in my arms, which seemed to wake him out of his trance.

"I need to feel you, please, Dante." He wrapped his arms around my neck, and as I turned into him he buried his face in my chest.

I felt his stubbled chin slide over my collarbone. I groaned, inhaling sharply. Who was the dominant and who was the submissive here? I wasn't sure who was in control anymore. He could have as easily been the puppet master pulling my strings, playing the boy who knelt at my feet, or maybe that was his charm; he was both. It became near impossible to say no to him.

"What happened?" I whispered into his neck.

"Kai," his voice broke, and his arms tightened around me. "I shouldn't have left yesterday. I thought he needed me. It was lies. He didn't need me, he's never needed me. I need to be here. I need you." Finally I was getting some truth. He looked into my eyes, and I couldn't be mad. Not seeing the hurt there. Something had happened between him and Kai, something he wasn't saying.

"This is where I should be," he said, and I wasn't sure I'd heard him right.

My stomach dropped. I wanted it, but could I handle it with strings? Could I send him home to his *friend?* Could I sit at home alone and give my heart to someone who would always return to another?

I pushed the thoughts out of my mind.

"I need to be here. Can I stay... Master?" He rubbed his jaw over the crook of my neck.

I all but dragged him into the house. He looked up at me

with his long lashes. Drops of water lingered in his tousled hair. It must have rained at some point while he sat out there. I realized he was soaked through to the bone.

"Let's get you out of these wet clothes."

He stood firm, not giving in to me as I tugged at his clothes.

"Only if you let me stay. I can't take it anymore. If you don't want me, tell me to go."

"You've been here with me."

"I don't mean like that," he replied.

"What are you saying? We can't do more." Frustration cut through me.

"I can. I want you inside me."

"You can't..."

"He told me I could...days ago."

My heart stopped for a second, and a nervous excitement settled in my chest. I forced the feelings away. I couldn't share. I made my voice calm.

"What did he say?" My shock was clear on my face.

"He told me to do what I needed to do to be happy."

"And you're just telling me this now." I wasn't sure what I should be feeling. My head was all over the place.

"I didn't tell you, because once we do, we can't go back."

I broke. The feelings I had been pushing aside came flooding out, and I dropped my lips to his. He didn't resist me, parting his lips and stroking his tongue over the seam of mine. I parted them willingly, welcoming his tongue into my mouth. He moaned softly, and I could taste it. I tilted my head to the side, deepening the kiss as my tongue brushed over his. Remi's fingertips pushed under my now wet shirt, and he dug his nails into my flanks. I growled into his mouth. My hands found his hair, and I yanked his head back, devouring him, taking everything I'd wanted and more.

"Stay."

His green eyes met mine, and he smiled.

"You're going to pay for that."

It broadened. "I know."

I rested my forehead to his, taking a minute before I gave into the desire eating away at me.

"This is a delusion. At the end of the day, it doesn't matter what we feel for each other, our worlds don't mesh. We both know you'll go back," I said the last in a whisper.

"Let's share the delusion for one night and face reality in the morning."

It was impossible to say no.

I had one revelation in the hell of this day: I liked him more than I should. I was fucked.

TWENTY · SIX

DANTE

I slammed him into the wall outside the playroom, kissing him roughly. He clawed at my clothes as I rubbed my groin over his. It wasn't enough. I wasn't sure anything ever would be. I'd craved this since the first time I had him stretched out on my table, and now it was going to take every ounce of control to not rush it. Grabbing him by the thigh, I pulled his leg around my waist. He locked his arms behind my neck and whimpered into my mouth.

"Like that do you?"

He nodded, too out of breath to form a reply. He reached between us and tore at the button on my jeans, trying to get them undone. I dug my fingers into his thigh, too consumed with his taste and the friction I needed to care what else he was doing. He shoved a hand into my boxers and closed his warm fingers around me.

"Shit." I groaned into his mouth as he bit down on my bottom lip.

"I need you inside me. It's been agony."

His pleading had the same effect it always did. I wanted to give him everything he needed. I grabbed at the belt to his slacks and pulled. Next was his button and zipper. I could be inside him in under a minute, but I made myself stop. This isn't how I wanted him. I wanted him wearing my marks when I took his ass. I wanted him floating, lost in subspace. He'd had what I assumed were hundreds of meaningless partners, and I wasn't going to be another notch in the bedpost. I wanted that connection we had when he was tied up under me. I wanted to hear him plead for it with his life. I could almost hear him offering me anything I wanted if I would just fuck him already.

My hand fell away. "Not here." I let him down to his feet.

His lower lip jutted out, and he whimpered. I held firm.

"Dante." His voice was laced with a deadly edge.

It made my cock twitch in his hand to hear the desire. "No."

He dropped to his knees before me and rubbed the scruff on his jaw over my base. I swallowed the moan in my throat, not giving him the satisfaction.

"Please, Master." He looked me in the eyes as he brushed his thumb over my head, bringing the tiny bead of precum to his lips. He sucked on his fingers, and I felt it in my cock.

I clenched my teeth, fighting back all the urges I had to grab a fist full of his hair and fuck his pretty mouth. Every moment with him was an erotic battle for control. Bliss.

"You will get it after I leave my marks on you, and if you give me any lip I'm going to make you wait." Even hotter than him on his knees with my dick in his mouth was the effect my words had on him. I could see his eyes blazing with defiance.

His lips pulled back as he growled low in his chest. I smacked his cheek. "We don't growl at our master."

He stiffened and parted his lips to take my head into his mouth. They closed around my girth, and he sucked lightly.

"It looks like you're not going to get my cock filling your ass tonight, my little defiant bastard."

He dragged his teeth over me as he pulled back, while teasing the underside of my shaft with his tongue. It was too much. I felt the last strands of resolve I had slipping. I yanked at his hair, tilting his head back just enough to get the right angle before I shoved my cock down his throat. His eyes bulged, watering as my tip hit the back. It took him a few moments, but he swallowed around me like a good boy.

I pulled back only to slam home again. He took me greedily, licking and sucking every inch. I could see in his eyes he thought he'd won. Looking up with his piercing green eyes, he was smug. I let him think it for another few moments, enjoying his warm mouth before I pulled back, putting my aching cock away before he could get at it again.

He stayed on his knees, mouth hanging open.

"You really think you're going to get what you want being so defiant? You have a lot to learn. Get to your feet and get your ass on my table before I decide to send you home to think about what you've done."

His mouth snapped shut, and he pushed to his feet one at a time. "You wouldn't." There was anger in his voice.

"Watch me."

He closed his hands into fists. "You need me just as bad as I need you."

"But I have patience." It was only half the truth. I'd have him today if he did what I said or not, but we'd ruin this if it came the wrong way.

I crossed my arms over my chest. Seconds ticked by. Finally, he removed his clothes, folding them and setting them by the door as I watched. Once naked, he stepped into the dark room, disappearing from my view.

I breathed. I could do this.

"Face up or down, Master?" The defiance had fled.

I flipped on the overhead light as I stepped into the room. He stood next to the stainless steel table, head bent with his eyes on the floor. He was a different person inside these walls. All the tension he carried in his shoulders had already melted away. I wondered whether he might have ended up a slave to someone, had he been born in a different life. My guess was yes. He was never so at peace as when he served.

I paused before I answered. I wanted both. Each position had its advantage. "Face up." I was going to be a greedy bastard today. I may never get an encore.

He stretched out on the cool metal, not flinching. His chest rose and fell, and the bare hint of a smile turned up the corners of his mouth. I couldn't leave it. It wasn't in me.

"Tell me what you need?"

His eyes flashed up to meet mine. "I need—"

I cut him off before the lie could leave his lips. "If you lie to me, there will be no play tonight."

"I need you." I was lost to the jade of his gaze.

"That much is clear. Tell me what will make you whole."

The turbulent sea thrashed behind his eyes. I knew he was at war with himself, fighting the answer.

"Don't hold it back." I wanted to hear the words.

"Take me, make me yours," he pleaded. "However you see fit."

"You've been mine awhile."

"Since the first time I knelt at your feet."

I mentally stumbled. I knew it had been a long time, but I never suspected he'd felt it from that first night like I had. His hands shook, and there were dark circles under his eyes nothing could hide. I bent to brush my lips against his ear.

"I'm going to take every part of you tonight. You're going to feel me on every inch of you."

A shiver ran through him. "Please."

There were toys scattered around my entire house, and the playroom was stocked with the best money could buy. I didn't need them. I was going to give him something completely unique.

I grabbed one of my stainless steel bowls and filled it with ice and then water. I set it aside and then found a lighter and two knives. I cleaned both knives thoroughly and then placed one in the ice mixture. I strolled back over to him to find him laying across the table fully naked. I resisted smiling.

"Hands above your head." I set the bowl between his legs.

He stretched out, tilting his hips while expanding his chest. I ignored the movement as I tied his hands to the end of the table with a simple hemp cord. Easy in, easy out. I'd want the access later, and I wouldn't have the patience to mess with cuffs.

"Good boy," I whispered as I pulled back, picking up the bowl.

"I'm always a good boy."

I picked up the cloth I'd brought over and draped it over his face.

"I want to see you." He pulled at the cords holding his wrists.

"You're not allowed to move unless I move you. I want you to stay exactly how I position you. I'm not binding your legs, but I will if you move." I was treading on quicksand thinking I wouldn't drown.

"Yes, Master." His words were moaned. I could tell he was already drifting close to subspace.

I adjusted him so his feet were on the table, spreading his thighs apart as far as he could comfortably hold them. His inked body was my own personal hell stretched out before me. I wanted to lose myself in him. I traced the outlines of some of his tattoos. He had so many. I wondered if they each had a meaning or if he'd submitted to every whim for new ink.

"I am going to play with knives. Do you have any objection?" I took the knife and dragged the point along the line of his hip so he could feel the cool steel.

His cock jumped. It was all the answer I needed.

"No, Master." His breath caught as he answered. I smelled fear, which was exactly what I wanted. "Remember, nowhere the marks can be seen, as we agreed on."

I removed it from his skin and held the candle under the blade, heating the length of it. I tested the tip on the back of my hand. It was warm, and I lowered it to the center of his ribs. "Your body is mine to do with as I will."

He flinched as he felt the steel. "My body and mind are yours."

I drew the flat of the blade down his chest, not cutting him. "Do you trust me?"

He stiffened. "I do..." he whimpered.

I lifted the knife to reheat it, this time waiting until it was hot. It would mimic the pain of being cut without opening his skin. A favorite game of mine, with none of the scarring of blood play. It also added a psychological element, as he had no idea what I was doing. I caught him under the bend of his knee, lifting his legs up before I pressed the metal to the curve of his ass. His back arched off the table, but he did his best to not move. His hands clenched into fists and then opened back up as he gritted his teeth.

I set aside the hot knife and grabbed the other out of the ice. I drew it along his collarbone. His chin tilted up and he hissed, cock standing at full attention between his thighs. The difference in temperature would fool his body into thinking more was going on. Precum leaked from his slit, dripping over his thick head.

"I need—" He didn't even know.

I took my time reheating the first knife, burning him lightly from shoulders to ass, even placing a few near the base of his cock. Tiny welts formed on his skin, making him even more beautiful. They would be no worse than burns from candle wax, but because he thought I was cutting him, I almost envied his high.

By the time I finished, he was shaking and breathing hard. I rubbed my hands up his bare body, stretching out to hover over him. I pulled the cloth from his face and lowered myself to whisper over his lips. "Tell me how you feel."

"I feel like I'm floating but at the same time I'm suffering in Hell."

"Hell?" I asked, taking a moment to study him. The lines in his face were relaxed as well as his muscles.

"I'm in a hell where the only way to quench my thirst is with your touch, and I don't think I'm ever going to escape."

"Fuck." It took every ounce of reserve I had to not lower myself to him.

He picked up his head and nipped at my lips. "Please. I

need to feel your skin."

Our eyes met. I hadn't intended on taking my clothes off. Making myself bare for him.

"That word." I stalled.

"Please," he said it again, drawing it out this time into a needful whimper.

My breath caught in my chest, and I slowly lowered my clothed body to his. As soon as we met, he lifted his hips to rub his cock over mine. I shoved my knees against his thighs, spreading him even more open for me.

"You are dangerous."

"Can I move, Master?"

I nodded, resisting the impulse to lower my mouth to his neck. He rubbed his cock into my jeans. I was already hard, and it was getting painful.

"Tell me what you want, Remi."

"I want you inside me. I want my blood and sweat to slick our bodies as we fuck." His voice was strained, and the sound drove me mad with desire. He was going to be the death of me.

I dropped my face to his chest and drew in a few ragged breaths. He still thought I'd cut him. I straightened and grabbed my shirt by the back of the neck and pulled it off.

His eyes raked down my body, and his breath hitched as his eyes landed on the scar on my chest. I let him watch as I removed my jeans and boxers. Now he was pulling at the ties at his wrists, the muscles in his shoulders tightening. I closed my eyes and climbed over him. With a quick flick of the knife, I cut his hands free and then lowered myself to him.

I'd never get over him. There wasn't a chance in this clouded hell.

He fisted a hand in my hair and pulled my head up.

"Fuck me."

TWENTY SEVEN

REMI

I pressed my cock into his, begging with not only my words but with my body.

He pressed his eyes closed and smiled. It was the most innocent I'd ever seen him. How had I gone my whole life without this? He tried to pull away, but I dug my nails into his back, keeping him right where he was.

"Please don't go."

"I need lube." He laid his forehead to mine and chuckled.

"It better not be far."

He held the bottle to the side of my face and only then did I let him have the few inches he needed to slick himself. He pressed his head to my entrance and paused.

"What are you waiting for?"

"Begging."

So fucking cocky, but I wasn't about to let any of my stubbornness show. I was too fucking desperate.

I moved my hands to his face so he'd look me in the eyes. I was sure he could feel my need. "Dante, if you don't fuck me I may die."

He pressed into me, pushing his tip past the resistance, and he didn't stop until he was buried inside me. Not giving

me a minute to get used to his girth, he pulled back and
slammed home again. My breath caught in my throat.
Never had I felt so connected to another person in my life.
He filled me so wholly and completely. I could have died
at that moment and been truly happy. Our bodies were slick
with sweat, and probably my blood, causing him to glide
over me with each stroke.

I had to have more friction. I lifted my hips, meeting his
brutal thrusts, grabbing his ass so he'd get deeper. I didn't
even care about getting off, having him there was better
than any orgasm I'd ever had. Then suddenly I was close,
I'd been fully aroused the whole time we'd been in the
playroom, but I thought I was a good boy and could go for
hours. Apparently not with *him* owning me so completely.

I groaned and pressed myself against the metal
underneath me, trying to get some space, any room to get
some control. I had to center myself as not to disappoint
him by coming and ruining the moment.

A hand closed around my throat. It shocked me, and I
looked up into Dante's eyes. He snarled, and the placement
of his fingers didn't help my impending release. His palm
wasn't tight, it was possessive. He owned me. My chest
heaved, and I melted under his touch. I was fucked. I was
going to lose it. I bit down on my lip, shaking as I held it
back.

"Stay with me," he commanded.

I looked up into his icy blue eyes and finally felt
centered. "I'm right here." I held his wrist, keeping it to my
throat.

"Don't pull back. I want you to feel me. Feel every welt
and mark as I claim you." His voice was steady and laced
with arousal. I did that to him. It was all me.

"I'm trying not to come," I gasped through my erratic

breath. "I want to be a good boy for you."

A sadistic grin curled over his lips. Fucking bastard. "Do you need to come, boy?"

I nodded, not trusting my voice. He slammed into my prostate, holding my gaze, taunting me.

"Please." I stretched out my spine, trying to pull away from him, but at the same time not wanting to go anywhere. I couldn't move an inch. "Please, Master."

"Come."

His words pulled my release from me, and I went from floating to unimaginable ecstasy. Lost in my release, his every movement magnified until I was raw all over. He dropped his face to my shoulder and bit down, pushing himself over the edge.

Dante collapsed on top of me, and I welcomed the weight. He stayed inside me, both of us regaining our breath, basking in the afterglow. He held me as I came down from my high, he held me through the surge of panic. I rarely had them when coming down, but this was too much, too real. I could lose him, and it might kill me. I wasn't even sure if he knew what was going on in my head, but his strong arms kept me close.

"Let's get cleaned up and go to bed." As he picked up his head I chased his lips, demanding a kiss.

He gave into my liberty, letting me taste him before he climbed off the table. I sat up slowly, sure I'd feel the cuts. My skin felt tight, it burned almost, further along in the healing process than it should have been.

"I think I needed that as much as you did." He brought a warm cloth over and began cleaning my skin. I melted all over again. This was a stark contrast. Where he'd been harsh before, now he was gentle. He kissed and cleaned each mark he'd left before applying a light coat of cool cream to the areas. "Such a good boy. *My* good boy."

A smile spread across my face. I felt relaxed, more relaxed than I'd felt in years. It was a gift. "You know what it's like to hear you say those words?"

"What?"

"I can't explain it. I never thought you'd want me. Use me like I was using you, sure, but—"

He half shrugged. For the first time, I let some of my vulnerability show through my mask. The pure submissive inside me, unadulterated.

"You know how perfect you are when you drop all your walls?" He pushed his fingers into my hair and yanked my head back so he could skim his nose up my neck.

"It's because you came in with your damn bulldozer and knocked them all down."

"I'm not going to apologize." He returned to the sink to rinse the cloth and then wash his hands.

"I didn't think you were, Master." I got to my feet slowly and smoothed my fingers down my chest, wanting to feel the cuts. "Where is the blood?" I searched my body, and there was nothing. Pink marks but not a single drop of blood.

The corners of his mouth curled up. "I didn't cut you."

Confusion washed over me. I'd been sure... "How the fuck?"

He held up his lighter and grinned. "It's amazing how the brain interprets pain with expectation. I didn't do anything worse than candle wax."

I groaned and gripped my cock as it started to grow hard again.

Dante smacked my ass as he walked past. "Down, boy."

I kept stroking myself. "Is that an order?" I'd never stop pushing his buttons.

He licked over his lips, eyes locked on my hand as it moved over my cock. "Don't you need to sleep?"

"It's overrated."

To be in bed with Dante with his arms around me was bliss. I was riding my high and release from earlier, but this was so much more. I now knew what Kai got out of our relationship even if he wasn't in love with me. I didn't know how I was going to function in my real life when I was forced to go back. I needed to go to Vegas. I needed to face whatever my father was fishing for, but it wasn't going to happen today. I could put it off for a few days at least.

I rubbed my face over his chest, savoring every moment of this. I would need to absorb as much of this as possible to get me through the days in Vegas. It was getting harder and harder to keep my mask up while I was there. My father noticed even the smallest slip. I was already dreading it.

"Tell me what you're thinking?" I'd thought he was sleeping.

"How I don't want to leave." I didn't risk a look at him. I wasn't sure what we were when we left the playroom. I had a place there, all the rest was new territory. Even when I'd been in his bed before, I'd been the submissive. This was so much more as he lay wrapped up around me, fully naked. I'd never been allowed to touch him like this. It scared me to be this raw with another person.

He was air, and I'd been drowning my whole life.

"Surely you want to return to your life?"

"Parts of me do," I said.

"And parts of you don't?" He was picking apart my

J.R. Gray

mind, and I wasn't ready for it.

"I guess."

"For a guy who's chosen to stay away as much as you have, it doesn't add up."

"I've never chosen to stay away." It was mostly the truth.

"You're dodging. Explain." He would pry the answers from me if I liked it or not. There was something about him that worked its way into my mind and opened up all the dark parts.

I sighed and pressed closer into him. "At first, it was because of Kai."

"Oh?"

"He doesn't have feelings for me." I'd never told anyone about our relationship. Kai, like me, didn't want our circle to know what he was.

"He has a submissive of his own you've said?"

I looked up at him. "He does."

"Does his submissive know?" His questions were so pointed. Nothing escaped him.

"He knows they aren't exclusive, but not that Kai is submissive nor that he is submissive to me."

Dante nodded, and I got a feeling he was disappointed. The feeling worked its way through me, making me feel sick from the inside out. He pulled away, putting a few inches of space between us.

"Are you upset with me."

"No." The word was cold.

I frowned and looked him in the eyes. "Then what is it?"

Dante shook his head. "Not a thing."

I could feel it, though. I knew there was something he wasn't saying, but I couldn't make him speak like he could me. I tucked in close to try and catch a few hours of sleep,

198

but he had changed. I could feel it in his fitful sleep.

We fell into a routine. Dante worked, and I played my part at the club keeping up appearances as his business partner, but the moment we entered his house, we were two different people. I was his, and I was never out of arm's reach. We christened every room in his house. The kinky bastard had toys stashed all over. No matter where I jumped him, he had a way to give me pain and make me fly. We started to sleep. Both of us had suffered insomnia for years, and here we were, sleeping late into the morning.

People were expecting me. My father had called three times, which is unheard of. Kai hadn't called, and I wasn't sure I cared. I wanted to vanish from my reality and make a new one here. It wasn't fair to him to think the thoughts I was thinking, and I hated myself a little for it, but not enough to leave.

My first mistake was getting out of bed to check my phone. It buzzed over and over until it fell off the nightstand. When I picked it up, dread punched holes in me like buckshot.

Kai: I know you're up. You're always running before the sun.

I glanced out the window. How wrong he was. There was something about coming clean with yourself and the universe about what you are which sets everything right.

Remi: You actually woke me.

Dante was snoring lightly as I slipped from the room to find coffee. I turned on the espresso maker I'd bought and checked the water, waiting for Kai to reply. I was already comfortable here. I'd bought clothes and filled drawers. Everything was new. I couldn't have taken anything from the place I shared with Kai. Even a mug would have been a drop of poison, a deadly reminder I couldn't hide here forever. I knew where the dishes were and where Dante liked his milk in the fridge.

Kai: He's changed you that much, has he?

I clicked the screen off and started on the espresso. My phone buzzed twice more in my pocket.

Kai: I don't think you've ever left me speechless before.

Kai: I haven't even seen you in over a week.

Another buzzed through as I was reading.

Kai: I was going to ask you to dinner, but I'm sure you're busy.

Remi: Dinner? I'm not in Cali.

Kai: I know where you are.

Ominous.

"I thought you'd abandoned me." Dante wore a lazy grin as he padded down the stairs in only his boxer briefs.

"I needed coffee." I set a cup in front of him and felt guilty about the messages on my phone. What had I become?

"You pay attention." He picked up the cup and brought it to his lips.

"Hmmm?"

"You know how I like my coffee."

"I do pay attention." I smiled into my drink. It was high praise from him, and I ate it up. I grabbed the Fruity Pebbles I'd bought out of the pantry and a bowl. "Want some?" I shook the neon box in front of my face.

He snatched it out of my hands. "Clearly not enough attention. What the fuck is this?"

"Breakfast?"

He stood reading the side of the box. "Did you even bother to look at all the chemicals they put in here? High

Fructose Corn syrup, hydrogenated oils, and colors." He tossed the box back to the counter and stuck out his tongue.

"It tastes good," I said with a mouth full of cereal.

He grabbed the bowl out of my hands and dumped it down the sink. "Let me make you some real food."

Both my brows rose. "I'm always willing to let you cook for me." It was half the reason I bought the crap cereal, not that I'd tell him that.

"I bet you are." He pointed to a stool, and I took the hint, giving him his space to work.

I didn't think I'd ever tire of watching him. He collected things from the fridge and set them on the counter. Then he got out bowls, whisks, spices, and finally the apron. It was black and well worn, and he tied it around his waist like he'd done it hundreds of times. I wondered if this too had something to do with his husband. He got to work in the kitchen, moving with ease.

He cracked eggs into a pan and laid out bacon on a baking sheet before sliding it into the oven. I pulled myself up onto the counter and sat to watch. The muscles in his back flexed as he mixed batter. Only the pleasure of watching him make me food kept me from dropping to my knees at his feet and begging him to take me. I'd never been so turned on by such a mundane task. Kai and I didn't even keep any food in the house except processed crap, as Dante called it. We ordered out every meal.

Dante took out strawberries and cut them methodically, placing them on the plate like it was a work of art. He held out the plate and a fork like what he'd done didn't mean a thing. I took it from him, and my chest tightened. I wanted to keep this man.

"Well? Are you going to eat?" He'd made his own plate and leaned back against the counter to eat, still in the apron.

"When I finish eye fucking you."

He put a bite in his mouth, chewed, then swallowed before he answered. "If you aren't gonna eat, I'll take it back."

I got to work on my food, too worried if I pushed it wouldn't happen again.

My phone rang. I picked it up, expecting to see Kai calling, but it was my father, again. I clicked ignore. Dante nodded with his chin in the direction of my phone.

"Why do you keep ignoring it?"

"Because I don't want to be pulled from my sanctuary yet."

He raised a brow, and I was sure it was because of my wording. "I've never been to Vegas. I'll go with you."

The panic must have showed on my face. He looked put off or stunned.

"It's not what you're thinking." Shit.

"You have no idea what I'm thinking." He went back to work on his food.

"Dante, we've had an amazing few days. Don't do this."

He wouldn't look at me.

"It's really not what you think." I was losing him. I could see him closing off.

"It's that I'm not good enough for your world. There is no reason to sugar coat it. I wasn't good enough for his either."

I laughed. I couldn't help it. It burst out of me, which only served to piss him off further.

"Did he tell you that?" I reined in my outburst. "Because it's not the truth at all."

"No, but I knew he felt it. I never went with him when he visited his family. I wasn't welcome, in fact."

His words made my chest ache for him. How wrong he

was about my reasons.

"It has nothing to do with you. My father would kill me if he knew I was gay." I'd never let anyone but Kai know the burden. I kept it so close to my chest it was a relief to say it out loud.

"Right." He scoffed.

I tossed down my fork and leaned over the counter. "I watched him put a bullet in between his own brother's eyes when he found out he was gay," I said it with spite as bile rose in my throat. I swallowed back the dry heave that came with repressed memories.

When I looked up he was staring. "You're serious."

I stared him down. "Yes."

His entire demeanor changed. "Shit." He came around the counter to take me into his arms. I melted. "How old were you?"

"Eight. I barely knew what attraction was. I was just starting to have those feelings. I'm so fucking lucky I'd never expressed it out loud." I laughed without humor and turned my face away from him.

He grabbed my chin and turned my face toward his. "So you ran away with Kai as soon as you could."

I nodded.

"And he has no idea what you and Kai are to each other?"

"None."

"No wonder you don't want to go back."

"Understatement of my lifetime. Not only do I not want to go back, I want to trade my life for another. I don't want any of what he has to offer. I'd escape it if I could."

Dante held me tight. It was almost as important as aftercare. Or maybe it was a sort of aftercare—one for getting things off my chest.

His phone started to vibrate between us, and he pulled back to answer it.

"Hello?" Dante pressed his phone to his ear. "Yeah, yeah. We good to go for tonight?"

He paused, listening. I wished I could hear.

"Yep, put me down." He paused again. "It's not a big deal."

"No flights are leaving Vegas," he said when he hung up. "Something about a fire in the air traffic control tower. So we are fucked for tonight's fight. I'm pulling guys, but I've got to fight. I know we made plans to watch it together, but it won't take me long."

My throat went dry. I knew the answer before I asked. "Who are you fighting?"

"Josh."

I was a fucking roller coaster of emotions, and I was too fucking afraid to tell him how any of it made me feel.

TWENTY EIGHT
DANTE

"You're tense." I'd done something. I had to have, because between him telling me what had happened and the phone call, Remi's whole demeanor had changed.

"I'm fine." He was lying.

I watched him, trying to suss out what the hell had happened. He was poker-faced. His phone went off again. He checked the message, not allowing his face to change, but he didn't realize he had a tell. His head tilted and dragged his teeth over his lips. It gave me all the information I needed.

"Put your phone down."

His gaze came back up, and he laughed. "Why?"

"Because I want you to."

He set the phone down and waited.

"On your knees."

He dropped.

I made sure to look unimpressed. "I really despise when you wear clothes."

"Should I remove them, Master?"

"Yes."

He unceremoniously stripped. He folded them and placed them on the floor.

"Much better." I dropped my gaze down his form, drinking him in. I felt his pride swell as I looked.

"What will you have me do?"

I took off my apron exposing my already hard cock to him. "I want to feel you gag."

He dropped to his hands and crawled forward. I was pleased with how quickly he'd learned my preferences.

"You're such a good boy. *My* good boy." I took myself in hand as he came up in front of me and brushed my tip over his lips. He parted them and waited. I grabbed a handful of his hair and pushed my cock between his lips. He took every single inch, greedily, until I hit the back of his throat. It was bliss, and I stayed there in his warm mouth as his eyes watered, and he swallowed around me, but it wasn't what either of us needed. A single tear streamed down Remi's face, and I tried to pull back. He grabbed my hips and took me further into his mouth to flick his tongue over my balls. My head dropped back, and a groan slipped from my lips.

I'd never expected to be in a relationship again, and certainly not with Remi, but he was who I needed. We pushed each other in all the right and wrong ways.

I broke his grip and yanked him off of me. "Stand up." I grabbed a counter height stool and set it before him. "Sit."

Without shame he did, backward, presenting his ass to me.

"Stay, I have things to get."

He raised a questioning brow but didn't ask. I knew what I needed. First twine, and plenty of it. I always had it on hand for meat—and things. Next I grabbed a handful of clothespins.

"Arms behind your back."

He did so but looked over his shoulder at me. "Why do

you have all this shit in your kitchen?"

I measured a length of twine. "This is used to tie meat." Starting at his wrists, I bound his forearms together, leaving myself a place to grip when I was ready.

"And the clothespins?" He drew in a breath through his teeth as I pinched the skin on his shoulders.

"Isn't it clear?" I placed a line of the pins across his chest next, and then for fun added a few to his thighs.

"Your use is, but not why you'd keep them in the kitchen." His words were jagged and spoken through groans. Every single one moved through me, not only making me harder, but feeding my mind.

"To keep bags closed, of course." I finished my line of pins from elbow to elbow across his shoulders and behind his head. I paused to drink in my work. He looked unbelievable. I stepped around him to open the dishwasher. From it, I grabbed a plug, and then my crop from the drawer of sex toys.

"What are you doing in there?" I could tell he was getting impatient.

"You mean you don't clean your sex toys in the dishwasher?" I held up a plug.

"With your pots and pans?"

I was horrified at the suggestion. "I wouldn't put pots and pans in a dishwasher, they'd get ruined."

"And you think it's a good place for sex toys?"

"It has a sanitizing setting."

"Will you just fuck me?"

"Oh, I'm not going to fuck you yet. Where would be the fun in that?" I coated the plug in lube and pressed the cool metal to his opening. "This may hurt coming out." It was slightly larger than a normal plug, but he could take it. I pushed it forward and watched him stretch over it. Remi grunted until it settled into place against his prostate and then he sighed.

It took a lot not to fuck him right there. I wasn't sure I'd ever get enough of him now that I'd had him. At first, I thought the desire was wanting what he wasn't offering, but now I knew there was so much more. Whatever he was, we were the same.

"Damn," Remi muttered.

"You look so fucking sexy like this for me."

I took the crop and used it to smack off one of the clothes pins on his chest. He clenched his teeth and grunted.

"Fuckin' hell, that hurts."

I hit the second. "Master?"

"Yes, fuck that hurts, Master." He lingered on the word, almost making it a protest.

I used the crop to knock off three more in quick succession. "I know."

He was breathing through the pain, and I let him have a few seconds to recover before I smacked the spot the pin had been. Remi pressed his face into the counter before him. I trailed my fingers down his spine, laughing to myself.

"Who was texting you this morning?"

"You know."

I did, but I wanted to hear him say it. I cleared the pins off his exposed thigh. "Answer the question."

He turned his head and looked into my eyes, not answering. I loved every single small protest he made, but I wasn't going to let it slide. I stepped around him to do the other thigh. I brought the crop down hard welting the already bright red skin. My cock was dripping. I needed him.

"Where did you learn how to do that?"

"It's a little trick I picked up from a Master I know in Chicago." I knocked the rest of the row off and lightly tapped my leather over his angry skin.

"It was Kai."

"What did he want?"

"Dinner."

"He's here?" I asked in a measured tone.

"I'm really sorry, he didn't ask." He pressed his face back to the counter, and his shoulders tightened up again. Now I knew why he'd looked so tense this morning.

"I think you need to stand up to him, but it's not my place. I expect to see you back before you go home." I leaned down and pressed my lips to his ear. "You belong to me. He can't take that away from us. Make sure he knows it."

I didn't linger. We both needed this. I took the clothespins off one by one with the crop, the satisfactory snap of leather against wood drowning out my thoughts. Slowly the tension in his shoulders left him, and he came back to us. His pouting helped because it meant his focus was completely on me.

We would both be tense tonight, and I needed to give us something to hold on to. Or at least, something for me to hold on to while he was off with Kai. I was beginning to hate the idea of Kai. He had this power over Remi, and it was deeply ingrained. I never expected him to give up Kai, but he had to learn to stand up to him.

His eyes drifted shut, and his head fell forward. He was floating. My chest swelled, and I grabbed him by the hair as I bent to kiss his jaw, his neck, and finally our mouths met. He responded, but he was slow to my aggressive come-on, clearly lost in himself. I bit his lip, and his eyes flashed open.

"Stay with me."

"I wouldn't be anywhere else." Even his voice was floaty.

"Good boy."

I withdrew the toy from him as I coated my cock with lubricant. When I forced myself inside, only the two of us existed.

TWENTY NINE

REMI

I stood in front of the Ritz hours later in the only suit I'd brought with me from Vegas. I was glad I hadn't left last week. I adjusted my cufflinks as I climbed the stairs, regretting this already. I was always going to be a disappointment because I could never be what anyone wanted me to be. Not at the same time. I was spread too thin and disappointing them all.

He was already seated, and I lingered in the entryway, ignoring the tiny woman who was trying to seat me. Kai played a tattooed surfer in our daily lives, but he came from as much money as I did, and his money was all clean, even if it was tainted in other ways. His light green button down hid all his tattoos except the ones above his collar. He was sampling wine, putting the ring wrapped around his left ring finger on display. It felt so wrong.

I brushed past the little woman, putting on my game face as I strolled to Kai's table. He stood as I approached and sat only when I did. Manners like those couldn't be forced out. He would always have old money stamped on his forehead. He told the waiter to pour me a glass of the white he'd selected, and I ignored it.

"Why are you here, Kai?"

"I figured you'd want to be asked to be my best man in person, and since I can't seem to catch you at *home,* I figured I'd come to you." He said home like it should make me feel guilty. It worked, but I didn't let him see it. My entire body went numb. We wore rings, we said we were engaged, but really they'd meant something entirely different to us when we'd got them. They were a commitment to put our friendship first.

Kai was doing what I didn't have the guts to do. He was leaving me first. I had no response. What could I say? Even knowing I'd thought about it first didn't make the pain any less. I was torn between who I was and who I pretended to be. The air I needed to breathe on one side and my best friend on the other. There would be no winning here.

"You're getting married? I've been busy. You know my father had me in Vegas."

"Yes, married, and, as I understand it you haven't been to Vegas."

My knees went weak. He'd talked to my father. "But we agreed."

"You broke it long before I did. Kyle asked me to marry him, and I said yes."

He'd seen right through my act. He knew how I felt. Mentally I'd left him long before he'd left me, yet he was the first to admit it.

"I haven't done anything. I still live there."

"Do you even remember the last time you were home?"

I set my jaw. "When you called me, broken, in the middle of the night and begged me to come home, only for me to find you'd made up by the time I got there? I'm not sure it wasn't more than a ploy all along."

I knew I'd shocked him. The look on his face was clear. "It wasn't a lie. We made up. I should have told you."

"You didn't tell me because you expected me to stay when I got there."

"I did." The set in his jaw told me he was still annoyed I hadn't. "I'm not going to live in that big empty house alone. Kyle wants this, and so do I." There wasn't a hint of defeat in his voice.

Silence engulfed us, and I picked up my menu. I wanted to ask so many of the questions I had no right to, so I ordered instead. I couldn't go back to Dante feeling like I was. He would read me like he always could. I had to get a handle on myself.

He rolled his eyes. "Remi, will you be my best man?"

I looked down at the tablecloth. "Yeah, of course I will."

There was another long silence before he asked, "Are you going to come home after you get this itch scratched—" He paused like he had more to say, but he didn't go on.

"It's not an itch," I snapped. "You know it will always be my home, but I deserve as much happiness as you do. You're getting married, for fuck's sake."

"Is it Cali or me that's home?" Kai asked.

I growled, "That you even have the gall to ask."

"You can't even answer."

"And you can't even acknowledge I deserve someone too."

He shrugged like the sassy switch he was. "You love me, but you've never been in love with me, and all the wishing in the world isn't going to change it."

"You're not in love with me either." As the words left my mouth I wasn't sure anymore.

I couldn't be in love with Kai, and I had tried. No matter how much I wanted to, I couldn't control my feelings, this obsession. I was never going to see him as a dominant. Not after he'd been on his knees for me. And there was no way he could handle me. We couldn't go back and forth. Our relationship would always be one-sided. He didn't need it like I did.

"You know it's not a presumptuous question to ask. You won't say who is home. You can dodge and not answer, but your actions scream it." His words stung.

"You moved in with him." I was tired of holding back all the things we didn't say. "There has never been an us. You don't want an us. You're only pissy because I'm with someone."

"It's not that. You've fucked half of the city."

Rage and hurt settled in my chest.

"It's different because I have feelings, even though you will never have feelings for me." He looked at me, his eyes telling me more than his lips ever would. I wanted him to admit it.

"You're just being greedy," I said between clenched teeth.

"Act like you don't like it." Kai threw his napkin on the table and stood. He got out his money clip and peeled off a few bills, tossing them down. "You want everyone to want you, but you don't want to give anything in return."

"I love it. I love our friendship, but it's nothing more."

He could have his happily ever after, but only if I stayed in his box so he could get the dominance he needed. It wasn't fair to me to never have what he already did, and he knew it.

"It was never more for you maybe."

I'd known it, and still it felt like a physical blow when he said it.

"I need to go, and you need to decide what's more important: your family and your business or kneeling at his feet." He stepped around the table.

"Where are you going?" I got in his face.

"You have some nerve causing a scene."

I gripped the edge of the table. If I wanted to cause a scene, I could have easily flipped it. "You're the one who wanted to do this in public."

"I'm going to sell the house if you don't make up your mind."

"You can't sell the house."

I clawed at my skin, like the act of it could remove the feelings inside me. If only I could dig deep enough or puncture something, they could all leak out. I wanted to get out of this hell in my mind for even ten minutes. But it was useless.

"What even are we anymore?"

"We are friends. We've always put that first."

He jutted his chin out. "I don't believe you."

"I've stayed too long. I won't next time. Kai, you're my best friend."

"I'm getting married. I'm not changing my mind."

"I never asked you to, but don't ask me to give him up."

Kai held out his hand for mine and raised his brows. "Come spend the evening with me then." When I took his hand Kai's face softened, and I knew he felt victorious. I'd let him have it. Why did it always feel like I was a status to everyone except Dante? Like I was a prize to be won.

He led me up through the Ritz in a blur. I didn't take note of anything, even which floor we stopped on. I sank to a seat on the bed once we were in the room, ignoring Kai's chatter about the suite. As much as he played the surfer, he was a rich boy, always would be. He fit my lifestyle in a way Dante never would. He did whatever I wanted. He was good for me, supported me, loved me.

Why couldn't I love him?

I was starting to feel like I was the deficient one. I'd been offered perfection in the form of a man who would kneel at my feet and love me for the rest of my life, and I wanted the asshole. The closed off, egotistical—

I pushed my nails into the base of my neck until I felt a hot stream dripping over my skin. I pulled my hand away to find it bloody. I hadn't even felt any pain. I couldn't even use pain to block him out. I was trapped in my own hell with no escape.

"Want to shower?" Kai was on his knees in front of me, unlacing my boots. Usually, I would have been aroused by the gesture, but I couldn't fake it today.

I shook my head. "No." I didn't have the balls to say what I needed to do. I was going to go back with Kai and take the easy road. Even Dante had seen it in me. I would keep doing it. It was who I was.

Kai shot me a glance like he could read my mind and got back to his feet. "How long is this going to take?"

I knit my brow, trying to process what he was saying. "How long is what going to take? What do you mean?"

"Never mind." He started to retreat toward the bathroom.

I shot to my feet and growled. "You don't get to blow this off. Answer me." I grabbed him by the shoulder roughly and turned him around.

I could see the fire building inside him. His voice dropped to almost a whisper, "How long are you going to let him affect you and us?"

Instead of allowing me to ignore it and carry on, there it all was, laid out.

"He's not a fling. As long as he'll have me."

He rolled his eyes and pulled out of my grasp. "So I have to clean up the mess and be punished for you needing to find something else."

I let my hand fall back to my side. I couldn't believe this. He had his fiancé and me still here, yet he was mad at me for being numb with an impending break up suffocating me from the inside. All the things I'd never said to anyone started to well up. I was about to burst. I had to get out of the hotel room before I threw away everything. I shoved my feet into my shoes and stalked toward the door.

As I yanked it open Kai said, "You would run away. All you ever do is run away."

It broke the dam.

"I was leaving so I didn't go off, but you know what? Fuck it." I slammed the door and rounded on him. "It must be nice to have everything you need in your little box with no issues, but I was never fucking allowed to be myself. You know what my father did. To his own brother." I nearly choked on the words as they came out of my throat. My eyes burned again.

"I love you, Kai, but I've never been in love with you. You make out you've been in love with me, but you've only been in love with the idea of me. You never cared what I needed, as long as you got yours. You get what you need from me, and you're loyal because of it, but you love Kyle." My breathing caught in my throat, and I wanted to hurt someone. I pressed my nails into my palms, trying to get a release through pain. "I've settled my entire fucking life. I've settled for what everyone else told me was best for me, and I really started to believe my own lies. I started to believe there wasn't love, or a connection, there was only mutually beneficial 'okay.' I didn't think there was a happily ever after in my cards. That true love was bullshit."

Kai leaned back against the door frame and stared at me. "You have always said it's you and me, to the end.

Friendship over cock."

"Yeah, I have, it was all part of it. Look where I fucking am. I'm here with you, not in bed with Dante." I regained just enough control to not finish the statement. I started to pull the door closed behind me.

"You're a coward, that's why you never get what you want."

I stopped and turned, looking him right in the eyes. "If you're making me choose, I'm staying here."

THIRTY

REMI

As I walked in the door I heard Dante shuffling around upstairs. I was hoping to find him in bed. I'd completely forgotten about the fight. Shit. I checked my watch, we'd have to leave any minute to be on time. Dread pooled in my gut, and I moistened my lips as I climbed the stairs, expecting to find him ready to fight. I wasn't sure I could watch him with Josh again. I felt ridiculous, I was the one who spent the last couple of hours with someone else, and here I was the jealous bastard.

I stepped into the room and around his large bed to find him buttoning up a shirt. He met my eyes in the mirror, a slight smile turning up the corner of his mouth.

"Why aren't you dressed to fight?" I absentmindedly adjusted my cufflinks as he put his on.

"I thought you didn't want me to fight?" He raised one brow and looped a tie around his neck.

Dante blew me away. He knew. I couldn't hide my smile. "I don't, but you didn't have a body?"

He was beautiful when he dressed up. A picture of refinement. Had I been allowed to be who I am, he would have fit nicely into my world. Better than Kai ever could. I imagined us living in a penthouse in Vegas. Dante sprawled out in an armchair overlooking the strip, me at his feet, his hand in my hair. In another life, maybe I'd deserve a happily ever after. There was only one way I saw my life going at this point. I could avoid it for a little while, but either I'd end up in Vegas as my dad's second, or I'd be in a body bag.

The bag had more appeal.

"Your guy made it." Dante's words pulled me from the bleak scene in my head.

"How does Josh feel?"

"He was resolved to get his ass kicked either way, so I'm sure he's fine with it." Dante turned on me after pulling on his coat. "Ready?"

I nodded, and he took my hand. It was almost like having a boyfriend. "He used to be your best, didn't he?" It was a strange feeling walking out to my Jeep hand in hand. One I'd never dreamed of experiencing

Dante took the keys out of my hand. I gave him a questioning look.

"If I have to ride in this piece of shit, I want to be in control."

We slipped into the seats. He still hadn't answered my question, and because Josh was a sore topic, I wasn't going to push either.

"He used to be. He's lost his confidence, and I don't know why."

I knew why, but I wasn't going to say it. I was tired of playing the role of the jealous bastard.

The club was packed, astonishing for a Thursday night. I noticed a few familiar faces from the Boston club, and I chuckled to myself. Dante was a superb salesman. I'd have to encourage him to keep going back, even if the place was painful. He kept my hand as we walked in. Him as if he owned the place, and me as his partner, not his submissive. He knew the right times to put me beneath him and the times to make me his equal without giving up an ounce of control. We strolled through the smoky bar, and I felt like a king. It was risky, but I was so far removed from my other life and I wanted it.

Josh blocked our path. He stood in low hanging shorts with his arms crossed over his wiry chest. "I thought we were fighting?"

"Caci's man made it."

Josh's scowl deepened. "I don't want to fight one of his jacked up fucks."

Dante enabled Josh as much as Josh enabled him. "It's set. I'm not dressed or warmed."

He squeezed my hand, and I knew he did it for me. My chest swelled with pride. He'd chosen me over Josh. Tiny tendrils of hope anchored themselves in my brain. I hoped as I never had before, against my better judgement.

Josh's eyes flickered to me and then back to Dante. They exchanged unspoken words, but I could guess the context. Dante tilted his head and looked down his nose at Josh. He held his ground for a moment then relented and stepped aside. It was like watching wolves vie for dominance. Dante lead me to his usual seat, and a girl appeared next to us. He ordered a bottle, probably to calm his nerves enough so he could handle watching Josh get his ass handed to him. Whatever he had to do, it still felt like I'd won.

Liv took the ring between the two fighters, and it was on. I knew the guy they'd flown in. I'd handpicked him on my last trip to Vegas. There was no way Josh could take him. The guy had almost laid me out with a single punch. I tried to repress the smile curling over my lips, but I couldn't help it. It was turning out to be a good night. Nothing was going to ruin it.

THIRTY ONE

DANTE

I had to ride a fine line, and it wasn't going to be easy. Remi needed to know what he was worth, and it was my job to take care of him, but I also didn't want to throw away my best friend because I'd picked my fuck buddy, which was exactly how Josh would see it. It felt like I was holding my world together with my bare hands as life tore it to shreds.

Josh didn't approach. It was a good way to start. He needed to see if his opponent would make a move and gauge his fighting style. He was a little heavier than Josh, so speed would be an advantage. I wanted to pick Remi's brain about him, but I resisted. The waitress came back with our drinks, and I sat back to sip mine. I was going to be the opposite of how I was at the last fight Remi had joined me for. Since he kept side eyeing me, I figured Remi was expecting me to become engrossed with Josh. There was little I loved more than proving someone wrong.

Josh engaged the fighter when he wouldn't approach. He landed a hit, coming away clean. Good start. The guy circled Josh, still not making a first move. Josh could use it to his advantage. I prayed he'd recognize the opportunity. Josh leapt forward, landing a few blows, then moved back, not giving the guy a chance to get at him without coming forward himself. Josh was fighting smart for the first time in months.

I turned to Remi. "How was dinner?" I saw in his eyes he'd hoped I'd forgotten or wouldn't ask. He had a lot to learn about me. I always asked if I wanted to know.

"It was heated. Kai is getting married."

I wasn't surprised. Kai was going to do anything to hold onto Remi, including faking a wedding. "How do you feel about it?"

"I'm... I don't know, but can I really blame him?" There was an undertone of context to his words he wasn't saying.

"You can't. Not if you plan on spending more time here, like you have been." It was leading, but I wanted the answer.

His eyes returned to the fight, and he watched for a few moments. "You owe me a truth."

"I haven't forgotten. I also owe you a night."

"The night is irrelevant." He was right. Nothing he would ask for would fulfill him the way making him do something I wanted did. He wanted me to take full command. Now that we'd fucked there was nothing he'd ask for.

"I want the truth."

I dipped my chin, encouraging him to proceed as I watched the fight out of the corner of my eyes. Josh had been laid out with one punch to the gut and was struggling to get up. I could not allow my attention to leave Remi. There are few moments in life we recognize as a turning point. A moment which will affect the rest of our existence. This was one of those moments, and I'd made my choice before Remi asked a thing.

"Do you want this to be more than us using each other?"

"This is the truth you want?" The back of my neck prickled. It had taken Masen two years to get the same words out of me. He had to chase them from me. I'd been reluctant to tie myself to any one person then, and I was even more reluctant now.

He nodded. "No dodging."

I sucked in warm air from the heated room then exhaled slowly, giving myself time. "There is more here than I've ever experienced before." I looked away. The words were painful as they came out. They hurt my soul, and what I'd had with Masen, but they were true. "I don't say this lightly. I was with someone I saw as my forever, and I never thought I'd recover after he left." I paused and held his gaze. "I don't know how to make this work or even what working would look like with us. I don't want to change you, and I don't want to change, but I think we can find some quiet in the chaos, some stolen moments."

I could see the change in him instantly. His chest swelled, and he sat up straighter. A smile spread over his lips, and his fingers tightened in mine. "Your Clouded Hell."

I nodded.

"I can't stay here for good. I think you know as much. I want to be here more. I want to be here as much as possible. I don't have a fucking clue how I'm going to balance it, but I'm going to figure it out. Kai said he was going to sell the house. I guess that's what really hurt."

I grabbed him under the jaw and pulled his face to mine. He'd have bruises on his jaw by the time I released him. "Let Kai sell the house."

He told me yes with his eyes, and I pressed my lips to his, inhaling him, claiming him, making him mine. I hated PDA, but marking him here in public, in my world, was important to him, so I did it. I could feel Josh's eyes on me. I could feel the anger pouring off him with every second I chose Remi. When we broke apart, I risked a glance. Remi sat back smug, while Josh sat in his corner looking right at me, with a fire in his eyes I knew I'd have to deal with later. Men were more drama than women ever were. At least Liv came out with what bothered her instead of stewing like these two did.

Josh got up when the bell rang and stalked toward his opponent. Something had changed in him. He didn't waste any time. It was clear his confidence was back, and he was going to beat the guy to shit.

THIRTY TWO

REMI

Dante had just said what may have been the best words I'd ever heard in my life, and I couldn't take my eyes off this stupid fight. A switch had been flipped in Josh. He was an animal, fighting like Dante did with no regard for his own safety.

The fight would be over in minutes if it kept on like this. I wanted Sam to hit him back, do something, but I knew he didn't have it in him. Josh was the underdog by far, and no one had expected this, so frankly, we stopped sending him hard fights. He'd lost even easy ones. With as hard as Sam hit, this should have been a no-brainer. He shouldn't have needed to defend himself. He was bloodied to a pulp and barely keeping his feet. I wanted to stop things, but instead I sat in horror and watched.

"Should we go?" Dante pulled me from my mind, and I glanced over at him.

"I want to see it finish."

He sat back and let me. I wasn't sure if I'd pissed him off. I'd worry about it later. Josh darted forward and hit Sam in the nose, in the neck, and then to finish him, hammered punches into his kidneys. Sam staggered and went down hard. Josh was on him, beating him into the mat. The crowd got to its feet, a collective gasp passing through it. Liv ducked into the ring to call the fight and pull Josh off of Sam.

Josh's chest heaved as he raised his hands when Liv got him off. He stepped back and looked me right in the eyes. His message was clear. He wiped his mouth and waited, baiting me. I stood and turned to Dante.

"I'm ready to go."

Dante looked between the two of us. "Yeah, I figured." He turned to lead the way through the crowd, pointedly not taking my hand or waiting for me. I couldn't blame him. He didn't understand the little war I had going on with Josh and probably never would. He was blind to Josh's feelings.

Josh stepped in front of us. "I found my confidence." He licked at the blood on his split lip, looking at Dante like I didn't exist. I didn't in his world. I was the competition, and you never gave leeway to the competition. It was one of my mistakes. One I needed to fix.

"You were amazing." The way Dante praised him stirred my jealousy.

I was the one he was taking home. I had to remind myself to keep it inside.

"Thanks. I'll call you tomorrow so we can get back to training." He stepped past us before Dante could reply.

It took every bit of my self-control not to tell Dante who he could practice with. I knew I'd sink myself if I tried. It was one thing to want him not to fight. I wouldn't ever be able to change who he was as he couldn't change me. There were things I was going to have to learn to live with.

Dante placed his hand on my lower back and leaned closer. "I think we both have some tension to release tonight. Hmm?"

I groaned. "Yes, Master."

Electricity flowed between us as we made our way into the house. The air was charged with both our need. He flashed me a single look as he took the stairs toward the playroom. I was right on his heels and stopped outside the door to undress. He was already inside readying his toys. I could see his shadow moving through the low light. My arousal stirred, and my mouth salivated. I needed a reprieve from the anger I felt toward Josh. I would catch hell for the way Sam was going home. Soon my father wouldn't be the only one calling me. I wasn't ready to face tomorrow. A good, long session with Dante would go a long way to giving me what I needed to cope.

My phone rang. I hadn't turned it off yet. I pulled it from my pocket, and the name on the caller ID made me sick.

"Answer it."

I met Dante's eyes. He stood just inside the room with his hands on his hips. I hesitated.

"You heard me. You can't run away from him forever. If you need to take care of it, do it then come back."

He was right of course, but I didn't want to leave.

"Hello?"

"You come today, or I'll come to you." His voice put ice in his veins.

"I'll catch the first flight."

The call ended.

I looked up at Dante and broke. He'd never made such a demand.

THIRTY THREE

REMI

My legs gave out, and I collapsed to my knees. Dante was there. He swooped in and collected me in his arms. I melted into him, pressing my face into his neck. I think we both knew this might be goodbye, and even if he didn't know, I'd show him what he meant to me.

He took me to his bedroom and laid me in the center of his bed. Piece by piece he stripped off my clothes. I'd never seen him so tender. I closed my eyes, reveling in the feel of him. When he pulled away my eyes snapped open, and I reached for him.

"Don't leave me," I begged, barely able to find my voice.

He reached down and pressed his finger to my lips. "Shhhh, mine."

I parted my lips and sucked on the pad of his finger. Fire flashed in his eyes, and my dick jumped, but he retracted his hand and got himself under control. He grabbed his shirt by the back of his neck and tugged it off, tossing it to the floor before working over the buttons on his jeans. He pushed himself out of them as he lowered his body to mine.

He was fully naked, and my hands were free. Not only could I feel every inch of him, I could explore. I grabbed his ass and held him to me, brushing my fingers along his seam. I wanted inside him. I wanted to live long enough where he'd let me. I could almost taste the closeness it would bring. It was easy to tell he wasn't the type to let someone fuck him readily.

He pressed his lips to my neck. I arched up into him. Even pressed together it wasn't enough. I needed more of him. The tender kiss turned rough as his teeth found my skin. He bit a trail down the column of my neck, and I was sure there would be bruises left in his wake. I breathed him in and wallowed in him, until there was nothing left in my mind but him.

His hands and his mouth explored my body, sending one message, every part he touched, he owned. I'd never felt so possessed. My breath caught in my throat as the memories threatened to work their way in. He placed his hand on my throat and his mouth next to my ear.

"Stay here with me."

I looked into his eyes and nodded. "Yes, Master."

"You're only in this room, nowhere else. Do you understand me?"

My panic started to recede. "I do." He had such a way of keeping me out of my own head.

He rested his forehead against mine. "This is important to me. I don't want your mind anywhere else." He cut off any reply with his tongue.

He pulled back too soon, and I noticed his belt in his hand for the first time. My skin prickled with anticipation. My cock stood straight up from my hips, begging for attention and leaking. His eyes dropped as if inspecting it.

"Take it in your hand. I want you to stroke yourself."

I did as I was told, and as soon as my fingers closed around my shaft I felt the sting of the belt. He painted my chest in welts until tears burned in my eyes and my cock was ready to erupt. My breathing came in forced gasps, and it was all I could do to not lose it.

"Stop."

I whimpered but let my hand fall away. I watched him, panting. He waited, letting me get control of myself, I was sure. He stretched out over me once more and reached between us, pressing his slick thumb against me. I let my knees fall open and welcomed the intrusion but it never came, he massaged around my opening, and then he was gone. I groaned.

"I need you." I didn't care how desperate I sounded. It was true.

"Patience," he said, and I felt what I wanted. "Come when you're ready."

I chased his mouth, biting down on his lip. "Thank you, Master."

I knew I'd said the right thing when he sunk inside me to his base. I dug my fingers into his back and wrapped my legs around his hips, keeping him there. He indulged me, keeping himself fully sheathed as he rocked slowly. I was shattered. I'd never be whole again without him. He'd stripped me raw, and I didn't think I could be any more bare to him until he kissed me.

I fell apart as he came inside me. I knew I'd never be the same.

I had to go home. I'd held him in bed a few hours until I had to catch my flight. He couldn't fix this. I wasn't sure I could.

"Fuck." Shoving my hand into my hair, I grabbed my bag off the floor, glancing back at him. Dante was sprawled out in bed, his breathing even. It was the most relaxed I'd ever seen him. The lines in his face were smooth, and all the tension he held inside himself was gone. I never felt as much from pure dominance. I had to submit to get a release like that.

Things grew dark. I envied him. My heart was black. I wanted it, this life I'd started. No, fuck that, I deserved it. No matter how hard I tried to play the part, it was a lie. A lie I was very good at, but a lie nonetheless.

If I stayed one more hour I wouldn't leave. I would throw away every damn thing I'd worked my ass off to be to kneel at his feet. I had far too much pride to do it. Then there was Kai. The look he would give me when I showed back up haunted me. I needed to rip that band-aid off.

I dressed without making a sound and was out the door, not giving Dante a backward glance. I'd lied to my father when I said I'd be on the first flight. I had to go to Kai first. I had to talk to him. I had to do something. I was choosing Dante, but I had to smooth things over after yesterday.

I went to the studio instead of the beach when I landed. I needed to hear the ocean, but I had to get this over with, and I couldn't do it at home. The breeze had a slight tinge of mold to it, and there were more houses with boards over the windows than not. I'd parked down the block, and I half expected the studio to be gone, but she was still sitting there as I walked up.

The tiny bell above the door dinged, and Kai looked up from the piece he was working on. His dark gaze tracked me for a few moments before he looked back down at his drawing table.

I waited for him to speak, taking a few steps into the small space. It was an old industrial building, turned into retail space. It had clean lines, with his art on the walls. All the furniture was repurposed wood and metal. I'd helped pick every piece as we funneled a lot of my earnings through the shop.

"I didn't expect you to poke your head out of your love nest for weeks."

"I was there for work as well as pleasure."

My words earned me another look. "The business was doing fine here. You can tell your father what you want, but you forget I live with you." His words were like ice to my veins.

"You act like I'm shacked up with a whore on some island."

"Might as well be." He set down his pencil and stood.

Snapping at him wouldn't get me anywhere. "Our numbers in Vegas have dropped for the third quarter in a row."

He laughed in the back of his throat. "So we go from making a shit load of money to slightly fewer shit loads?" He rubbed his fingers over his forehead, something he did when he was frustrated with his submissive.

"You know what it's like for me." I turned away to look at the new piece of art he'd hung while I was gone. I had to think it was pointed. It was a two-foot heart with a nail through it, and the drops of blood dripping from it were all blurry images. No one else would be able to tell what the images were, but to me each one brought to mind a time and place.

"There are times I forget. You play the part so well I've believed it at times, but no, now I see how you're slipping. It's affecting everything. It's why I told you to go."

"Then stop making me feel like shit for it."

He picked up a pencil and leaned over his calendar like he was going to write something down. "Only if you stop calling it business. Call your prostitute what he is." He squeezed the pencil in his hand until it broke.

"Prostitute?" I knew what he was getting at, but I wanted him to say it out loud.

"He's beating your ass, and you're paying him, what else would you call it? Ok, it's not cash you're paying him, but I can bet you're cutting him a deal. I can't imagine the rednecks down there are worth anything close to what Vegas is." He straightened up, coming just two inches shy of my height. He was California blond, exactly how a surfer should look.

"Like it or not, this guy is good business." I reached in my messenger bag for the numbers I calculated on the plane. I tossed it down on top of his drawing. "Vegas is saturated, we needed a new market, and this one pays more."

"Just like you to start a fight, and next you'll walk out the door." He pushed the folder off his desk into the trash, where a portrait of me also resided.

"I'm not leaving." I stood my ground. "I catch hell from you, and you're a Goddamn switch yourself."

Kai set his mouth in a line.

"You have Kyle any time you want. Anywhere you want. I don't have a best friend who will top me in my own house." I'd come here trying not to lose my temper, and I'd already failed. I smoothed a hand over my shirt.

"But you do, you just don't trust me."

I couldn't argue with the truth. "We've gone 'round and 'round with this. Why is it so hard to let me have what you do?"

"Because I'm in love with you. It's hypocritical, and I know I don't have the right. We've always had an agreement, but at some point that went out the window. I'd offer to give up Kyle, but I know that wouldn't do anything either, and I love him too. There isn't a win for me here. I lose you either way because I've never been enough for you." Each word cut me. He'd been holding it in a long time.

"You should marry Kyle. You'll be happy with him. I'll still give you what you need."

Tears glistened in the corners of his eyes. "You've got to go. I have to work." He turned his back on me. "I have someone coming to list the house tomorrow."

"Do we really need to sell it?" I stepped forward, wanting to give him comfort but not knowing how.

"I can't look at it anymore. I can't be there. I need to start over. There is too much of you there."

I knew when I was being dismissed, so I walked out.

I couldn't face my father yet, so I went to the beach house to say goodbye. I lingered there, hoping Kai would change his mind, come back so we could talk. The tide rolled into the beach, bringing with it a stiff breeze. It blew my hair back and chilled the night. The beach was deserted, and my board taunted me from where it hung.

I was shocked he wasn't there. Kai rarely slept over at his submissive's place. He didn't believe in giving them such liberties. This from the guy who lived with his dominant. We were all hypocritical in our own right. Every single one of us. I'd venture to say every single human on this planet was in one way or another.

"Fuck it."

I grabbed my board off the rack and took the stairs down to the beach two at a time.

"By yourself?" his voice came from behind me.

"Yeah, I might as well." The sand was warm under my feet, and as much as I'd thought about staying in NOLA this past few weeks, I didn't think I could give up my addiction.

One of the metal chairs scraped against the deck, and I knew Kai had taken a seat. "Did this guy feed you stupid pills?"

I paused and turned around, frustration dripping from my words. "Dante. His name is Dante."

"You may have to be respectful, but I don't."

I growled under my breath. "You need to be respectful of me, boy."

"Yes, Sir." There was an edge to his voice, one I knew well.

"You're pathetic," I said.

"I know."

I glanced over my shoulder at him.

"You have a phone call. He doesn't sound happy." I could have slapped the smirk off his face.

"The house line?" I hoped it was Dante.

He shook his head, and I realized I'd left my phone charging. "Who?"

"Guess."

"Dante?"

"Your father. He's been looking for you. He called the shop a few hours ago."

"I can't go to him like this. Not after..." I couldn't bring myself to say breakup.

Kai looked me over. "You better do something before he comes looking for you. He said he would be here in the morning if you weren't there tonight."

He was usually right, but I didn't want to go to him.

"Hello?" I answered the phone.

"I would have thought you could afford a watch."

"I had an issue I had to handle." I had to make up an

excuse. Kai stepped inside looking almost smug at my pandering.

"Enlighten me to what is more important than what I need you for."

"I'm driving to the airport now. I'll explain when I get there."

I couldn't shake the feeling I was driving to my funeral.

THIRTY FOUR

REMI

My first stop was the room under his penthouse. The hotel boasted a few, one of which my father owned. I tossed my bag on the bed and arched my back, looking out across the strip. No one here would ever know my name like they did my father's, and I was okay with it.

I changed into something he would find presentable, a charcoal pinstriped suit, suspenders, and a light purple shirt as well as my gun from the room safe. I never carried in Cali, life was different there. I was a different person there, and still yet my father's reach had prevented me from being myself. The last thing I did before leaving was take off my ring. Kai's ring. I thought maybe I should leave it there for good.

I sighed as I stepped in the elevator and put on my face.

When I stepped out on his floor I could hear the yelling. It wasn't at me. He wasn't expecting me yet, I had to remind myself. I reached for the handle and walked into chaos.

"You taint my house with this?" Frank Caci stood over a man on his knees. Frank was spitting in his face with each word. Frank's 'muscle' stood to the side with a gun pointed at the guy's head.

Walking into the room was like walking into a thick fog of tension. Tears streamed down the guy's face. I could see from the back of his head it was one of my second or third cousins. The one who ran my father's chop shop. One of the jobs I would have started in had I stayed in Vegas. The work was pretty easy as far as our industry went. Mario was a little older than I was, and I didn't know him well. He was scared for his life, as he should be. Frank had no qualms about putting a bullet in the back of anyone's head. Bile rose in my throat as I remembered the first time I'd walked in on a scene like this. I had to grip the back of the chair to keep my feet. This probably had nothing to do with Anthony and why my father had killed him, but it brought a wicked sense of déjà vu and guilt to the surface.

"In the penthouse?" I made a sound in the back of my throat, playing off my fear as disgust. I'd learned how to act since I was old enough to remember. Always assessing him and giving Frank exactly what he wanted.

"Nice of you to finally show up." Frank didn't look at me. "You cross me by bringing cops into my place?" Frank spat as he spoke. He tossed down a bag of coke. "And what the shit is this? Not only is the DEA up my ass now for your backdoor dealings, but the shop will be closed for months. Where do you expect me to do my business? Do you think these places grow on trees, so when you fuck it up I can just pluck a new one out of thin air?"

"It wasn't me. I swear it, Uncle. I wouldn't be doing that under your nose." His tears, mixed with snot from his nose were dripping down his face. Frank would probably kill him even if he hadn't done it, just for acting like a pussy.

"Admit it, or I'm going to hang you over the balcony by your balls," Frank snapped.

"It's fifty stories, and your balls aren't going to hold

you," I said, feeling bad for Mario.

He fell forward sobbing that it wasn't him, over and over. Frank waved, and he was removed from the room. I had made myself numb to such things. The last time I opened my mouth, I got a broken cheekbone as a reward. An eight-year-old doesn't make that mistake twice.

"Where you been hiding, kid?" My father had walked to the window. He was looking out over his empire. He didn't own anything with his name on it, but everyone here knew it nevertheless.

"I've been expanding. You should be proud." I prayed he wouldn't question it, although I stopped believing in any kind of God years ago. If there was one, he'd forsaken me.

"Why you need to play around with this crap is beyond me. Aren't you done playing with toys and ready to take on your responsibilities?" He turned, but not all at once. He had this practiced, daunting, slow turn meant to intimidate. It still got to me, even if I didn't let it show.

He wore a ring on every finger. It was cliché. His tanned fingers were as fat as sausages. He never had to hit anyone anymore, but he'd done so much of it in the early days all his knuckles were oversized.

It was worthless to bring up how much money I made playing with my toys. "I like what I do."

"You mean you like fucking off with Kai on a beach in California." Both his large brows pressed into his wrinkled forehead. "What else could you be doing to keep you so busy?"

"Kai enjoys the beach, but he works as much as I do at the shop. The shop that launders a great deal of your money, so don't put it down." Did he know where I'd been going? "Kai won't leave Cali. We own the shop together.

Life is slower there."

"That's because he's a fucking hippy." He laughed. "I'll get him a shop on the strip, and he'll make ten times what he does from the hippies in Venice."

I held up my hands. "You've talked to him. You know how he feels." I loved laying the blame on Kai when he wasn't here, but when the house was sold my excuses would end.

I pressed my eyes closed for a moment, not allowing myself to remember.

"Yeah, yeah, yeah. Maybe when you give him a nice big ring and a penthouse so he can retire he'll come with you."

I blinked and my heart stopped before Frank cracked a smile. God, he was joking.

"This isn't why you summoned me, is it?" I was annoyed I was here and not in bed with Dante.

He held his hands out to the side. "I need you to run a bill through the shop for me again this month. It can't wait."

I stifled a groan. "I'm already running too much through the shop. If I do any more I'm going to have the IRS up my ass."

He turned back toward the window. "I have a job which needs to be done. Can you buy another shop?"

I considered the idea. "These things take more than a few days to set up, Frank. They have to have licenses. It's not like opening a laundry."

He pointed a finger at me. "If you think I don't have to jump through as many fucking hoops as you do."

I held up my hands. "That's not what I said. I'm saying it's a process."

"Shorten it."

I brushed my fingers over my facial hair. I didn't launder money even close to the scale he did, as he did half the cities, and I only did mine and what he needed on the side. "I might have a friend who can run some. I'll ask around." I shouldn't bring Dante or anyone else I gave a shit about into this. Hell, I needed to keep Frank as far away from Dante as possible. If he smelled the dominant on Dante, I knew what would happen.

"Chris," Frank said and one of the muscle stepped forward with a suitcase.

"I'm not going to take it now."

Frank rolled his eyes. "He acts like doing me a favor is so much to ask," he said to no one in particular. "Like I didn't put clothes on his back and food in his mouth."

"Pop." I hated when he made me feel like this. I would fight a war in my head for days over pleasing him.

"No, no." He threw up his hands. "Not like I didn't loan you the money to move to California with the hippy so you two could chase *his* dream."

That was the story we'd fed him, when in reality I'd begged Kai to go along with my story. He'd wanted to live in Venice, but it was me that needed to get out of Vegas. I would be dead if I'd stayed, there was nothing I was more sure of.

"I wanted to make myself like you did. I wouldn't be respected if you'd just handed me everything. I've done a damn good job too."

"You've done that. It's time to find a nice girl and settle down."

"Or six?"

He scoffed and rolled his eyes. "A first wife will only keep you happy so long. My generation wasn't like yours. Classy women weren't just giving it away. You had to give them diamonds." He had six ex-wives, and the last was still trying to use the courts to get his money. She was too stupid to realize that like any good businessman, he had an iron-clad prenup, and his 'assets' were piles of fake debt. All the real money was in the mattresses, literally in some cases. "You're having dinner with me."

I resisted the urge to press my hands into my eye sockets. Dinner wouldn't be until nine at the earliest.

"I see your reluctance." He paused, looking me over. "Do you have somewhere you need to be?"

I plastered on a mask. I curled my lip up slightly and shook my head, playing it off.

"Oh shit, I forgot. Let me send a gift."

I barely controlled the shock on my face. What was he talking about? I was going to look like the idiot if I didn't figure it out soon.

"You don't need to send a gift," I hedged.

"But of course, I do. I know how Kai can be." He picked up his phone. "Can you send Kai a gift, like a watch or some of that lobster I had the other night?" He hung up the phone, probably before his secretary could answer. "Dates are important to that boy. Even if he says they aren't. He's like your mother." He held a finger out at me like he always did when he was going to lecture me. "I'm shocked he let you out of the state with it being tomorrow."

I still hadn't any idea what he was talking about. "Is it tomorrow already?" I was going to put my foot in my mouth if I didn't get out of here. I was already pissed he'd called me here just so I could launder cash. "I've got to get going if I'm going to check in on my guys before dinner."

"Sure, sure." He looked me over again. "What are you going to do when Kai moves out?"

"Can't hurt to live alone." The question was leading.

How did he know about Kai moving out? How? I hated playing from behind. Now I had no excuse to stay in Cali. It took me a minute but I put it together. He knew Kai was getting married. "Did Kai invite you?" I hadn't even seen an invitation.

"The kid practicality lived with us in high school, are you really surprised he'd invite me to his engagement dinner?"

I choked. Kai knew how Frank felt about being gay. My head was spinning.

"I'm glad he's found a nice girl to settle down with. It's a shame I can't get away."

I blinked. So Kai had told everyone he was marrying a girl? I wanted to laugh. Maybe he'd get his trust fund back. I shook my head, glad I didn't have to fight that battle. It was easier for everyone here to believe Kai had ended up with a woman. I wished I could do the same, but I didn't have the lie in me.

"There's something..."

I raised a brow and put on my best face. "Something?"

"You look different." He ran his tongue over his teeth making a sucking sound. "I've been hearing whispers."

Ice ran through my veins. "Oh?"

"You haven't been spending time in New Orleans have you?"

I struggled to take in enough breath to get words out. "I have. My new business venture is there."

"Hmmm... I see." He stared me down. I didn't give in. My entire upbringing had prepared me for this moment. "You better watch what company you keep. You wouldn't want anyone talking."

"There is nothing to talk about."

Both his brows rose, and I felt sick. What could he

possibly have heard?

THIRTY FIVE

REMI

I was jittery on the plane and not much better by the time I landed. Waiting for my rental was hell. I kept replaying the conversation Dante and I'd had over and over. It shouldn't have felt like he was running to Josh as soon as I left town, but it did nonetheless. If I was honest with myself, I'd done the same. I'd run to Kai to smooth things over. I tapped my fingers on the counter waiting for the paperwork. He'd just told me he wanted me a day ago, and here I was with my chest aching because he was out with his best friend. Why did feelings destroy all rational thinking?

Josh gave me this feeling, like he was waiting in the wings to swoop in and be the hero Dante needed as soon as I fucked things up. It was a weight on my shoulders. One I was already sick of. I slid my hands into my pockets and rediscovered the napkin the flight attendant had scrawled her number across. It was flattering, all the ego boost of flirting without any of the unnecessary attachment. Which I needed after the wringer my father had put me through.

The inadequacy that had been ingrained in me my entire life was rearing its ugly head. I usually ran home to Kai. Dominating him always made me feel like more of a man.

Pathetic. I was pathetic, stuck in this toxic idea of masculinity. I wanted to slit my wrists knowing how stupid I sounded. At least no one else was subject to the inner musings of my mind.

At long last I was handed my keys, and I practically sprinted toward the now familiar row of cars. My Jeep was there. It was about time I bought one here, but it seemed like too much of a commitment to put on Dante. I was never any good at relationships, and the in-between stage where you didn't know where you stood was the worst. It was risky to move too fast and risky to move too slow. We were something, he told me, and I had to hold onto that to tide myself over. I headed toward the bar, the last place I wanted to be at one in the morning. I'd been dying to get under Dante in the playroom since I'd stepped foot in my father's penthouse. I needed a release to calm my nerves.

I walked into the place expecting the worst. It wasn't a fight night, so the place would be slower and at this hour, maybe nearly dead. I was right. I scanned the room. My gaze was drawn to Dante in a moment. He sat at his table in the back with a small group. They were laughing, and Josh had his arm on Dante's shoulder.

All the anger I'd built up in Vegas now had a focal point. It would be so easy to lose my shit. I reined himself in. It wasn't the time or place for this. I crossed the room, and Josh noticed me first. Our eyes locked, and Josh flashed a grin before he laid his head in Dante's lap. Dante's eyes flashed, and he grabbed a handful of Josh's hair, yanking him up.

"Behave, boy."

That one word unraveled my composure. All the doubt built and broke me. I stopped in my tracks, reaching into my pocket to close my fingers around the number I'd saved. I didn't know why I had, but now I was glad. Dante looked up, meeting my stare. He cocked his head to the side and beckoned me forward with two fingers. Josh watched my every move, not making an effort to get the hell away from what was mine. I still wanted Kai in my life. He was my best friend, and I hadn't even told Dante everything. How could I expect Dante to be exclusive to me? He couldn't read my mind. He had every right to have his hands all over Josh.

Dante said the word 'come,' coyly.

"I'll need a little more than hair pulling if you want me to come," Josh said, earning laughs from the other people at the table.

Dante smacked him and tried to slide out of the booth. Josh grabbed him by the jeans, pulling him back to a seat. It was such a small gesture, but it broke the dam.

Fuck. This. Shit.

Dante caught me at the door, grabbing my shirt to easily spin me around. I didn't have the strength to fight him, too desperate for his touch.

"What the hell?"

"Boy?" I said under my breath. My pride held me back.

"Boy?" Dante returned the word with a raised brow.

"You called *him* boy," I said the word as if it tasted bad.

"Who?"

Was Dante so casual with a word I cherished?

"You called Josh boy." My hands shook as I threw Dante's arm off. "I'm going."

Dante growled. "You fucking know it doesn't mean anything. He's a friend, nothing more."

"Does he know that?" I asked.

"He's always known. He's never hit on me."

I looked over at Josh who wore a shit-eating grin.

Bastard. "I don't think he does." I had to get out of here before I lost it even more.

THIRTY SIX

DANTE

"You can't seriously be doing this?" I grabbed both of his hands so he couldn't get any further away from me. If Remi could see inside my mind, he'd know I didn't have eyes for anyone else. He'd be able to see Josh's behavior did nothing for me. It annoyed me.

"Doing what? Having feelings?"

"You're overreacting," I said, calmly.

"That word, you throw it around like it's nothing, but it's everything to me."

I could see the hurt etched in his features.

"Why are we fighting?" Suddenly I was exhausted. "No, honestly, what are we fighting for?"

He paused. "What?"

"Are we fighting for or against this? Because I don't know anymore." I wanted to take him in my arms. "Does it have to be so hard?"

"Can two people so different really be together?"

"If they decide to make it work, yes. There isn't a magic holding people together. It's dedication. Love isn't sparks flying. Love is sticking it out when it's hard. Love is staying, and most people bail when it's hard. My husband did. He couldn't stick it out 'til the end. He couldn't stick it out. Couldn't give me the 'til death do us part he stood in front of everyone and promised me faithfully. If you can't either, leave now." I couldn't be left for the second time. I couldn't invest what I did with Masen and have it all fall apart. I'd already lived through it once. I didn't have it in me to do it again.

"I don't want to leave."

He surprised me. I wasn't sure what to say.

"Speechless?" The bastard grinned, all crooked. God, he was beautiful.

"No."

"You so fucking are."

"Why do you have to ruin the moment by speaking?" I asked.

"You'll get used to it."

I groaned and distracted him with my mouth. He parted his lips, letting my tongue slip between them. I tasted him and moaned. He nipped at me before pulling back to whisper something.

"Hmmm?"

"I win," he said a little louder.

"I should not touch you for a week for that comment."

"But you won't," he said sing-songy.

"Are you so sure?"

"You want inside me too bad to resist." He was right, of course, but I wasn't going to tell him that.

"I can get off without touching you, and I can make sure you don't get off."

He reached between us and grabbed his dick. "You're evil."

"You just said you were staying. Regretting it?"

"Not even a little." He released himself and slid a hand around the back of my ass.

I dipped my head to nip at his jaw. "You're a bigger masochist than I thought."

"Or maybe I know you're not as scary as you look."

I growled, and he laughed.

"Can we go home now?"

I liked that he called it home. "Tired?" I asked.

"Not in the slightest. I need you."

"I think we should sleep. I'm beat." I wanted to get a rise out of him. I knew what he needed.

"I liked you better when you didn't sleep."

When we got home I didn't take him to the playroom, I took him to the bedroom. We stood in the low light and stripped each other. There wasn't any rush, and we took our time. My fingers drifted over the lines of his weary body as he stood before me unashamed.

"You're beautiful," I whispered as I brought my mouth down on his skin.

He wrapped his arms around me, bringing our bodies together. His cock met mine, and he rocked against me. The friction drove me insane with lust. I dug my nails into his ass to get more leverage. My mouth watered for the taste of him.

"Lay back on the bed."

He clutched at me as I pulled away, but I planted a hand on his chest to keep our bodies apart.

"Do as you're told."

He groaned. "Yes, Master."

He stretched out like silk draped over the sheets. I made myself wait a full minute before I was on him. I didn't need anything but my hands and my mouth tonight. I was going to torture him with pleasure and denial, one of my favorite games. I pushed his thighs apart as I settled between his knees. I bit the hinge of his hip before turning my face to flick my tongue over his dick laid over his stomach.

"No coming." I scraped my teeth over the underside of his head, causing him to hiss in pain.

His hips lifted off the bed as my mouth worked, biting sensitive areas, then soothing them with my tongue. He'd be begging for my mouth or my cock soon enough. His fingers slid into my hair. Not a demand, but a suggestion. One I ignored.

His phone started to ring. He didn't move from where he lay, so I continued my play. I slid my fingers into my mouth, moistening them before I circled them around his entrance. I ran the pad of my thumb up his taint, massaging the area, making his cock jump. I loved the effect I had on him. Every reaction was raw and needy.

My mouth hovered over his straining length when I heard it again. I sat back and met Remi's gaze.

"Leave it," he begged.

I strolled over to his slacks lying on the floor and picked them up. Digging around in his pocket I found his phone. Six missed called and one voice mail.

"This is out of control."

"I can't help it. He's not usually like this." There was a hint of something to his voice. Something he wasn't telling me.

"Do you think he knows?" I asked.

"How could he?" Remi sat up. "Let me have it."

He didn't have a password on his phone so I played the voicemail on speakerphone instead of handing it to him.

"Did you fucking sneak out in the middle of the night?"

"Did you?" I asked.

He nodded. The voicemail went on, "We have business to discuss. I'll expect you here before sunrise. I will come drag you out of the Inferno if I have to."

Something wasn't right. "I thought you hadn't told him about here?"

"I told him about the venture, but nothing of you or your bar." There was an edge in his voice.

"Do you think he knows?"

"I was just there. There is no way he does." Remi brushed me off. He ran a hand through his hair. "But I better go."

"It's after two."

"If I push it he'll come here. We don't need him in our business. It was a mistake to leave, I just needed the release. I didn't think he'd notice. I thought I'd have time to get back."

I turned around and nodded. "Go then." He pulled a shirt on. "Drop me off at the bar on the way. I'll go give Liv a hand."

I could see he was disappointed. I was too.

Remi's phone rang again, this time he grabbed it out of my hand and answered it.

"I have an emergency. I need all my men around me. I need you to stand by my side."

I stared at Remi as he listened. He said he'd be there, then hung up.

"See, it has nothing to do with us." He pressed his lips to mine. "I'll be back in a day or two. I'm sure he's overreacting. It's probably a turf war."

"Don't get yourself killed."

"I won't."

THIRTY SEVEN

DANTE

I held out my drink for her to refill. Liv did so then took a seat next to me.

"I promised myself I would never have feelings again."

She tugged my head into her lap. "He's not worth your hurt, Dante."

I closed my eyes. "I'm not hurt. I'm worried. What if he doesn't come back?"

She sighed, and I ignored it. I knew he'd never be her favorite person. "I don't think anyone can stay away from you."

I scoffed. "Masen did a damn good job of it."

"He put a bullet in his brain. He just didn't have the balls to do it in front of you. Stop blaming yourself for him."

"You honestly expect me not to?" I fought the urge to get up and walk the fuck out. She couldn't judge me. No one could. I did my fucking best.

"And you're an idiot for having feelings still."

"Thanks, that's what I need to hear right now. I fucking know I'm an idiot."

"You've been destroying yourself for months over him." Suddenly we were talking about Remi again. "You think I like watching him take every last good part of you and ripping it to shreds? I just don't think he's the staying type."

I could feel her eyes on me. I opened mine to look up into them. "No, I'm sure it sucks to watch, but it also fucking blows to have to live like this. It's not what I wanted. I never wanted to feel like this again." My hands balled into fists at my sides. I needed pain. I needed to let the pain consume me and purge these damn feelings. The best thing about physical pain was its ability to drive everything out of the mind and set you free.

"Don't do what I know you're going to do." I knew she wasn't going to fight me on it, but it was more like she felt like she had to say it.

"I don't know why you waste your words."

"Sometimes I wonder why I ever do with you. Your stubborn ass doesn't listen to anyone."

I lifted my shoulders. There was no denying it; it was the truth. I made my own choices. I always had.

"You've got to stop punishing yourself at some point for his death."

"I'm not still punishing myself." I didn't know if my words were true. Maybe I was still punishing myself. Maybe it's why I avoided a relationship for so long.

"You deserve to be loved, Dante, by someone who isn't ashamed to get on his knees for you. By someone who isn't going to play head games." I hated hearing the pity in her tone. It was worse than knowing I fucked up. I had, and I would live with it, but I didn't need this from her. I would take the blame for my actions. I didn't need anyone's pity.

"Not everyone can be openly submissive and like the way people look at them. It's like being gay. Not everyone will look at you the same, and I understand how he feels." I sat up and brought my glass to my lips, taking a long pull.

"Stop making excuses for him. If he can't woman up like so many female submissives do every day, then he doesn't fucking deserve you." She paused. "Do you think it was easy for me to come out? To tell people I was going to be the ultimate bitch and trade my dick for heels? He has no excuse. There is nothing wrong with being a submissive."

She was right, of course.

"I need to call Josh." I pulled away from her altogether as she tried to grab at my shirt.

"Why do you need to call me?" a voice said from the back entrance.

"Because I need a good ass kicking." I pulled my shirt off my back without turning to look at him.

"Not this again. I thought we were done with this two years ago."

I ducked into the ring and rolled my neck. "It's therapy. I have to keep it up for my mental health."

"I feel like this is the fucking opposite." His words said no, but his actions said yes. He stepped into the ring, discarding his own shirt. "You know I hate hitting you when you won't fight back. At least throw some punches."

"I'll do it during our next fight if you won't, and then you'll have no control over it." A low growl built in my chest.

His upper lip curled up. "You wouldn't."

I pushed my tongue into the inside of my cheek. We both knew I would.

"Dante..." There was an edge to his voice.

"What are you going to do about it?" I crossed my arms over my chest and stared him down.

He came at me, throwing a slow punch I could have easily ducked. I didn't, but he pulled it at the last minute to barely graze my cheek with his knuckles.

"Just fucking hit me." It was too close to a beg for comfort. His eyes went wide.

"Bastard. Fight me back and I'll kick your ass, but I won't just stand here and beat you again." His chest heaved. "In fact, I know you're just doing this to pick a fight with him. I'm not going to be the wedge between you any longer. I'm worth more than that."

"I've never once fucking used you." I looked to Liv for support, and she stayed silent.

"You have, and it's not cool. I love you, man, but you self-sabotage more than anyone I've ever met. You don't give at all. It's your way or no way. It sucks to deal with it as your friend. I can't imagine what Masen went through. Maybe he left for a reason. He was going through hell, told you he was dying, and you wouldn't hear of letting him end his suffering gracefully. The only person you thought of was you and your pain. Now you're going to do the same to Remi. We can't all live our lives to your expectations."

"How long you been holding that in?"

He shrugged.

I looked at Liv. "You too?"

She didn't say a word.

"Fuck both of you."

I wasn't going to be judged for what I needed, or who I was. "Then I'll get it tonight." I was out of the ring and halfway up the back stairs before either of them could get a word out. I grabbed a bottle from the freezer on the way and had it open as I stepped into the morning light. We'd sat there so long the sun had come up. I couldn't remember when I'd last had a meal. I hadn't had more than alcohol in days. Probably not the best diet, but I couldn't bring myself to care at all at the moment.

"Dante." He'd caught up with me, and Liv wasn't too far behind.

I didn't look back. I kept my head down and crossed the parking lot. I had no idea where I was going. I had the whole day to kill before the fight tonight. There was no way I'd sleep worrying about Remi. I had to find a distraction. "I don't want to hear it. If you don't want to do it, I'm not going to make you."

"You can't imagine what it's like to have to do that for you." He stopped halfway across the lot.

I turned slowly, meeting his gaze. "I would do it for you if it's what you needed. I guess we just have a different idea of friendship."

"That's not fair."

"But pulling you out of the gutter at six in the morning is? Having to tell your mom I took you to rehab for the third time." He had no fucking room to talk. We all had our vices, but at least mine didn't hurt anyone but myself.

"You've done plenty for me, but this isn't good for you, just like drinking ain't good for me." He clenched his jaw. I knew he wouldn't back down. He'd found principles since then, and he didn't owe me anything.

"I told you, I'm not going to push." I returned to my path. "Don't cancel the fight. That's an order."

I got on my bike and drove toward home. The cool morning air brought clarity where I'd hoped to stay in the fog. I didn't want to have to blame myself for Masen leaving. I'd blamed him for so long it had become a crutch.

There wasn't much I hated more than feeling like I'd made a fool of myself. I'd gotten as bad as Josh was with his drinking, only my drug of choice was pain. I was driving Remi away with Josh, and I was driving Josh and Liv away by having my head up my ass. I had some major shit to fix. I just didn't know how.

I pulled my bike into the drive to find a stranger sitting on my porch.

THIRTY EIGHT

DANTE

"Can I help you?" I asked.

He picked up his head out of his hands and looked me in the eyes. Bile rose in my throat. I'd seen him before. I knew who he was.

"No, not really. I just had to meet you." The expression on his face said it all. I felt lower than dirt.

I extended my hand. "Dante, and you are?" Since we'd never met face to face I didn't know if he knew my name.

"Kai." After we shook, he pulled his hand back and rubbed it over the back of his neck. "I don't even know why I came here."

"Probably the same reason I've almost gotten on a plane to Cali myself." I stepped past him and opened my door. "Come in and have a drink."

He lingered, and I thought maybe he was going to leave so I pushed inside. He didn't owe me anything. I was curious, but that was my normal. I had to figure out every angle of a situation.

I took out two glasses but only filled one with ice and Jack. When I turned back around, he was standing there. I could see why Remi liked him. Tattoos with a clean cut look and an angled nose he'd probably broken at some point.

"Do you have anything else?" he asked when I grabbed ice for his cup.

I raised a brow but pulled the vodka I kept for guests out of the freezer. I left Remi's tequila where it was, guessing he wouldn't want that.

"I'll take the tequila."

I was even more surprised and exchanged the bottles before filling his glass with it.

"You don't have to keep eyeing me like that. He always smells like whiskey when he comes home. I can't stomach it anymore." He brought the glass to his lips and looked me over as he drank.

"I'm surprised to hear it, as he drinks his body weight in tequila every few days while he's here." I set my drink aside, suddenly not thirsty.

"But he sweats Jack. I don't know why. It's like you've marked him." He looked at the floor and shook his head. "You know I shouldn't be jealous. I think Remi's fucked every single person and half the married people in Venice, but you're different."

I lifted one shoulder. "I've been told I'm addictive." It was the truth. I just never let anyone stay.

"So is he."

I laughed and scrubbed a hand over my face. "You don't have to fucking tell me."

He nodded. "I've never seen him return it. Usually, he's bored as soon as he gets them."

I picked my drink up, musing over his words. I knew why he kept coming back. He didn't have me. No one would ever have me.

"It was easier to share him when he never went back for seconds?" I wanted to understand him. Both of them.

He didn't answer right away. "I don't even think it's that." He didn't explain further. I was going to have to pry this out of him.

"What is it then?"

"Why do you think I'm here?" He chuckled. "I'm trying to figure it out. Maybe it's that you give him what he gives me, and I could never do that for him."

"Why not? You're a switch."

He shook his head. "He doesn't see me that way."

"He's one of those." I knew why. It was clear when I thought about it. Status was everything to him. He would never bend a knee to someone he saw as weak. There was a part of him that hated his submissive side, so in turn, he saw his submissive as weak.

"Mmmhmm."

I didn't even have to say it.

"Has he convinced you to move yet?" Kai walked around the kitchen looking at every little thing. Probably judging my less than lush lifestyle.

"Move?" I glanced around my place. "I'm not trading the place I have for a condo."

He turned around and cocked his head. "I didn't mean for a nicer place."

"He has a pretty good idea I'm not leaving here."

Kai just shook his head. "You don't know him as well as I do."

I crossed my arms over my chest, leaning back into the counter.

"You're right. I may never," I returned. "I wasn't sure he'd even come back."

"Okay." He set his half-empty glass on the counter. "He's never going to want to be on a leash there for you, but he'll miss the ocean. He won't stay away from it."

"You can't know that. He's happy while he's here."

"I know he is. But he'll miss it. Mark my words."

I wanted to ask him what he really came here for. I wanted his blessing. I wanted him to back off. There wasn't any way I'd ever get rid of him. I wasn't a jealous person, which was in my favor, but I didn't want to always have to be battling Kai.

My phone started buzzing before I could reply, and Kai's followed shortly after.

Remi: You mean the world to me. Remember that.

I frowned at my phone, and looked up to see Kai with the same expression. "That isn't a message from Remi is it?"

He knit his brow. "Yeah, but it's really not like him."

I turned my phone around to show him the message. Kai held out his so I could see the message he got. They were almost identical. Dread closed its cold fingers around my neck.

"Was he having issues with his dad?"

"Yeah, he'd been avoiding him, but he's been there a day or so. It's got to be smoothed over by now."

I shook my head. "He was there only about twenty-four hours. He was here until late last night."

Kai shook his head in return. "Then he was only there half a day at most. He was at our place until yesterday morning."

"Do you think his dad is pissed?"

"I've seen him pissed. There is more to it than that." Kai wrinkled his forehead.

I typed out a message to Remi. He couldn't just leave me with that and expect me not to panic.

Dante: Don't do this to me. I'm already worried.

Remi: Remember the story I told you? It's happening.

I'm sorry.

My heart stopped, and my gut heaved. "He can't fucking do this to me." I dialed his number. It went straight to voicemail. His phone was off.

I held out my phone for Kai.

"We'll never make it there on time." I tore at my hair. This would kill me. His father might as well kill us both. Or better I'd go there and end his father, then have the luxury of having his people return the favor. It was time to be done with this petty indulgence people called life. I was long past weary. I was going to set things right before I went to my final resting place. Maybe I'd get lucky and I'd meet him again in the afterlife. In our own little shaded spot in Hell.

"I'm going." I grabbed my keys off the table.

"To your death?"

"Yeah."

Kai paused and looked at me and nodded as if accepting me. "I'm going with you."

THIRTY NINE

REMI

They were waiting when I landed. A car sat ignored by the patrolling cops with two of my father's men standing outside of it in full suits. By the perspiration on their brows, they'd been standing a while. I approached the car with my mask in place, but I knew what it meant. Adam held the door open for me, and there was pity in his gaze. I wanted to punch him in the face for the look, but I knew it wouldn't do me any good. My fight was with my father. As soon as I was settled in the back seat and we were on our way, I dug out my phone and sent two texts.

I knew Dante wouldn't be happy about the texts I'd sent him, but he deserved to know what happened to me after the way Masen had left him. I'd turned off my phone after and regretted it almost instantly. I had way too much time in the early morning traffic on my way here to think, and now I wanted to feel his words. Maybe it was early enough he'd be able to move on. He deserved as much. I was ready to go. I couldn't live a lie anymore. If he didn't ask me outright, I'd decided on the way here I was going to tell him. I was done with coming here. I was done with playing his games. He'd either let me walk out of here and expect nothing more from me, or he'd kill me.

After allowing me to change, they kept me in his office until my father decided to show. It was a scare tactic. He wanted me afraid when he arrived. All the waiting gave his victims time to think about what they'd done. I wouldn't give him the satisfaction. I took a seat on one of his sofas and closed my eyes, forcing my mind back to Dante.

"It's time for you to come clean." He was imposing behind his desk. He held very few meetings in his penthouse. He liked to keep business to the strip club or one of his restaurants. This felt different than every other time I'd been in his house, even after growing up here.

"Come clean?" I took a seat, crossing my ankle over my knee, acting calmer than I felt. My heart was racing, but I'd had many years of practice covering it up for this man. He couldn't unsettle me yet. I would do this on my terms.

He opened a drawer and withdrew a picture, setting it on his desk. I didn't lean over to get a glimpse of it like he wanted me to. I waited until he pushed it over with a fat finger. I picked it up and glanced down at it like it was the most unimportant thing in the universe.

"You had me followed to the Boston Club?" It was a shitty cell phone picture taken in the dim light after I'd beaten Dante. I had my winnings piled in front of me with a big grin on my face. "I wasn't aware not telling you my every move was lying to you."

His scowl deepened, and he withdrew a second photo. It was me and Dante chest to chest in a corner. It was too dark to make out our faces, but my tattoos were a dead giveaway. He placed another photo on top. It was us much closer. He dropped photo after photo in front of me, and my stomach turned. Dread settled in my gut. He knew. This is what I'd been running from my entire life. I knew I couldn't avoid it forever, but I didn't think I'd die before thirty.

He turned and looked out across his empire. "I offer you this city on a silver fucking platter, and you piss it away for nothing."

There were more, hundreds more. He dumped out an envelope of them. Most of them were from the fight the other night. I'd been holding Dante's hand all night. Shit, he'd kissed me in public. It was evident after he'd found out about the Boston Club he'd hired someone to follow me. I'd never suspected it in the least. How long had he been sitting on this?

"What is the explanation for this?" He wanted an out. He wanted me to lie to him. I didn't have it in me anymore. After this, I could look forward to a lifetime of being followed and checked. He'd make me move back to Vegas and marry some poor girl.

My chest ached, and my mouth went dry. I had a choice to make. I could save my life and end it in the same breath, because if I moved here it would be over. I'd be a ghost without the pain and control. I'd be lucky if I lasted six months before I killed myself. I might as well have him do it for me. I wanted to go with my dignity intact.

"It's exactly what it looks like."

He took his time coming around the desk. He grabbed me by the shirt, picking me up and throwing me backward. I barely kept my feet under me.

"What did you just say to me, boy?" That word coming from his mouth filled me with rage. He had no right to use it.

"I'm gay."

It felt like I'd cleansed myself in holy water when I said

it. The weight came off my chest, and I was free. Soon to be dead, but I could enjoy the fleeting moments of freedom.

"You're confused."

I wasn't going to backtrack, but maybe he wouldn't really kill me. If no one here ever found out, maybe he'd get over me living in Cali and staying out of his town. It was worth a shot.

"I'm not confused. I've known for a long time. I don't plan on telling anyone. Let me go back to my life and forget I exist."

"You're my only son."

"There are three or four of your heavyweights you could hand everything off to. There are others from the family. Just let me go."

He rubbed the corners of his eyes with his thumb and first finger, and it looked like he was considering it. Maybe all I needed to do was face my fear. If I could face him, I could face Kai and Dante and tell them both what I needed. I sucked in a breath and waited for him.

He turned his back on me. I should have run. I should have gotten the fuck out of there, but the sick and twisted part of me that's always wanted his approval waited. He slid open the top drawer. The only thing he kept in that drawer was a Remington 911. My blood ran cold. I'd known what the consequence of my admission would be, and it still shocked me.

"Ashamed isn't even the appropriate word, boy. That's what you like to be called, isn't it?" He spat on the floor at his feet. "Disgusted about covers it."

"Father."

"Don't call me that again." He looked right at me but through me, like I didn't exist anymore. "Get on your knees."

I'd spent my whole life denying I loved to be on my knees and this is how it would end. I did as he asked. It was the perfect way to go. I turned my face away and closed my eyes. I held an image of Dante's face in my mind. I could die with him in my heart and in my head.

"Fucking coward." He slid the magazine home and pulled the slide back, cocking the gun.

He was right. I opened my eyes and turned back to face him, staring down the barrel of the gun. If it was my time, then it was my time. I'd abused the rules enough, and I knew what was coming to me.

"I may be a submissive, but I'm no coward." I stared into the same eyes I looked at in the mirror every morning. Whether he wanted to admit it or not, I was his blood, and if he was going to put a bullet in my brain he was going to have to look into his eyes to do it.

"Motherfucker." He dropped the gun and went to the side table where all the liquor sat. He poured himself a warm scotch and water.

I waited there, on my knees, half wishing he'd get it over with. I shouldn't have turned off my phone. There were so many things I wanted to tell Dante and Kai. My eyes burned, and my throat closed. I didn't give a shit about anyone else, but I loved those two.

I rubbed my sweaty palms on my jeans. Killing was such a fast thing in the movies, I shouldn't have to sit here and agonize over how they'd find out. How long Dante would wonder if I'd abandoned him like his husband?

"Will you fucking do it already." My mouth always got me in trouble, but I couldn't sit here anymore. I'd rather see Dante as the blood ran out of my body ruining his floor.

He turned around, sharply. "You want this?" His hand

shook as he brought the gun up to aim at the crease in my
brow. It was only a second of doubt, but I'd seen it.

"I want you to stop controlling my fucking life. I want
to be out from under you. I've been scared my entire damn
existence you'd find out, and now you know. I'm free, and
if I have to die for it then let's get it the fuck over with."

"You're proud of being a fucking faggot?"

I laughed, full body. It was sick and twisted to laugh
with someone holding a gun in my face. I'd probably lost
it. Jesus, fuck, there was a good chance I had PTSD from
my childhood. It was a miracle I hadn't killed myself or
anyone else up to this point. If anyone was going to get
taken down for my life it was going to be me, and I was
going to go out on my own terms.

"I'm proud I can take a dick like a pro, but that's not
even the half of it. I'm a little bitch on top of it. I like to get
beat." I grabbed the bottom of my shirt lifting it up to
expose my chest. I had fresh marks from Dante. If I had to
die for who I was, I was going to lay it all on the table. I
straightened my shoulders so he could see my chest. Then
I thought better of it and climbed to my feet. "If you're
going to shoot me then I'm going to look you in the eyes
like a man when you do."

"You're not a man." His hand shook as he stepped
forward. He steadied himself and pressed the nose of the
gun to my forehead. I scowled at him.

"This notion of men is all in your head. I'm more of a
man than you'll ever be." I leaned forward, pressing my
forehead into the cold steel. I never thought I'd be so calm
facing death.

I looked into his blue eyes and saw none of myself
reflected back as he lingered. I wasn't sure what he was
waiting for. If he was expecting some profound moment

before he blew my brains out on his carpet, he wasn't going to get it. Seconds ticked by, and neither of us moved or blinked. Maybe he was waiting for me to retract it all. To offer to move home and be who he wanted me to be. I was long past it. Before Dante, I might have done exactly what he wanted, now there was no going back. Faced with mortality, my focus became clear. Life was too short to live a lie.

"I should have shoved your mother down the stairs when she was pregnant with you. I knew as soon as that Gypsy whore told me she was pregnant you would be fucked up."

"I knew Mira was my mother." The tiny bit of information settled a part deep inside of me. I wouldn't appease him by asking what'd happened to her. I could rest easy knowing I wasn't a product of him and his wife.

"Your blood is tainted."

"Tainted by your blood. I'm guessing the only reason I'm not insane is because of her." I couldn't believe he wanted to drag this out further.

"The reason you're queer is because of her. Fucking queer—"

I grabbed his wrist jamming the gun into my head. "Damn right I'm queer, in every sense of the word. It's more likely I got it from you, you homophobic bastard. I bet it's why the entire family has this macho attitude. You're all hiding it. I bet you dream of a dick in your ass. You're the only coward in this room. You can't even shoot me." I tightened my grip around his wrist, not letting him free. "END ME."

He struggled to pull his hand out of my grasp. We fought over it, I reached for the trigger and he grabbed my hand. I looked down the chamber, staring death in the face, and I realized I didn't want it to end. I wanted to go climb back into Dante's bed and spend the next week there. I wanted to talk to Kai, lay it all out there. I had so much unfinished business. I was going to get through this even if I left my father dead in my wake. This might be the only chance I get.

I shoved him back, letting go of his hand as I did. He stumbled, tripped, and I saw something flash in his eyes. The tell. He was my first subject to study. I'd sat in on all his meetings since I was a kid. I knew when he was lying to someone or when he planned on double-crossing them. It was there. His nostrils flared, and he pulled the trigger.

The world slowed, and I watched the bullet coming toward me. There was nothing I could do about it now. I held on to Dante and Kai as the metal buried itself into my flesh, ripping and tearing me apart as it did. My legs gave out, and I collapsed to the floor.

FORTY

DANTE

Four hours is an eternity. I felt the weight of every second as I sat beside Kai in first class. I hadn't even glanced at the price of the tickets or brought anything but the clothes on my back. Remi was slipping through my fingers. Every second that went by felt like another drop of blood spilling from his veins. It was losing Masen all over again, but worse. At first, I'd thought Masen had just needed some time. But as the days grew into weeks without a word from him, I finally realized he wasn't coming back. I'd had time to come to the worst conclusion. Time to process, not that death was ever easy, but this, knowing there wasn't a damn thing I could do. It was Hell.

Kai laid a hand on my knee. "Dude, you've got to sit still. You're going to give yourself a heart attack." I saw everything I felt in his eyes.

"I'd be pacing the fucking plane if it wouldn't get us kicked off."

He sat back and looked out the window. "We'll be landing any minute. We are assuming the worst. He's probably fine."

"I know you don't really believe it."

He sighed. "I don't, but I think you may be the only

person who will be hurt worse by him dying."

I wasn't sure I could handle it at all. A few things had come into focus over the last few hours. If I was going keep existing as I had, why was I bothering? I wasn't happy. I just trudged on in a meaningless fashion. I now had a purpose, and it was revenge. I was going to hunt down that bastard and have him taste lead.

The plane landed, and we got into a cab, driving straight onto the parking lot Vegas calls a highway. I checked my watch. "What the fuck is this shit? It's too early for there to be this much traffic."

"Welcome to Vegas. Off the strip it calms down, but with the year-round tourists, shit is always like this."

I banged my head into the rest in front of my face. When the cab finally rolled to a stop in front of a high rise, I threw cash at the driver and climbed out. I stared up at the massive building. We didn't have a clue where Remi would be. Kai informed me his father owned tons of places around the city and did most of his business in them, but this was where Remi always came first.

Kai took care of the doorman and put his key into the elevator, pressing the button for the floor below the penthouse. The elevator took years off my life getting to his floor. His hands shook as he unlocked the door. He pulled it wide, and I stepped past him, my heart in my throat.

Things were strewn around the place. The shirt he'd left in lay draped across the back of a chair. His keys lay on the counter next to his wallet and a glass of water. Drops of condensation dripped down the surface, pooling on the granite countertop. The ice wasn't more than half melted. He'd been here recently. I grabbed his keys.

"You know him better than I do. Where would he go?"

I squeezed them in my hand until the metal broke my skin.

Kai's eyes fell to the glass, and he rubbed a hand over the back of his head. "He might have gone upstairs. His father would be just finishing his 'day.' He likes to watch the sun rise from his penthouse, and he takes only personal meetings there until he's ready for bed, but if he—" He couldn't get the words out.

"It's here. We'd be stupid not to check it out before we looked elsewhere."

Kai nodded.

"Do you think he has a key?"

"There is full access to upstairs from this floor and vice versa. It's one of the reasons Remi wanted to get as far away from here as he could."

I dropped the keys into my pocket and followed Kai toward the door. "Wait."

Kai looked back at me.

"Does he keep a gun here?"

He exhaled slowly and turned to open a drawer in the kitchen. The only thing in the drawer was a stash of weapons. "With who his father is, of course he does. Remi is always armed when he's here."

"Would he have shot his father?"

Kai shook his head. "I don't think he has it in him."

I grabbed a gun, checked the mag, and slid it into the waistband of my jeans as we waited for the elevator. Kai hit the penthouse button, and we waited to the sound of smooth Jazz in an almost cliché way. The doors slid back to a front entrance. I'd never seen so much luxury in my life. Art on the walls and gold vases sitting on end tables that probably cost more than my place.

"I've only been here a few times. I have a few excuses, but if he's here I doubt he'll tell us shit," Kai whispered as we walked into a formal living room. Not a speck of dust or a pillow out of place. He turned down a hall which opened up into an expansive room overlooking the strip with the same view as Remi's place below.

"Hey! The fuck you doing here?" A huge guy in a suit was in our face obstructing our view.

Kai held up his hands. "I'm Remi's business partner. I have my own keys. The boss here?"

A second guy joined the first, and they exchanged glances. There was something they weren't saying. Panic blossomed in my chest, eating its way up my throat. The smell of iron reached my nose, and my heart rate accelerated. I scanned the room looking for any evidence.

"The boss is out right now. He had a meeting, and some people are coming to redo his floors. We ain't supposed to let anyone inside," thug number one said.

"You've got to go. Give the boss a call," thug number two added.

My eyes landed on hair, barely visible around the edge of one of the sofas.

"Alright, we'll catch up with him. Thanks." I grabbed Kai's arm as he said the words. He glanced over at me as I withdrew the gun from my waistband.

"I don't want to have to shoot you, but I will. Both of you hand over your guns." I pointed the gun right at the men.

"What the fuck is this?" thug one asked.

I chambered a round. "I'm not kidding, hand them over. I know Remi's over there. You're waiting for a clean-up." I wanted to see his face. I had to touch him one last time. I had to tell him what he'd meant to me, even if he might not hear it. If there was any chance I could give him in death what I couldn't give to Masen, I was going to do it. Then

I'd torture them until they gave up their boss' location. I could do a lot with a stove and a knife. Once they gave me what I wanted, I'd slaughter him using Kai as my easy in. Against his will or not.

I was almost drunk on the idea of inflicting pain. I had to make other's feel what I was feeling. I shoved the gun into Kai's hands and shoved passed them, selfishly leaving Kai to deal with them.

There he was, slumped over in a growing sea of red.

DANTE

There was too much blood. I fell to my knees beside him, gathering him in my arms, coating myself in the process. Pain split me in two as I cradled his lifeless body. My body shook with sorrow, and I let my mind go to the darkness.

"Is he?" Kai's voice was raw. I knew he was somewhere close behind me, but I couldn't look away, I couldn't see anyone but Remi.

"Shoot them both." I choked back a sob. "Wait. Don't kill them." My thoughts were splintered. I tried to rein myself in. I had to do this right. I wouldn't get more than one chance at a man that powerful. "Shoot them in the knees."

My mind was torn between mourning and the icy need for revenge taking over my body like a poison. I kissed Remi's forehead then each of his eyelids and finally his lips before I laid him back.

"Where's the kitchen?" I asked Kai as I sat back on my knees. I cataloged the things I would need to get the party started on these two and then what I'd need for their boss.

"That way." Kai pointed.

I was about to get up when I saw a flicker. It was no

more than a muscle spasm in a dead body, but it worked its way through me like a bullet, tearing apart my mind, making it impossible for me to move as I watched him.

Again his eyes flickered then blinked. His chest heaved and blood leaked out of the corners of his mouth. He tried to make his mouth form words, but he had no breath to birth them. I dropped my face next to his.

"Remi!"

He grabbed me with one arm and held on to me. I picked him up and hauled us both off the ground.

"Kai, he's alive. I don't know how much longer he will be, but we need to get him somewhere."

He spun around. "We can't take him to a hospital. There will be too many questions. With his father's contacts, we'll go to jail."

"He's fucking bleeding out. I don't care."

"I used to be a medic in the army," thug number two commented. "We were told to let him bleed out while we wait for clean-up, but if you order me to help, I will."

I laid Remi on the sofa, but he clung to me. I sized up the guy as he walked over. "If you hurt him, so help me God, I will make sure the last days of your life are worse than any hell you might believe in."

"I believe you, man. I like the guy, I was just following orders."

"Geo, grab the first aid bag. We've got to get the bleeding stopped." He went to work tearing off Remi's shirt. "Where is he bleeding from?"

"I have no idea."

Geo came over with a kit. "Adam," he said as he held it out.

Adam tore it open as he found the wound. It was an open hole leaking blood in slow spurts at the bottom of Remi's ribcage. He took out pads and pressed them to the wound.

"I think it went through, but you're going to need to get him someplace," Adam said.

"We've got to take him to the hospital, Kai."

Remi shook his head. He grabbed my shirt. "I'm fine," he hissed.

"You have a fucking bullet through your lung. You're not fine!"

"It's but a flesh wound." He barely winced as he said it.

"If I wasn't so fucking worried I'd smack you and tell you to go home with Kai," I said through my teeth, trying to focus on Remi as well as the guy patching him up.

"Please." It was barely more than a whisper, but he forced a smile through his pain.

"I think he's in shock." I looked to Kai for support.

Remi was mumbling again, and I put my ear next to his lips. "I got a guy. Tell Kai to call."

"Where is your phone?"

"Pocket," he said then started coughing.

I dug in his pocket and extracted his phone. "Kai, he said he has a guy on his phone."

"Douglas?" Kai asked already flipping through Remi's contacts.

Remi nodded as best he could. Seconds felt like hours as we waited for Adam to get him in a condition we could move him. I dropped my face to Remi's chest, inhaling his scent. He placed a hand over the back of my head, holding me there.

"I've got him patched up." Adam got out a shot, and I grabbed his hand before he could stick Remi.

"The fuck is this?" I squeezed his fingers, crushing his hand.

"Painkillers. Look at it yourself."

I looked at Remi, and he nodded gritting his teeth. I let go of Adam, allowing him to give it to Remi.

"We've got to move." Kai held his hand over the phone speaker. "Out the back."

"This isn't going to be fun, but I should carry you, Remi."

"Put my jacket on him." Adam slid it off his arms and helped me put it on Remi before I picked him up. "Listen, I like you, Rem. Don't come back. He won't quit."

"Thank you." I looked Adam in the eyes, and he nodded.

"No problem."

Kai led the way to a service elevator, and then we were speeding toward the ground.

"If I have to die, it's much better to be in your arms than on the cold floor in a place I hate," he said through ragged breaths.

"You're not fucking dying."

"No promises." He tucked his face into my chest and let his eyes fall closed.

"Don't you fucking dare."

FORTY TWO

REMI

An excruciating twenty-minute car ride later, we pulled up in front of a nondescript house in the middle of the suburbs I knew well. Dante came around and opened the door to the SUV, but I waved him off. I was his submissive, but I'd never been weak for him. Today I was weak.

"I'm walking." My voice was less than a whisper.

"Suck it up, and let me carry you."

"I lost all of my pride today, so let me have this." I closed my eyes and swung my legs out of the car. I gripped the handle with my good arm to help lower myself out of the car. My vision swirled, but I waited until it passed. Dante scooped me up. I had no energy left to protest. My body was failing.

We made it from the street to the front door, how I don't know, but I was ushered into the clinic and onto a gurney. The entire inside of the house had been gutted and turned into a state of the art clinic for those of us who couldn't step foot into the hospital.

Dante hovered as the doctor examined me. The doctor was cold and didn't say a word as he worked, not caring if he was hurting me as he rolled and prodded. I didn't make a sound, gritting my teeth and bearing it.

"It looks like the bullet went all the way through, but I'm going to need to open him up to make sure nothing vital was hit."

Dante met my gaze. "You trust him?"

I nodded. The doctor put a mask over my face, and I looked into Dante's blues, in case it was the last time.

"I'll be here when you wake up."

FORTY THREE

DANTE

Remi slept off and on for the next few days. We were transferred into one of the rooms in the house, which I was sure was costing Remi an arm and a leg. But we were well hidden and safe for the moment, which was all I cared about. The sun filtered in through the window, causing Remi to stir. His dark green eyes swirled with the chaos he was.

I'd finally figured it out, the key to happiness was choosing each other. Everyone had baggage, life was hard, but if we continued to choose each other day after day we could make it work.

"I missed you." His voice was raspy and strained.

"I haven't left." I scooted closer to his bed and took his hand in mine.

"I was never supposed to fall for you. You were a fix and nothing more."

"But here we are," I replied, leaning down to kiss his knuckles.

"Where do we go from here?"

"I'm sure as fuck not moving to California."

"I didn't expect you to." He offered me a smile.

"Let's go home."

"For clarification, do you mean NOLA?"

I gave him a pointed look. He laughed and winced, then closed his eyes again to drift off.

"In the smallest ways, in those early hours, I realized I loved you for a million different reasons, and none of them for the face you put on. I love you for who you are when you're stripped raw."

DANTE

EPILOGUE

DANTE

It was good to be home. As much pain as I realized this house gave me, it would always be home. Remi was asleep in my— In *our* bed. He'd insisted as soon as they'd cleared him to travel. Kai had wanted to drive him to Venice but Remi wouldn't allow it. My heart warmed as I watched him breathing. How trivial a thing breathing was. We all took it for granted day in and day out, but now the most important thing in my world were those breaths. I'd almost lost them. What would I have done? I wasn't sure I should let my mind go there. I couldn't allow myself to dwell on it.

I pressed my palm to my chest. It felt like I had a rock sitting just under my ribcage. It had hardened there as Remi fought for his life before my eyes, and I wasn't sure it would ever go away now. I dreaded the day he'd go back to California. Not because Kai was there. He still wasn't my favorite person in the universe, but I could live with him. My real fear was letting Remi out of my sight. Not leaving his side was the only reason I hadn't gone on a killing spree. I suddenly had an urge to clean up the streets in Vegas.

"Why aren't you in bed." His breathing hadn't changed.

How long had he been awake?

"I got up to get a drink, and I didn't want to disturb you. I know how much pain you've been in." I'd been so restless the last few nights and every movement made Remi ache.

"I can't sleep when you aren't here." It was the truth of course. I'd walked in on more than one nightmare. I was starting to wonder if he'd had them before me.

"I'm sorry." I shook off the stiffness in my bones as I climbed from my chair.

He grunted as he rolled to make room for me. I offered a hand, but he wouldn't take it. The sliver of moonlight reflected in his gaze as he looked up at me. "Don't be sorry."

I stripped off my shirt and shorts before slipping in next to him. There wasn't the space between us there used to be. It was easier to get close to him without the invisible barrier. He'd stripped himself raw and offered himself for death. It had changed him. I pressed my lips to his neck as his hand slid up my arm. His fingers lightly played over the ink I had there.

"What is this?"

"You've seen it before."

"You're not the run out to get a giant tattoo type, It must have a meaning."

I smiled into his neck hoping he couldn't feel it. "You already used up your truth."

His chest rumbled as he growled at me. "We—this— we're more than those games now. Do I still have to drag every single bit of information from you?"

My cock pressed into my boxers as he scowled at me. I'd never get tired of getting him riled up.

"You asshole."

"What?" It was impossible to keep the hint of laughter

from my voice.

"You're getting off on this."

My smile spread, taking over my entire face. "I am."

"Explain the tattoo."

I let out a breath I hadn't realized I'd been holding. "It's a long story."

"It's a good thing neither of us has shit to do." He pulled back a little and our eyes met. He took a breath like he was formulating more, but slipped his hand into my hair and brought our foreheads together instead.

"Well that was easy."

"I'm not letting you win," he retorted.

"It feels a lot like a win."

He was quiet for a few moments, but it wasn't an awkward or an angry silence. We were comfortable with each other.

"I want to know you. I don't just want the Dante the rest of the world gets. I want more than the bits and pieces you give away when you're feeling generous."

It was so hard to do this, harder than he or even Masen would ever understand. Everything in me told me to make a smart ass remark and leave it at that, but deep down I wanted more too. More than I'd ever wanted with anyone else. I had to pry open my soul and let him see inside.

Fuck, if only it weren't so painful.

"I never thought I'd live past thirty. I thought I'd end up killing myself with my vices long before I reached what I saw as adulthood. The track record in my family makes it even harder to believe I'd live into old age." I hated talking about my childhood, more than just about anything. "With as stupid as I was as a kid, it's a wonder I wasn't dead before eighteen."

He couldn't help but fill the pause. I wasn't surprised.

"What does this have to do with the tattoo."

"Patience is something you need to learn."

He laughed and then winced. "I know."

"I didn't have any tattoos when I met Masen, I'd never found anything I wanted on my body permanently."

"Which is why I'm surprised you have one at all."

"Masen changed me in a lot of ways. I never thought I was good enough to be with anyone, and I stayed away from relationships until him, but him and I— he changed me. We had a lot of philosophical conversations and I came to realize I don't have to be anything more than I am. I don't have to become what my predecessors were, we aren't predestined for anything. We choose who we become, and up until that point I'd given myself a lot of excuses, assuming I'd become what I hated no matter what I did." I trailed my fingers over his chest and the splattering of ink there. "He had a lot of tattoos like you. All of them could be hidden by a suit for his job, but he loved them. I watched him get more than a few, and after one particularly deep conversation I knew what I wanted."

"Go on." I wasn't going to get away with anything with this one. It was a contrast to Masen. Masen would have let me be and drawn out the information slowly letting me do it on my own time. Remi was too demanding to wait.

"The universe is infinite. We aren't even as significant as dust in the grand scheme of things. We live and die in the blink of an eye to the universe. It was here long before man, and it will be here long after man. I've never bought into the big man in the sky thing, but I do believe and always have that there is something greater than ourselves. I guess, to me, the universe represents that. It's my reminder that in this vast space, life is what we make of it and we choose our own path. I'm responsible for me, not for my parents choices, so I've tried to do right by it and do my own little part. My bar puts food on the table for a lot of people. I could get by with a lot less help and I could make a lot more money, but these people, my people, needed it after Katrina." Words stop coming and we drifted back into silence.

In the darkness, his lips found mine and we kissed. There wasn't a rush, it was slow, but we kissed until we were both breathless and then we kissed until the world seemed to right itself. My hands wandered the planes of his muscles, touching as much of him as I could, carefully avoiding the tender areas. I was lost to all but the feel of him. How my skin heated and buzzed under his touch. We broke apart and his lips formed a smile against mine.

"How come you never got it finished?"

I thought I wouldn't want to tell him, but I found I didn't mind. "I'd always go with him, to his guy, and I couldn't fucking look the guy in the eyes after Masen left. I just couldn't fucking walk into the shop with the memories and get another damn session done on it."

"Will you let me?" He propped himself up on his elbow, breathing through the pain taking a closer look at it. When he'd caught his breath he leaned over and clicked on the bedside lamp.

I hesitated. Did I even want it finished? Could I go down this road and find peace at the end of it. I was so used to the abrupt ending of the tattoo, almost like a metaphor for my relationship with Masen. Remi tugged at my arm, urging me forward. I let him move me. He studied the back and pursed his lips.

"What? It can't be fixed?"

"No, it's great work, and I want to complete it for you. Please."

The words stuck in my mouth, but I forced them out. "Okay."

He sat up and tried to swing his legs over the bed.

"Where the fuck are you going?"

"To get my stuff."

"It's two in the fucking morning."

"So? It's not like we were anywhere near going back to sleep. I've been sleeping for days. Let me do this."

I let him go, resisting the urge to follow him, or help him. I'd quickly learned he needed to do things himself. So I waited for him to come back and my hand found the lump in my chest again. I hadn't even realized, the ache happened to be right under the scar there. I was glad he hadn't asked about that one yet. That story might be a little harder to get out of me.

He retuned with a bag, flipped on the overhead light and then and sat on the edge of the bed. "It's going to have to be short sessions until I can sit for longer."

"Right now?" I stared at him. "Do you really carry it with you?"

"Every where I go. You never know when you'll need to tattoo."

I laughed. "Can't you pick up new equipment if you need it."

He paused looking up from the assembly of his gun. "How dare you. I'm an artist. A gun is as personal as paintbrushes. You can't just use any old one." He scoffed at me and went back to work.

"Paint brushes are personal?"

He just groaned. "Don't you fucking start."

I figured it would be better to not goad the man taking a needle to my skin and instead laid out on the bed when he told me to. He was quite thorough in cleaning my back and setting up the little thimbles of ink. I didn't even ask him what he was going to do. I wanted him to paint me like he looked like he'd been painted. I wanted his art etched into my skin.

"I'm going to freehand it. It's going to look a lot better if I draw it directly onto your skin instead of on paper."

"I trust you," I murmured.

He paused with a sharpie above my skin.

"What?" I looked over my shoulder at him.

"You trust me?"

"I do."

His smile said more than words could as he went to work.

The buzz of the gun started soon after, and the burn lulled me into an almost sleep like state. The pain took the edge off the anxiety I'd been feeling. It made me less murderous which was an added bonus I hadn't expected.

He pulled and stretched my skin as he worked. I never wanted him to stop. I felt him in my skin, down to my bones. He was there, inside me, and he would stay there forever. It was like he was closing an old wound for good. I pressed my eyes closed, happy, really fucking happy, for the first time for as long as I could remember.

This book never would have happened without the amazing people behind me, helping me do what I do. I'd like to thank my amazing betas, Karen, Sal, Karen, Jen, Lili, and Kerry, to my PA Dawn, my epic cover artist and formatter at Rebel Graphics, my editor Silla, to Kerry for helping with all the formatting ARCS and help with anything I need as well as countless voxer walk throughs, to the girls at The Literary Gossip for handing promo, to Judith for her exceptional spotlight post skills, and to Jen for putting up with me and making me rewrite my blurbs six-hundred times—Lobster, to N and my kids for tolerating my hours and hours of work.

But most of all to those of you who pushed me with negative comments, and hate. This one is for you.

GRAY

Made in the USA
Middletown, DE
12 March 2018